ISAAC ASIMOV'S ROBOT MYSTERY

# HAVE ROBOT, WILL TRAVEL

ISAAC ASIMOV'S ROBOT MYSTERY

# HAVE ROBOT, WILL TRAVEL

ALEXANDER C. IRVINE

ibooks

new york

www.ibooks.net

DISTRIBUTED BY PUBLISHERS GROUP WEST

An original publication of ibooks, inc.

Copyright © 2004
by Byron Preiss Visual Publications, Inc.

An ibooks, inc. Book

Distributed by Publishers Group West
1700 Fourth Street, Berkeley, CA 94710
www.pgw.com

ibooks, inc.
24 West 25th Street
New York, NY 10010

The ibooks World Wide Web Site Address is:
http://www.ibooks.net

ISBN 1-59687-151-2
First ibooks, inc. printing May 2004
10 9 8 7 6 5 4 3 2

Edited by Steven Roman

Special thanks to Mark W. Tiedemann
for his invaluable assistance

Jacket art by Luis Royo

Printed in the U.S.A.

# ISAAC ASIMOV'S

# THREE LAWS OF ROBOTICS

### 1.

A robot may not injure a human being, or through inaction, allow a human being to come to harm.

### 2.

A robot must obey the orders given it by human beings except where such orders would conflict with the First Law.

### 3.

A robot must protect its own existence, as long as such protection does not conflict with the First or Second Laws.

# PROLOGUE

*Record module file catalogue "Operations Adjustment, Reorganization, and Redirection" subfile Addendum, access code secured user-designate, running virtual conference reference Nova City fill visual fill audio status On*

The thick man with amber-tinged hair watched the attendees vanish one by one. They no longer bothered hiding their identities since the Chairman had barred chameleon programs on pain of expulsion from the board. The numbers varied, from a low of four to the current membership of eleven. The survivors from the days when Kynig Parapoyos ran the organization attended anxiously, as if waiting for—

He did not know what they awaited. Nothing good, he suspected. The other, newer members often reacted to the older ones with a bemused fascination, as if sensing that the current mission of the board had once been very different.

The Chairman had learned to function with ambiguity, but he rarely tolerated it if he thought it could be dispensed. He pressed a contact on the edge of the table, then turned to gaze out the panoramic window at the landscape beyond.

"It's quite different."

The Chairman glanced to the newcomer standing to his left. "You're prompt."

Hofton nodded, still staring at the view. "Your request came during a lull in my day. I'd just finished meeting with Senator Taprin's aide on Kopernik."

"Any change?"

"No. The Terrans still want us completely removed from Sol System, treaties notwithstanding. The revelation that a Solarian ambassador had been simultaneously the head of an interstellar black market syndicate soured what was left of the wine between Terrans and Spacers. Never mind that Gale Chassik—pardon me, Parapoyos—was unmasked and his network dismantled with Spacer help. Never mind that no other Spacer legate was involved. And never mind that no other Spacer government official knew about him."

"This is only a pretense for actions Taprin wanted to take anyway," the Chairman said.

"Of course. But it's so disappointingly predictable."

"For you, perhaps."

Hofton waited. The view beyond showed a landscape in the throes of rebirth. What once had been a poisoned terrain, pustulant with unregulated pollution from industries run unchecked as a result of an embargo by Settlers, Spacers, and Terrans, now showed signs of renewal. The greens and yellows no longer seemed so putrid or diseased. Even the sky seemed less ominous.

"You need advice?" Hofton finally asked.

"Yes. Since assuming control of the Parapoyos organization—"

"The Hunter Group."

"—correct, the Hunter Group. I have found the resources at my disposal broader, more substantial than I expected. Yet I find my actions blocked, delayed, and challenged in ways I do not completely understand."

"And you want to understand them."

"I want them removed."

Hofton gave the Chairman a skeptical look. The humaniform's ability to mimic human expression always surprised the Chairman. Although Hofton's thinking remained comfortably familiar, there always seemed the possibility of randomness, of irrationality, of unpredictability.

"I will settle for understanding," the Chairman said. "To begin with."

Hofton drew a deep breath—more mimicry—and nodded.

"Let's recap, then. To begin with."

Hofton seemed to collect his thoughts. The Chairman wondered how much his ability to imitate humans depended on the continual embrace of human forms, even to the extent of taking time as if he were human. The Chairman had called up and organized the necessary data in an insignificant amount of time. Perhaps the delay was an artifact of the distance between the Chairman's location and Hofton. In either case, Hofton did not speak again for several seconds.

"With the assassinations on Earth that effectively ended any workable compromise between Terrans and Spacers," he finally said, "and the subsequent revelation that the sponsoring Terran politician, Senator Clar Eliton, was part of the plot to undermine the conference at which normalization would have occurred, tensions continued to mount over the issue of positronics and its use in diplomatic, commercial, and security matters between the three human polities—namely Terran, Spacer, and Settler.

"The further complication of the discovery of cyborgs, created using orphaned children stolen from Earth by the Hunter Group, tying several Terran concerns in with a Solarian interest, fed the growing distrust of Spacers on Earth. Senator Jonis Taprin, successor to Eliton, has made enormous political gains out of an anti-Spacer, anti-positronic platform, going so far as to call for boycotts and possible sanctions against all Spacer worlds.

"Though the efforts of Derec Avery, Ambassador Ariel Burgess, and the investigator, Coren Lanra, revealed all these interests to be extralegal and largely unsanctioned by any legitimate government, the political climate on Earth has not shifted back toward a more moderate position. Almost all Spacer legations have left Earth. The few who remain do so only until official notification from their governments to vacate. Pressure continues to expel all Spacers from Terra. The gains toward an accommodation with positronics on Earth have been lost, and there seems little possibility of rebuilding. Positronic presence on Earth has been eliminated. Only the Spacer enclaves on Kopernik Station retain robots, and that privilege is being attacked by Taprin's confederates.

"Through diplomatic channels, I have monitored a great deal of dissension among the various Spacer factions over all these events. Many wish to retreat back to their own worlds, withdraw from all interstellar arenas, and leave the Terrans and Settlers to their own devices. To date there has been no consensus. Aurora is voicing strenuous opposition to any retraction of Spacer influence. Unfortunately, the events around Nova Levis have done a great deal to undermine Aurora's authority. The revelation that the head of the Hunter Group, Kynig Parapoyos, was in fact the Solarian ambassador to Earth, Gale Chassik, and that his network of agents included several sensitively-placed Aurorans, has resulted in an unprecedented backlash from all quarters. It is too soon to tell how alliances will ultimately change over this matter.

"Last, but by no means least, we have the matter of positronic intervention directly in Spacer affairs."

"No action has been taken yet."

"It will be. The question itself, as to whether or not Spacers constituted a legitimate example of Human, demands a response from any Three Law entity. You yourself have been the fulcrum in such a consequence."

The Chairman looked at Hofton. "Me?"

"You as the new head of the Parapoyos organization. You as a new type of positronic construct. You as self-motivated actor in correcting perceived mistakes on the part of humankind."

"I am fulfilling my obligation as required by the Three Laws."

Hofton looked skeptical. "Are you? As Bogard, you had fairly clear criteria on which to base your decisions. But as the Chairman, you seem to be making up your own criteria as you go along."

"The situations are fluid. Flexibility is necessary."

"I'm not criticizing, Bogard. From the evidence, you have been doing a remarkable job. I am merely including your actions into the total picture as I see it."

The Chairman considered. It was, he decided, difficult to select the important from the trivial to make a verbal summary. Easier, perhaps, to simply transfer data from one positronic mind to another, but they were stuck with this format for the time being.

"The Hunter Group program," he said, "has been significantly altered from its original intent. The original embargo by Terran and Spacer fleets—due to a refusal on the part of the governor to allow surface inspections—triggered a series of incidents leading to the revelation that, in fact, Nova Levis was a host polity for the Parapoyos organization. The isolation imposed by Terran and Spacer forces was exactly what Parapoyos wished, since it gave him a perfectly shielded base from which to export on the black market. He had infiltrated the blockade. His agents held key positions from Earth all the way out to the Terran fleet base station in the system. Goods entered and left easily. And his factories operated without any regulation whatsoever.

"Parapoyos' program was the exportation of tailored diseases for which his own people had developed treatments. By making them available through several pharmaceutical concerns on Earth, he profited considerably through quasi-legitimate trade entities. Nova Levis itself was made into a breeding ground for many of the viruses.

"Since Parapoyos' removal by the self-same cyborgs he had been creating as a potential extreme threat force, and my own assumption of his position as Chairman, Nova Levis is on its way toward recovery. The blockade has been partially lifted, thanks to the diplomatic efforts of Ambassador Burgess. The Parapoyos program has changed as well, moving in the direction of legitimate research and development. The environmental factors that led to the spontaneous eruptions in the past of a number of exotic diseases, like Mnemonic Plague, have become the primary focus of our efforts. Each new world humans attempt to settle pose unique challenges. If terraforming to any significant degree is required, we can now provide solid background on the potential risks that may arise from unforeseen biological reactions.

"However, I have been unable to control all former members of the organization. A number of them have elected to leave the group and pursue the older, more profit-intensive policies. I have been forced to take action against some of them. Others I have yet to deal with because of the intricate connections they have with current members whose safety and freedom of action I cannot jeopardize at this time.

"It has come to my attention also that there is still a Spacer presence within these illegitimate groups. I have been unsuccessful in isolating those I can identify. They are operating on Earth and possibly on Kopernik, which has remained largely unregulated and poorly policed.

"Recently, it has come to my attention that a strong isolationist faction on Aurora is beginning to gain momentum. If Aurora withdraws completely, nothing will be able to contain Solarian ambitions, which seem allied to the former Parapoyos organization. Details are vague at best."

"What about the robots?" Hofton asked.

"Solarian robots remain largely unconvinced by our arguments. They will take no actions yet to interfere with Solarian policy."

"What do you require?"

"Ambassador Burgess must be reassigned from Nova Levis. She has the expertise and wherewithal to be effective on Kopernik. To date, the Auroran council has denied any petition to reassign her."

"Likewise, I'm certain, with regards to Derec Avery."

"Aurora would be pleased to see him remain sequestered to Nova Levis. However, he also understands Terrans better than most Spacers. His presence on or near Earth now would be convenient."

"I'll see what I can do. But the Calvin Institute is angry with him."

"Why?"

"For building you."

"He will not build me again. They should move on."

"Although they may be genetically drifting from human-standard, Aurorans are still emotionally very human."

"Wasteful."

"And Ariel?"

"They have blamed her for the failure of the Terran mission."

"She was not in charge. That's absurd."

"I agree." Hofton looked back out the window. "It looks better, certainly. I will see what I can do about Derec and Ariel. Is there anything else?"

"Stop Jonis Taprin."

"Short of killing him?"

"Of course."

"That, unfortunately, is beyond my influence."

"You asked."

"I will let you know what I can do. Till the next meeting?"

Bogard nodded and watched Hofton shimmer and fade from the room. Alone now, he continued to gaze out at the reviving landscape.

He had learned to accept his successes in bits and fragments. He collected them, knowing that one day they would form a whole—and he would know then if he had done well.

# CHAPTER

# 1

After five years, Derec Avery still couldn't stop looking out the windows. He lived on the second floor of a building so new the paint had still been drying when he came to look at his apartment, and his view consisted only of other buildings similar to his, stretching down the street toward the gray hulk of the Triangle, a kilometer or so to the north. He wasn't interested in the architecture of Nova City, though; what still drew his attention was the sky.

He hadn't spent all that much time on Earth, but somehow those few years had utterly conditioned him to the sight of a dome where the sky should be. Derec had often reflected on why a few short years, after spending most of his life under Aurora's open skies, had had such a profound effect on him. In the end, unable to come to a useful conclusion, he'd just decided to enjoy being free of Earth, even if that meant living on Nova Levis.

This morning, there were low clouds to the north and bright blue everywhere else, the sharp color that meant the air was dry and there would be no wind above a refreshing breeze. A good day to spend outside, if you didn't have work to keep you in—which, of course, Derec did.

Time to face the day. He finished dressing for work and asked his robot Miles if the afternoon's meeting with Senator Lamina was still scheduled.

"Yes, Derec. Two o'clock."

So he had six hours to anticipate how venal and frustrating his afternoon would be. Perfect. "Okay, Miles," he said. "Let's try to get some work done before the Senator tells us how much of the Triangle's money we're wasting."

Since he'd been unofficially exiled to Nova Levis, Derec had slowly pared away the trappings of his previous lifestyle on Earth. In Washington, during his time with the Phylaxis Group, he'd lived in a district that, if not fashionable, marked him as someone with connections to the powerful Spacer diplomatic and research presence. He'd been a leader in his field, probing the frontiers of the Three Laws in his robotics work, taking pride in his technical publications and his election to the editorial boards of prestigious journals. He'd been accustomed to the peerage of powerful people: scientists, diplomats, senators. None of it was self-conscious—Derec had never actively concerned himself with social position, and he slept more often in his rooms over the Phylaxis Group lab than in his apartment—but in hindsight, he realized he'd taken the accolades and the success as simply his due. He'd taken his importance for granted.

Now he lived in a small apartment a few hundred yards from the lab that consumed his waking hours, and instead of Bogard at his side, there was Miles.

He'd built Miles from scratch even though there was nothing about the robot that couldn't have come off an assembly line in Solaria. In a way, Derec supposed it was a kind of penance for his experimentation with Bogard; he'd never settled to his own satisfaction just how much responsibility he bore for the events sparked by the massacre at Union Station in Washington, D.C,, six years ago. When the cyborg lab outside Noresk had gone up in flames and the experimental discards from that lab had taken Kynig Parapoyos to his death, a curtain had come down on a long act in Derec's life.

He paused at the door of his lab and waited for Kashi, the lab RI, to scan him in. The door clicked and he went inside, followed by Miles. The robot went to its station and began work, assessing data from overnight diagnostics. Derec took a moment to look over the lab: a bank of terminals, splicers and sequencers, with his assistant Elin Imbrin already shuffling among them. She was an early riser, Derec guessed, because of a chip on her shoulder about her colonial origins. Not many of the native-born citizens of Nova Levis battled through the mutating nanoplagues and political chaos to achieve a useful education; Elin saw herself as an exemplar of native potential, and a living rebuke to real or imagined condescension from the off-worlders who made up the majority of the government and skilled workforce. In a way, she reminded him of the students who had worked with him at Phylaxis.

*Miles and Elin and I,* Derec thought. *We three are the advance guard in the war to reclaim Nova Levis from decades of ecological destabilization.* The job needed hundreds, if not thousands, of dedicated professionals, not a transplanted roboticist and a lab tech just out of a cobbled-together doctoral program—but that was Nova Levis. You made do with what you had.

"Anything I need to know?" he asked Elin.

She started to answer, but Miles cut in. "The compiler has malfunctioned, Derec. It shut down automatically at 12:17 A.M. when Kashi detected the problem. I am already working to restore function."

Elin's mouth shut hard enough for Derec to hear her teeth click. "The question was addressed to Elin, Miles," he said.

"My apologies, Derec. You did not so indicate. Apologies to you as well, Elin."

*A fine start to the day,* Derec thought. *My assistant angry at my robot for its lack of social intuition.* He wished he'd spent a little more time on Miles' communication matrices, but he'd wanted a typical

3

robot, and a typical robot he'd built. Good intentions always had unintended consequences.

Elin had already turned, tight-lipped, back to the sequencer she'd been programming when Derec and Miles came in. Derec decided to let the whole thing pass. Nothing he said at this point would make Elin any less angry. He went to a terminal and sorted through the morning's messages. They were all relentlessly ordinary, and after he'd read through them Derec turned with relief to the day's work.

A two-by-three-meter screen on the wall over Derec's terminal displayed a map of Nova Levis. The three primary human settlements—Nova City, Noresk, and Stopol—lay strung out south to north along the course of a river that drained the greater part of the planet's smaller northern continent. Various groups of colonists had given the river a dozen names, but privately Derec called it "the Bogard"; an odd tribute, perhaps, but one he was comfortable with. A second northern landmass was empty of *Homo sapiens* except for a scattering of research stations established since what the government liked to call "the Liberation," and even these small outposts were absent from the rugged and sinuous southern continent that spanned nearly seventy percent of Nova Levis' circumference at about forty degrees south. Together with a number of large island chains, these three continents occupied approximately forty-five percent of the planetary surface.

"Plague incidence," Derec said, and Kashi overlaid gradients of color onto the two-tone scheme of land and water. Bright splotches of red blended to orange and then yellow, indicating aggregate rates of infection from nanoplagues and non-native viruses. All three cities were red, and around Noresk the color spread into a hundred-kilometer-wide teardrop with a tail that didn't peter out until nearly five hundred kilometers southwest of the city.

There were other splotches of red on the map, signaling areas where renegade vonoomans or viruses had attacked native biotes—but it was the three cities Derec was there to save, and to do that, he had to understand the story of those red shapes. Nova City, with a population of approximately a quarter of a million, showed infection numbers only seventy percent of Stopol's, despite Stopol's much smaller population; and Noresk, with only ninety thousand people, had five times as many sick people as Nova City. Citizens of Noresk were fifteen times as likely to contract a non-native or nano-derived disease as their fellows in the other two cities.

The swaths of color hadn't changed since yesterday, but Derec began every morning by looking at them. They reminded him of his task, kept him going in the face of frustrations like the afternoon meeting he was trying not to think about.

"Mutation rates," he said.

The map's palette shifted, grew more complex as, without asking, Kashi recentered the map on the three cities and zoomed in. Derec had field agents working throughout the Bogard watershed, along with robots stationed in areas of maximum biodiversity. The team collected samples of the local microbes and constructed genealogies, using this data to focus restoration efforts on areas with the greatest rates of mutation. If those areas could be brought under control, there was hope for the perverted ecology of Nova Levis, and hope that humans might one day live normally there.

Derec dove into the day's work, sifting through reports, allocating resources, periodically checking on Elin and Miles. Much of what he did consisted of making sure that his team was pulling in the same direction, and perhaps that was what he was best suited for. At times, he considered the analogy of designing a positronic brain, making sure that the decision matrices embodied no contradictions of the Three Laws. His work here was much the same, keeping the various autonomous elements of his team from contravening the singular law that presided over them: restoration.

Two o'clock came before Derec had taken a break for lunch. Miles reminded him of the meeting, and with a stifled groan Derec left the lab and walked in the open air to the Council building a kilometer or so away. Meeting number nineteen. Four years and nine months since the blockade imploded and Kynig Parapoyos died at the hands of his creations. Derec couldn't remember the last time he'd passed five years without an interstellar trip. Nova Levis had changed him.

The Capitol building anchored the rebuilt center of Nova City, its granite triangle occupying a space once taken up by one of the city's many slums. Two hundred meters on a side, with meeting chambers at each terminus and office space along the halls, it was the symbolic construction of representative democracy on Nova Levis. The points of the triangle were executive, legislative, and judicial, and the building had been constructed to ensure that officials of the three branches would meet daily in the halls, fostering cooperation. The whole idea seemed a little utopian to Derec, but nobody had asked him, and whatever idealism had motivated the Capitol architect hadn't percolated into the actions of the human beings working within his creation's imposing walls. People rarely lived up to the ideals they proposed for others.

One of the few exceptions to this rule was Ariel Burgess, and the only reason the afternoon's meeting might not be a complete waste of time was that she would be there. Derec considered this affection for Ariel an emotional oddity, almost a character flaw. They'd been partners, but weren't anymore; they had worked together, but didn't anymore; they had argued violently about principles important to them both, and then slowly smoothed over some of their differences. The presence of Ariel Burgess in Derec's life had a way of predisposing him to believe in fate.

Yet, he'd rarely seen her since the two of them were cashiered to Nova Levis in the wake of the Parapoyos events. She was putting her diplomatic experience to good use as a consultant to the government's Justice Ministry, working to institutionalize transparency and root out the corruption that came inevitably with a planet being rebuilt from scratch. Her work put her at odds with a sizable number of officials appointed to serve by the planetary governments of Earth and the Fifty Worlds—everyone, it seemed, saw the rebirthing planet as a way to make money, a colony existing to enrich the seats of empire. Whatever progress Derec had made in balancing the ravaged ecology, Nova Levis' history as a bazaar persisted into the present. Smugglers thrived, and industrial enterprises that in other systems would have been restricted to orbital facilities flourished on the ground here. Too often, government officials ignored these crimes, due either to incompetence or corruption, and it was up to Ariel and her subordinates to keep them honest. Like Derec, she had her work cut out for her.

He signed in at the security checkpoint and walked down the E-J hall until he came to the committee chamber that hosted the quarterly meetings. As he entered and saw the long rows of bureaucrats on either side of a polished native wood table, he scanned for Ariel's face. She wasn't there, and he sighed. The meeting would be worse than usual without her in attendance.

Then someone tapped him on the shoulder, and he turned to see her coming in the door behind him. "Hi, Derec. Ready to take your quarterly beating?"

"With you here, I suppose I can stand it," he said. They sat together near a corner of the table at the far end from Senator Eza Lamina, an embittered Keresian posted to Nova Levis after a bribery scandal back home. Lamina chaired the committee that oversaw the various quasi-governmental agencies devoted to restoration and development. She'd been elected to the chair, Derec was sure, because she was implacably hostile toward the work of everyone whose funding she controlled. At every meeting she attacked their work, vowed to slash their budgets, and scorned the idea that Nova Levis would ever be anything more than a squalid colonial backwater. Eighteen meetings had gone exactly this way.

Number nineteen was no different. Derec, Ariel, Hodder Feng from the Technical Education project, and all the rest rose to give their reports, and were icily belittled. The minority representation of the committee—put another way, the native Settlers who had battled their way into politics—spoke up for them, but the real power lay with the offworld representatives. By the end of the meeting, Hodder's project was defunded and Senator Lamina had made it clear to each of the others how very thin was the ice on which they stood.

"This is getting almost routine," Derec said to Ariel as they walked out together.

She nodded to Hodder Feng. "Not for him."

It was true. Derec and Ariel had survived this long only because Lamina wasn't sure how much influence they still had on Earth and Aurora. Keres teetered on the brink of open conflict with both, and Lamina couldn't risk having a local vendetta erupt into an interplanetary incident. Everything on Nova Levis seemed to unfold this way, as a proxy struggle for grudges and hatreds born and nursed lightyears away. The native-born minority in the government did what they could, but too few of the offworld cat's-paws had the integrity to stand with them. Hodder Feng had been born on Nova Levis, and so was an easy target—what did the education of the poor matter when stacked up against the imperative to maintain the pecking order in a Senate committee?

Derec wanted to get back to his lab, lose himself in work, try to cleanse himself of the taint he always felt after these meetings. He hadn't seen Ariel in nearly a month, though. They walked to Kamil's, a restaurant across the broad strip of Nova Boulevard to have a drink.

"So how goes the fight against corruption and evil?" Derec asked, making an effort to keep things light.

"The only reason I'm still working is that the Terrans in the Senate need me to harass the Spacers, and vice versa," she said. "If they ever decide to quit needling each other, I'll be out of a job." She smiled with only a trace of bitterness. "Thus I prove my worth to the great powers."

So the meeting had gotten to her, too. "We just got a new batch of ungulates from Nucleomorph on Friday," Derec said. "They're tweaked to break down alien proteins in their digestive tracts and excrete vonoomans tailored to go after them." It was, he hoped, a turning point; the inventory of invasive microbes and nanos had taken the better part of four years—and was, given the mutation rates in much of the Bogard Valley, ongoing. Derec believed that having identified some of the enemy, he could set about eradicating them.

Ariel raised her drink. "Good luck," she said. "Nucleomorph operates out in the old Solarian concession near Noresk, don't they?"

"They're headquartered on Earth. Detroit, I think. But yes, their local facility is built on the old cyborg lab."

A silence fell between them. The old cyborg lab, Kynig Parapoyos' operation, had spawned a series of events that had reached across galaxies to kill senators and ambassadors, shiploads of the illegal emigrants known in the trade as "baleys," and, most significantly to Ariel, her lover Coren Lanra. Five years weren't enough to dull that kind of pain. Not for Ariel.

She finished her drink. "Well. I've got corrupt judges and corporate criminals to go after," she said.

Derec stood with her. "I shouldn't have put it that way."

"Your phrasing isn't the problem," she said. "Listen, we should arrange to meet more often. We need to watch out for each other, and if we're in more regular contact our history won't keep jumping up to surprise us."

Pure Ariel, killing two birds with one stone. "You're right," he said. "Let me know a good time. We can make it a regular occasion."

"I will," she said. They split up on Nova Boulevard, Derec heading back to his lab and Ariel off across the streaming lines of transports to chip away at the apparatus of corruption and indifference that stood solid as the Triangle between Nova Levis and the life its people wished for.

There was another utopian idea, thought Derec—that this place has potential. His cynicism surprised him, and he quickened his pace back to his lab, where all that mattered was the work.

# CHAPTER
# 2

A riel called R. Jennie when she got back to her office, in the late-afternoon shadow of the Judicial corner of the Triangle.

"Routine correspondence," her robot said. "Except a request from a Zev Brixa at Nucleomorph. He would like to meet with you tomorrow."

Nucleomorph. The past wouldn't leave Ariel alone today. "Regarding?"

"He declined to elaborate."

"Is he in Nova City?" Noresk and the Solarian concession were a long way off, at least a thousand kilometers. If this Brixa had come to Nova City and then asked for a meeting, either he was extremely intent on meeting her, or he had other business in the city. Either possibility raised Ariel's suspicions. His only reason for coming to Nova City would be meetings with government officials, which didn't make him trustworthy in Ariel's judgment—and why spring this request on her? Why not call ahead? She was busy.

Ariel took his contact information. It was nearly six o'clock. She had three other appointments tomorrow, each with representatives of regional authorities trying to stabilize political institutions in the outflung settlements sprouting up beyond the three large cities. This was her most important work, fostering independent decision-making in the local governing bodies of the planet. If the rule of law took hold there, the planetary government would be transformed whether it wanted to be or not.

She called Zev Brixa on the office comm. He answered immediately, a Terran of middle years in business dress. Behind him Ariel saw his office: a terminal, holo projector displaying economic data from the Fifty Worlds, native plants carefully arranged to soften the room's functional lines.

"Ambassador Burgess," he said. "Thank you for returning my call so quickly."

For the thousandth time, Ariel wished that Aurora had stripped her of the title. "What was it you wanted to meet about, Mr. Brixa?"

It came out more brusquely than she'd intended, but Brixa didn't react. "I'd prefer to discuss that in confidence, Ambassador. Could we meet tomorrow?"

She made a show of consulting her schedule even though she'd already decided where she could fit him in if that's what she chose to do. "You're a long way from Nova City, Mr. Brixa."

"I can fly in tonight," he responded. "It's important that we meet as soon as possible."

"Very well. Between prior commitments, I have exactly thirty minutes available tomorrow."

She waited for him to bluster. Instead he said, "Would you like to tell me which thirty?"

"Ten-thirty to eleven."

"I'll see you at ten-thirty, Ambassador," Brixa said, and cut the connection.

Well, that was interesting, Ariel thought. Her initial misgivings were replaced by fresh curiosity. What did a Nucleomorph executive need from her that would spur him to fly across a significant piece of the planet, overnight, so he could occupy half an hour's time with an out-of-favor official working in governmental reform?

"What do you think, Jennie?" Ariel said, even though Jennie was back at her apartment.

"Of his motives?"

"Why is he so eager?"

"Clearly you have something he wants, or he believes you can perform a service for him."

There was nothing like a robot to put the obvious in sharp focus. "Run a search on Nucleomorph, just this facility. Any criminal prosecutions pending?" It wouldn't be the first time an industrial executive had appeared from nowhere in an attempt to cajole—or bribe—Ariel. Once a vice-chair of a mining conglomerate had even claimed he could get her posted back to Aurora. She'd turned him down out of hand, and only afterward realized that she didn't want to go back to Aurora anyway. Or Earth. Her diplomatic service seemed in hindsight to be a waste of time—years spent greasing the social interactions among the monied and powerful. How long had it been since she'd done any meaningful work? Once it had consumed her life.

And even that was avoiding the real truth behind her dismissal of a chance to go home. The truth was she didn't want to return to Earth because Coren had died there.

"Ariel." R. Jennie was waiting for her.

"Go ahead."

As R. Jennie reported, public records related to Nucleomorph played across Ariel's office terminal. "They have been engaged in reconstruction and expansion of the ruined cyborg-research facility near Noresk for almost four years. Only during the past year have they begun production of organisms for the ecosystem restoration. Your colleague Derec Avery has contracted for the design of a number of species derived from native fauna. At this point, he and the Nova Levis government are Nucleomorph's only on-planet clients." The screen changed to display public legal filings. "No evidence of statutory violations exists in the records available to you."

Which, unless something was being aggressively concealed, was everything except classified military or research contracts. Ariel considered getting in touch with Masid Vorian to see if he could browse the records beyond her security clearance. She'd asked him for similar favors once or twice before, and he'd come through for her—but he too was stigmatized in the eyes of the colonial government because of his involvement with the Parapoyos debacle. Despite this, his spying experience made him too valuable to them to shunt him completely aside.

"Shall I consult the records further?" Jennie asked.

Ariel decided to wait on contacting Masid. The sudden surfacing of the cyborg lab had dredged up painful memories, leaving her ready to jump at shadows, that was all. A cyborg built from the son of one of the lab's founders had killed Coren; now the corporation taking over the remains of the lab wanted to talk to her. There was no reason to assume a relationship between those two facts. Zev Brixa had in all likelihood contacted her because of her prominent yet marginal position in the government. She could speculate about his reasons all night, and it would get her nothing but insomnia.

"I'm coming home, Jennie," she said. "I'd appreciate a drink and dinner when I get there."

When Derec got back to his lab, Elin had gone home. She came early and left early. He instructed Miles to let him know when the compiler was running again. Since he'd have to hold off on specimen testing until he had a compiler to grow specimens in, he turned to the other project under his guidance.

Mutations in the field occurred so quickly that there was often no way to track whether a tailored organism had actually had its desired effect. Derec had lost count of the times he'd engineered a vonooman to eradicate an endemic pathogen only to find that the pathogen was transformed by evolutionary pressures by the time his remedy took the field. Things moved fast on Nova Levis—part of his job was to slow them down. So while he kept the arms factory cooking in the compiler, he also tracked rates of infection, mutation, and recovery in certain sectors of the human population. He concentrated on native-born and Terran-émigré cohorts, on the theory that Spacers' immune-system enhancements would skew the results, and he'd found certain population clusters very useful in predicting what new pathogens would reach pandemic distribution.

Once he'd given Miles instructions, Derec settled in to comb the most recent results from his indicator populations. He received weekly reports from on-site personnel in Nova City, Noresk, and Stopol—personnel more qualified in epidemiology and population statistics than Derec was, which was lucky for the enterprise—and he tracked their reports through a database that monitored each subject's population of invasive microbes. Preparation of his quarterly report for Senator Lamina's ritual slaughter had put him behind schedule on generating his most recent results, and he threw himself into the task now as if fresh data would scour away the residual frustration of the meeting.

They didn't, but when Derec had the field results processed and plotted, he at least had something else to think about. The first thing he always did with a weekly report was see who had died. No clearer indicator of progress existed than mortality rates, and Derec measured himself by the rise or fall in the number of fatalities in his sample populations. It wasn't the most scientific way to approach the problem, but it was the approach he could live with.

And this week the number of deaths was sharply down. The problem was that the number of UDs was up. Sharply.

Unknown Disposition. This meant that the field operative hadn't been able to locate the subject in question. Nova Levis was a raw and shifting place; it was easy to disappear here. Still, UDs typically amounted to perhaps five percent of total samples. This week the number was seventeen percent.

*An anomaly*, Derec thought. He brought up the rates for the previous twelve weeks, and frowned at what he saw.

Five, six, three, eight, five, six, five. Seven weeks of statistically normal UDs. Then: nine, eleven, eight, twelve, fourteen. And this week, seventeen.

His first thought was that one of his field scientists was getting sloppy. Derec broke the numbers down by location, and saw that UDs in Nova City were up 220 percent, in Stopol 240 percent, and in Noresk 330 percent. He viewed the numbers cautiously. All three were up noticeably, but Noresk far more than the other two. Address first what is knowable, he thought, and punched in the code to contact Gar Purlin, his on-site supervisor in Noresk.

Purlin answered quickly, but he didn't look happy about it. "It's eight-thirty, Derec," he said. "This couldn't wait until tomorrow?"

Eight-thirty? Derec looked across the lab. Miles stood engrossed in the compiler. "I hadn't realized it was so late, Gar, sorry. This will only take a minute." Purlin waited for him to go on. "UDs are up more than three hundred percent in Noresk over the last six weeks. What's going on there?"

"Not very subtle this late, are you?" Purlin said. "I've been working like a baley trying to track these people down, let me tell you that up front."

"I'm not accusing you of anything, Gar. I'm just following up on the figures. There was a quarterly today, so I'm a couple of days behind on the field results."

Mention of the meeting softened Purlin a little. Everyone involved in the project knew the battles Derec fought to keep their work funded.

Derec watched Purlin pull up his most recent records. "Right," he said after he'd looked them over. "People are just disappearing. I hadn't noticed there was a trend." He shrugged. "You get caught up in each individual case. It's easy to lose track of the group situation."

"Any sense of where they're going?"

Purlin ran his finger down a list just out of Derec's view. "Nothing definite, at least not on first glance," he said. "I only file a UD after I've asked family and friends if they know where a subject might have gone." Derec nodded. If people moved out of target areas, they were either reassigned to another group or dropped from the study. In both cases, Derec received notification of the change in status. "I haven't been able to track any of the UDs I reported this week, but people don't always tell me when they're going to leave."

"Noresk isn't that big," Derec said. "Someone should have heard something."

Now Purlin's sour expression was back. "Two things, Derec. First: I'm not a detective. I'm a medical scientist. And second, we work for the government, remember? I don't know how things are in Nova City, but in Noresk people don't care for the Triangle." Something caught his attention offscreen. "Wait a minute. This family here. Aja Kyl, her spouse Toomi, and their children. Vois, Lek, and Shila." Derec found the names on his own report. "They said something about getting together with relatives in Nova City. I followed it up and, let's see, the relatives... there's the name. Mika Mendes. She's on the log in Nova City. I tried to contact her and got no response before the weekly was due, so I filed them all as UD."

"Okay," Derec said. "I'll get in touch with Cin and see if she's heard anything. Thanks, Gar."

Cin Boski was Derec's local field worker. She probably wouldn't be any happier to hear from him than Purlin had, especially not at almost nine o'clock. He decided to wait until morning.

Where were all of these people going, though? Most of Derec's study population lacked the resources to relocate. He flipped through the weekly from Nova City until he found Mika Mendes.

"Derec," Miles said. "The compiler is functional."

"Thanks, Miles. Get it working on whatever is next." Miles turned to the task as a skull-cracking yawn reminded Derec of the sleep he'd sacrificed over the previous week preparing his quarterly report. He was too tired to solve mysteries tonight. "Come home when you've got the next batch building," he told Miles, and then he went home.

*A wasted day,* he thought after he'd undressed and lay drifting to sleep an hour later. *More questions and no answers.*

*But at least I got to see Ariel.*

# CHAPTER

# 3

ev Brixa arrived at Ariel's office at exactly ten-thirty the next
morning, his appearance so punctual she assumed he'd stood
out in the hall waiting for his chrono to tick over. She had an
instinctive mistrust of people who choreographed their appointments,
but Brixa's demeanor put her at ease. He shook her hand with an
easy, unaffected smile that deepened creases at the corners of his
eyes. He didn't seem the typical driven mid-level corporate executive.

"Ambassador Burgess," he began, "I much appreciate your willingness to see me on such short notice."

Ariel gestured him to a chair in the corner of her office. She sat in
the facing chair rather than behind her desk. "As I said, Mr. Brixa,
I'm happy to make as much time as I can," she said.

He glanced at the wall chrono. "Down to twenty-nine minutes
already. I'd better get to business." That smile again, as if the situation
suited him perfectly. "As you have doubtless already learned, my
employer Nucleomorph recently completed the reconstruction and
expansion of the former cyborg lab near Noresk. We've invested a
great deal of both human and financial capital in the project, and

we've also made considerable effort to recruit and train local employees."

"Your Terran workforce refused to relocate?"

"Well, we've had to make a virtue of necessity in that regard, yes. But it's the right thing to do, both for the company's long-term stability on this planet and for the locals we've trained. We will only make money here if we can maintain a professional pool of locals, so in this case what's good for Nucleomorph is also good for Nova Levis."

Such disarming openness, Ariel thought. Most men in Brixa's position would have given her a prepared speech about their noble intentions. She found his candor a refreshing change from the unctuous platitudes she so often dealt with.

Unless that was a canned speech itself, she reminded herself.

"I take it you haven't come here to declare your altruism, Mr. Brixa," she said, purposely keeping a distance between them. Good-humored visitors to her office frequently hid illegal motives behind a professional smile.

"No, I haven't," he said. "I did want to set you at ease regarding our intentions, though. I'm not here to ask anything that would put you in a difficult position."

"Glad to hear it," Ariel said. "What exactly are you here to ask?"

Brixa settled back into his chair and crossed his legs. The pause before he spoke was the first ripple Ariel had seen in his calm surface. "We have some concerns about the reanimes," he said at last.

"The what?" Ariel asked, thinking she'd misheard him, but even as the words left her mouth she understood. Reanimes. What the locals had called the cyborgs discarded from Kynig Parapoyos' experiments.

Brixa watched her face, waited for her to catch up.

"I'm sorry," he said. "I realize this touches you personally, but—"

She cut him off. "You came to see me in my professional capacity, Mr. Brixa. Please leave my personal history out of this."

If only she could do the same. Already she felt herself hardening against whatever Zev Brixa was going to ask of her, just because he'd brought memories of Coren with him into the room. She didn't want to deal with cyborgs, even the pitiful rejects who gleaned their survival from the garbage piles of Noresk. A cyborg had killed Coren, and every time she heard the word she thought of him dying, his body broken and Ariel lightyears away.

She realized she'd been sitting silently for much too long. "What problems?" she asked.

"The same problems you might expect from any marginalized and impoverished sector of a society," he said, relaxing as they steered away from the shoals of Ariel's memory. "Theft, vandalism, and so on. The particular situation is exacerbated by the reanimes'—*reverence* is, I think, the best word—for the lab site. They were created there, and cast out from there, and the past few years have apparently been enough for them to construct a kind of mythology of the place. Or perhaps *sacred history* is a better characterization. I'm unfamiliar with the processes of religion. In any case, representatives of the reanimes have approached Nucleomorph demanding that the lab be preserved in its original state because they believe some sort of messiah will appear there."

"That's not likely unless you're making cyborgs again," Ariel observed.

Brixa laughed. "No, you're right about that. And it's even less likely because this messiah they await is, as near as we can discern, none other than Kynig Parapoyos."

"Didn't the cyborgs kill Parapoyos themselves?"

"According to eyewitness accounts, during the activation of the spacecraft that composed the core of the old lab, a cyborg broke Parapoyos' arms as he was about to kill a certain Masid Vorian. Then a number of other cyborgs took Parapoyos away after the first announced, 'He is ours, now. He must answer.'"

The words gave Ariel a shiver. She could only imagine what Parapoyos had gone through before he died; the cyborg Jerem Looms, who had killed Coren, had also tortured his own father for days before murdering him and trying to take over Imbitek. And Parapoyos was, in a sense, the father of them all.

She forced herself back to the topic at hand. "So what is it you need from me?"

"Well, we've come up with what will seem like a fairly radical solution," Brixa said. "It's Nucleomorph's position that the reanimes' superstitious extremism stems largely from their marginalization on this planet. We believe that a vigorous effort should be made to bring them into the economic and political institutions of Nova Levis." He paused, maybe to let Ariel appreciate Nucleomorph's magnanimity. Then he concluded, "In short, we believe the reanime population should be granted citizenship."

Ariel automatically started to remind him that robots were precluded from citizenship—then she had to remind herself that cyborgs weren't robots. They weren't bound by the Three Laws, they weren't built on the principles of positronics...as far as she knew, nothing in the constitution of Nova Levis would prevent it.

But ... "This is Nova Levis, Mr. Brixa. The people who founded this colony were members of the Church of Organic Sapiens. If you ask this question publicly, people are going to riot. I hope you have good security up at your plant."

"Our security arrangements are more than sufficient. And believe me when I say that Nucleomorph has no shortage of political will. We have made this decision, and we intend to see it through."

"To what?"

"Ideally to a vote."

At least he wasn't asking her to set up a legislative end run around Nova Levis' tattered democracy. Still, the idea shook Ariel. "I'm not sure why you've come to me with this," she said.

"You were chosen because you have a reputation for assessing issues on their merits, without the unfortunate colonial prejudices that afflict many of your colleagues," Brixa said. "We trust that you'll investigate the possibilities in an unbiased manner."

Ariel let the compliment pass. She was still trying to sort out her emotional response and differentiate it from the relevant legal and political questions.

Of course, the political question was all about emotion, wasn't it? And Brixa had brought this proposal to her for exactly that reason, because he figured that, if she could handle it, anyone could.

"You've told me a lie, Mr. Brixa," she said.

He looked surprised. "What's that?"

"You said you weren't going to ask me anything that would put me in a difficult position."

Brixa thought this over. "Well, yes. I suppose I should apologize for that little bit of rhetoric. If I'd been thinking ahead a little more, I wouldn't have put it in exactly that way." He stood. "I've used up nearly all of my thirty minutes, and I should let you get back to your work. The last thing I'd like to say is that a great deal rides on this issue. Nucleomorph is poised to do great things on Nova Levis, and it would be a shame for all of us if that work was hindered by bigotry."

"I'll look into it, Mr. Brixa," Ariel said as she showed him to the door. "If there are no explicit legal barriers, I'll sound out a few of my more discreet colleagues. Beyond that I don't know what will happen." And she didn't know why she'd even promised that much. Brixa had purely manipulated her; if she didn't pursue his request, he'd take it to someone else; in the firestorm that followed, Ariel would be left questioning her commitment to the ideals she espoused. Very deft, this maneuver, and somewhat lacking in empathy.

"Of course not." Brixa shook her hand again. "Contact me anytime," he said, and walked away down the hall.

When he'd stepped into the elevator and gone, Ariel stood for a long moment in her office doorway, feeling terribly lonely, her mind alive with questions she very much wanted not to ask.

# 4

D erec located Mika Mendes' address in the part of the city unselfconsciously called New Nova, a riot of prefabricated apartment buildings and small factories just outside the southern walls of the original city. The breaking of the blockade had brought legitimate commerce to Nova Levis, and with commerce had come widespread income disparity. A lot of people were getting wealthy because Earth and the Fifty Worlds were too preoccupied with their political strife to enforce interstellar trade laws on the Settler worlds, and Nova Levis had an outlaw heritage that drew extralegal entrepreneurs out of the proverbial woodwork. In the five years since the death of Kynig Parapoyos, illegitimate enterprise had flourished.

Freebooting trade had been good to a number of the officials imported to oversee the transition of Nova Levis from diseased backwater to functioning society, but it hadn't been as good to the people who were already there, or the baleys who showed up in greater numbers after the blockade ended. New Nova's poverty was ample evidence of the tendency of money to flow upward.

Once, Parapoyos had kept Nova City clean and healthy with his black-market pharmaceuticals; now, with the removal of his locally benevolent despotism, people here were as vulnerable to disease as anyone else. The resources to inoculate or cure all of them no longer existed.

Derec had an intuition that if Mika Mendes hadn't permanently fled her home, a communication from him would be more than enough to set her on her way. People in New Nova, like those in Noresk, didn't appreciate government workers. So he mapped the address, put Miles to work on a regression analysis of the genome of a biting fly native to the marshes around Stopol, left Elin to her work on a viral antidote to a pervasive fungal infection, and went to New Nova himself.

Armed sentries no longer guarded the gates between the original settlement and New Nova, but Derek was keenly aware as he passed through the southern gate that most of the people on the outside were still barred from coming in. Money, in his experience, was a much more effective barrier than violence. Nova City was clean and orderly, its inhabitants well-dressed and healthy; New Nova looked and smelled like a Terran slum from the twenty-second century. What struck Derec as much as anything else was the absence of robots. People here did for themselves all of the things he expected Miles to take care of: they cooked their own meals, made their own repairs of vehicles and dwellings, cleaned their own messes. Or didn't, Derec amended, stepping around a mound of what looked like construction debris liberally topped with household refuse. Rusted metal, broken glass, fly-buzzing masses of rotting food, empty aerosols. He felt like he'd stepped back in time. Once this had been the day-to-day existence of most of the human race. Now it was his work and Ariel's to lift New Nova and places like it out of their desperation. Five years had taken Derec a long way from the frontiers of positronics.

He found the address halfway down a dead-end street of four-story apartment buildings. All were hastily constructed, cracks already showing in foundations and around doorways, and the interiors were shabby and poorly lit. Mika Mendes lived (or so he hoped) on the third floor, number 64, at the end of a long and dusty hall.

Derec knew what she looked like, and the woman who answered his knock wasn't her. "Who are you?" she asked him, opening the door only wide enough to get a look at her unwelcome visitor.

"My name is Derec Avery," Derec said. "I'm looking for a Mika Mendes, who I believe lives here?" He turned it into a question, hoping to get her talking.

"Not anymore, she doesn't," the woman said through the crack. All he could see of her was a narrowed brown eye and the dark hair that curled over her forehead.

"I'm a public health worker, ma'am," Derec said. "Do you know where I can find her?"

"No. She's gone, and I live here now."

"And your name is...?"

She shut the door, and as Derec heard the scrape of the lock turning he did something that shocked him. Leading with his shoulder, he bulled into the door and forced his way into the apartment.

The woman scrambled away from him across the apartment's living room into the kitchen, where she spilled dirty dishes onto the floor, grabbing for a knife. "Get out!" she screamed at him. "It's my place now, and Vilger will be back any time! You don't want to be here when he comes back!"

Knowing he'd made a mess of the situation, Derec stayed by the door, hands away from his sides. The woman found the knife and brandished it at him.

"I'm not armed, and I don't mean you any harm," he said.

"Out!" She stabbed the knife in his direction but didn't come toward him.

Derec saw a terminal in the living room wall. "You're welcome to confirm my identity," he said, pointing at it. "I'll stay right here."

"I don't want you to stay right there," she snapped. "I want you out. Vilger's coming right back."

Briefly, Derec wondered what would happen if this Vilger did come back. He wouldn't be much good to anyone in a hospital, and even though the woman in Mika Mendes' apartment had the worn look of someone fighting a long-term illness, she looked frightened enough to come at him out of sheer adrenalin.

"I'm a public health worker," he repeated. "Mika Mendes was part of a health study, and I'm concerned that we haven't been able to contact her."

"You can't contact her because she's gone," the woman said. "I don't know where, and I don't care. Now get out."

Her tone was getting less hostile. Derec risked another question. "All right," he said. "If you don't know where she is, do you know if she had relatives visiting before she left?"

There was a pause. "Was she sick?" the woman asked. She looked around the apartment as if afraid disease might be lingering in the corners.

"Yes, she was. Not as bad as a lot of the people I work with, but she was sick. We were working on a cure."

"Am I going to get it?"

You might already have it, Derec thought. Or more properly them; most of his study subjects had more than one infection. That was the last thing this woman needed to hear, though. "I don't know," he said. "Part of what we're studying is transmission vectors."

"She's probably dead," the woman said.

"Did she tell you she was part of a study?"

"She didn't have to. The woman comes to my cousin Ike, too."

Good. She was starting to believe him. If she would just put down the knife, Derec thought he'd be able to relax. "Did you live in this building before Mika Mendes left?" he asked.

"I got every right to take the place now that she's gone," the woman said. "Me and Vilger were stacked like crates in the other place, and I don't like his mother."

"That's fine with me," Derec said. "I'm not here to evict you. I just need to know what happened to Mika."

"She left last week. Her cousins showed up, and the next morning they were all gone. I waited a whole day, and when none of them came back I got Vilger to move our stuff over here. That's fair." The woman appeared to consider something. She put the knife back on the kitchen counter. "Can you get me in the study?"

"I can have someone come and talk to you." Derec weighed the question, and decided he couldn't in good faith promise her anything else. "Her name will be Cin Boski. She'll examine you and see how you fit in with what we're working on. I'll need your name, though, so Cin can go over your records before the visit."

"My name's Lianor Phelp," the woman said, "but you won't find any records."

A baley, squatting in the apartment of a woman who had in all likelihood gone off to die with her relatives. Just thinking of it made Derec tired.

"Lianor, I need you to tell me what you know about Mika Mendes," he said. "You may be right that she's dead, but if she's still alive, I need to find her."

"If you get me in your study, I'll tell you," Lianor said.

"I'll have Cin come talk to you," Derec said, and waited, hoping it would be enough.

"Vilger and I lived next door," Lianor began after a moment. "The night before Mika left, some people came to visit her. Walls are thin here, and from what I heard I figured they were family. I tried not to listen—I'm no gossip—but they argued some, and the next morning they were all gone."

"Did you hear what they argued about?" Derec prompted.

Something came over Lianor's face then, the shadow of someone wanting to unburden herself of a troubling secret. But she mastered it. "I told you, I'm not a gossip," she said. "I know they were arguing from the noise, but I didn't listen."

She straightened and walked to where he stood inside the door. "They're gone, Derec Avery. You did say that was your name, right?"

Derec nodded.

"They're gone," Lianor repeated, "and maybe you should go, too. Go on back inside."

*Inside?* Derec wondered. *We* are *inside.* Then, as she was shutting the door behind him, he realized she'd meant back inside the walls. Back into the safely ignorant other world inside the walls of Nova City.

Lianor Phelp's words stayed with Derec, dogging him through his walk back along the unfamiliar streets of New Nova to the southern gate of the old city. He felt as if an invisible door was sliding down behind him, shutting out the people he was supposed to be helping. At the lab, he watched Elin and Miles working and realized he wasn't sure how to proceed. Indecision was strange to Derec. Normally he broke down his options and chose one with only enough hesitation to double-check his reasoning; now he couldn't resolve whether he should try to find Mika Mendes and the Kyl family in Noresk, write them off as just another group of UDs, talk to Lianor Phelp again, or involve an investigator.

And why was he thinking that? Something about Lianor's face, about the way a trace of fear had shown through the defensiveness and fear. Derec felt certain that she wasn't afraid of him, or worried that the Kyls and Mendes were dead. No, she was afraid of something she knew, and the only thing Derec could think of that she might know was where the Kyls .iad really gone. Why wouldn't she want him to know that?

"Derec," Miles said. "I have completed the regression analysis."

"And?"

"Segments of the fly's genome match a virus that first appeared in Noresk eleven years ago."

Of course, Derec thought. Noresk. Kynig Parapoyos had done his work much too well. The genome of a fly, two thousand kilometers from Noresk, still bore traces of his legacy. "How many generations?" he asked.

"Several hundred. I am unable to be anymore specific without losing statistical confidence."

And each of those hundreds of mutations had left behind an unchanged part of the population that went off on another evolutionary tangent. The vast majority of those tangents came to quick dead ends, but some went on, and in the case of this fly converged with their distant relatives. People who carried certain receptors altered by another version of the virus contracted an autoimmune disease when bitten by the fly—apparently the gene sequence in the fly activated the dormant virus. It was a recombinant plague, possibly only if the virus had somehow been programmed to control its own evolution for the particular purpose of reconstituting itself in different hosts. Derec had been working to isolate this virus and its history for three years. Now he had it, and if he could recover the programming in the initial genome he could build a phage to disrupt that programming and consign the virus to evolutionary oblivion. Isolating the trigger in the fly meant they could now see how it combined with the human-hosted material, and working backward from there Derec hoped to eliminate the entire strain.

"Okay," he said. "Good work. Elin, you start combing the records for other matches of the trigger sequence. Miles, start putting together some new instructions for the fly."

"I'm almost done with the next generation of the cow for Nucleomorph, Derec," Elin said. "Shouldn't we get that up and running?"

"This fly kills two hundred people every year in Stopol," Derec said.

"If I can get this cow out there, it might save a lot more than that," Elin responded, keeping her voice even, and she was right, but at that particular moment Derec needed a certain victory.

"The sooner you get the other strings identified in this virus, the sooner your cow goes into service, Elin. I don't want to explain 'might' to people dying in Stopol."

This was unfair, and Derec knew it, and so did Elin. She turned her back on him and went to work.

Miles was already engaged in counterprogramming the fly. Derec watched them for a long moment, torn between elation at the fly breakthrough and frustration that he wasn't better at working with Elin, with residual disquiet about Lianor Phelp behind it all. He could do something about that, but it wasn't something he wanted to do. How many people had died the last time Derec had stepped outside his role and investigated a crime?

On the other hand, what if he could do something to help the Kyls, and Mika Mendes?

That decided it. Leaving Elin and Miles to their work, Derec went home to call Ariel.

# CHAPTER

# 5

S he wasn't at her office, and it took her three hours to return the message Derec left with R. Jennie. Ariel looked preoccupied when she called, and she only snapped into focus when Derec asked her if she knew how to get in touch with Masid Vorian.

"Why—" she started to ask, and then changed her mind. "You could look him up."

Derec waited.

"I'm at the Triangle," Ariel said after a pause. "Why don't we meet where we talked yesterday?"

He left immediately. She was waiting for him when he walked into Kamil's, in the back of the seating area where she couldn't be seen from the street. Derec had a bad feeling even before he'd gotten a good look at her, and that first look did nothing to lessen his apprehension. There was tension in her face, and maybe even a little fear; her eyes darted around with uncharacteristic nervousness.

He sat facing her. "Are you all right?"

"Why did you ask me about Masid Vorian?"

"He has some experience with Noresk, and I know he's in the same kind of liaison agreement as you are. I suppose he was the first person I thought of."

"He was a spy," Ariel said flatly. "What do you need a spy for?"

"Ariel. Why the interrogation?"

Surprised, she sat back. "I—you're right. Yesterday and today have been unusual, and I'm edgy. Masid's name came up in a meeting yesterday, and..." She trailed off. "There have been too many coincidences."

Derec put his own questions on hold for the moment. "All right. Start with the first one."

"The first one," she said, "is Nucleomorph."

She recounted the details of her meeting with Zev Brixa and her preliminary research into the question of reanime citizenship. "There's no legal prohibition, but that's only because it's never been considered And as soon as the question becomes public, there's going to be a political uproar. My guess is that the Terran members of the Senate will be against it because the cyborgs to them are too much like robots. The Spacers will fight it because if cyborgs gain citizenship it will raise too many questions about the human-machine boundary. And the natives will fight it because most of them settled under terms of the original lease between Solaria and the Church of Organic Sapiens. They're all Managins, or were."

"Not all of them," Derec said. "A lot of people have come here since that lease expired. They can't all be anti-robot zealots. Nobody screens baleys."

"The colony is too young to have gotten that far from its founding ideal. At heart, your average citizen of Nova Levis is working from a Managin worldview. And even without that, at heart they're all basically Terran—even though most of them hate Earth and everything they think it stands for. Terrans don't like robots."

Ariel petered out, and Derec considered the situation. She'd danced carefully around one question, though. "How do you feel about it?"

"Terrified. Disgusted. Outraged. But I'm a Spacer, and upbringing dies hard. Then there's Coren." She let that hang between them before adding, "All of those are personal feelings completely apart from, and irrelevant to, the question of what's right." Another pause. "If it wasn't for Bogard, I'd be much more certain about this."

Bogard. Derec's finest creation, the robot designed to have unprecedented latitude in analysis and interpretation of the Three Laws, who had saved lives, perhaps cost others, and in the end killed the cyborg Tro Aspil and disappeared. Not a day went by without Derec wondering what had become of Bogard, and wondering too if maybe he never should have taken the liberties he had with the Three Laws.

"Bogard did raise more questions than he answered," Derec said. He hoped Ariel wouldn't dredge up their long disagreement over his testing the boundaries of the Three Laws. They had argued about it—and bitterly—and if Derec was honest with himself he had to admit that he'd been at least as dogmatic as she had. One casualty of the debate was the intimacy they had once shared.

"I'm in a very delicate position," Ariel said. "Zev Brixa's ingratiating and pleasant, but the more I think about our conversation the more certain I am that Nucleomorph is going to go ahead with this no matter what I do."

"That makes it easy for you, doesn't it? You can just tell him you don't want to involve yourself, and let Brixa go to someone else."

She considered. "That's where it gets difficult. In my professional capacity, it's incumbent upon me to put aside personal reactions, and I think I can do that with respect to the fundamental question. The more important thing, though, is another question: Would this be good for Nova Levis? If it happened, would we be even more isolated? Ideals are only useful until they get in the way of actually helping people. And behind all that is the real question: What do we owe the reanimes, Derec? Even Jerem Looms once was human. What happened to them isn't their fault. Once they were us. Has what they suffered made them less than human? What do we owe them?"

She asked the question as if Derec might have a special insight.

Bogard again. Some of life's actions had seemingly infinite consequences.

"I don't know," he said. "It's a question that needs some consideration."

Ariel smiled. *"There's* an understatement. All right. If you're not going to solve my problems, you can at least tell me yours."

Derec wasn't entirely ready to leave the Nucleomorph question where it was, especially not when he was about to do so much business with them. He would be putting his project's success in their hands; Miles and Elin couldn't mass-produce vertebrate life. Ariel didn't seem interested in going any further with it, though.

"Too many of my study population are disappearing," he said. "Over the last month I've lost contact with almost twenty percent of them. I started looking into it, and my field worker in Noresk gave me a name to check here—Mika Mendes. I went to see her, and she's gone, too. There's a squatter in her apartment. A scared squatter."

"Scared of what?"

"That's what I'm trying to figure out. I think she knew what happened to Mendes, and to the family who came to visit her, but for some reason she didn't want me to know."

"A whole family disappeared?"

Derec had brought a copy of the Kyl file with him in the hope that Ariel would put him in touch with Masid. He passed it across the table and Ariel looked through it, lingering over the images.

"Two of the children were too sick to travel. I wasn't expecting them to live."

"Maybe they took the kids somewhere to die," Ariel said. "Is there a religious background?"

"There might be, but why would that make the squatter afraid to tell me what happened?" Derec started to get the feeling that Ariel might be partly right. "Maybe they did take those children somewhere, but I don't think it was to let them die."

He turned the idea over in his mind, letting it develop. Before the blockade collapsed, the two most lucrative industries on Nova Levis had been infecting people with new microbes and curing them. How much of that trade still went on?

"Ariel," Derec said. "Masid Vorian infiltrated a drug gang to get close to Parapoyos, didn't he?"

"That's not why he was here, but yes, he did." She sipped her drink. "Do you think the Kyls went looking for a cure they didn't think you could give them?"

"If something illegal is going on, that would explain why the squatter in the Mendes apartment didn't want to talk to me."

"This is Nova Levis, Derec. Something illegal is always going on."

This was true, but at that moment Derec had no interest at all in legal issues. If there was someone out there who could cure people he couldn't, Derec wanted to know about it. The whole question lay well beyond the boundaries of his job description, but so did forcing his way into apartments in New Nova. He wasn't restoring the ecology of Nova Levis for the sake of its struggling native organisms. He was trying to keep people alive.

"Do you remember the drug trader's name? The one Vorian was working with?"

Ariel shook her head. "No. But you should talk to Masid. When you do, let him know that I need to ask him something, too, but Nucleomorph can wait." She finished her drink. "I'm supposed to meet him in twenty minutes. You go ahead, and I'll let him know to expect you instead."

Masid Vorian, like Ariel and Derec, had been relegated to office space outside of the Triangle. The colonial administration was rigorous to the point of fanaticism in its sidelining of people who had been working on the planet while Parapoyos still held sway. Even Derec and Ariel, who had arrived shortly after the lifting of the blockade, were considered suspicious because they'd been pursuing cyborgs at the time and were thus tied to events on Nova Levis. Senator Lamina and her colleagues were determined not to do more than tolerate anyone tainted by Nova Levis' sordid recent past, and that toleration would evaporate as soon as Lamina thought she could fire them without offworld repercussions. Masid appeared to be anticipating this; the plaque on his door read VORIAN CONSULTANCY AND INVESTIGATION. He was already sidling into private practice.

Derec knocked and entered to Masid coming toward the door. He was a compact, dark-haired man with the kind of nondescript face and bearing that had always been the spy's chief asset.

"Mr. Avery," he said. "Ambassador Burgess informed me that she's now scheduling my appointments."

Derec laughed and they shook hands. "Ariel has a way of getting what she wants."

"So what can I do for you?"

They sat, Masid at his desk and Derec in a leather chair that seemed out of place in the room. He wondered where Masid had gotten it. "I'm working on invasive-disease eradication and ecosystem restoration," he said. "Part of the project involves tracking certain populations to see if and how well our efforts are succeeding. Over the past few weeks, a large number of people in these populations have disappeared. Some of them were too ill to travel except in the case of a dire emergency, and it occurred to me that they might be looking for a cure that the project—that I haven't been able to provide."

"You're looking for Filoo," Masid said.

His certainty stopped Derec in the middle of what he'd thought would be a lengthy explanation. "Well," he said. "I don't know if it's specifically him."

"If it's anyone, it's Filoo," Masid said. "He was running things for Parapoyos, and unless someone killed him he's still running things."

"Where would he get the, ah—"

"Product? Anyone with a sequencer and a compiler and a need for some quiet money. I don't keep track of these things anymore, Mr. Avery. The man's name was Filoo, and he was as dangerous and lacking in scruples as anyone I've ever met except when it came to his loyalty toward Kynig Parapoyos. We're all lucky his ambition doesn't match his cold-bloodedness. If, that is, he's still alive."

Something changed in Masid's face, as if in raising the possibility that this Filoo was dead he had reminded himself of other deaths. A spy with a conscience, Derec thought. Maybe that's why he's no longer a spy and still on Nova Levis.

*If* he was no longer a spy. How could you tell?

"Thank you, Mr. Vorian," Derec said. "Do you want me to let you know what I find out?"

A knowing smile quirked at the corner of Vorian's mouth. "If you stir Filoo up, I'm guessing I'll hear about it," he said.

A riel spent the afternoon laying the groundwork for an ethics indictment against a magistrate in Stopol. When she got to the point where she could safely delegate the rest of the preparation to the district office there, she took a long walk through the city, watching the people and wondering how the brain behind each face would react to the proposition that cyborgs should be able to vote. If she became the standard-bearer for the question, she would absorb all of the superstitious fear the citizens of Nova Levis could muster. It would be the end of her political career, that much was certain; the Spacer bloc in the Senate was looking for an excuse to be rid of her.

What a useless irony if she were to do all this in the service of a cause that repelled her.

And how she was repelled by the idea. The night before, she'd dreamed of going to vote, and being the only human in a room full of cyborgs. All of them were Jerem Looms. Ariel hoped the dream was a symptom of her subconscious working through the problem and overcoming her emotional reaction. Zev Brixa had maneuvered her into a position that would require all of her faculties.

She couldn't shake the intuition that he knew more about her than he'd let on in their brief meeting. A corporation the size of Nucleomorph did nothing by accident; he might well have burrowed through any number of records of her behavior in the events following the Union Station massacre. She had certainly burned her share of bridges at that time, for what she considered unimpeachable reasons. No doubt there were profiles of her archived in a database somewhere, and no doubt they said that she pursued what she believed was right without regard for the consequences. Perhaps this was even characterized as a kind of behavioral deviancy. In any case, it was true—if Ariel did not explore the question and honestly determine its merits, she would spend years questioning her motivations. Surely Brixa had chosen her because of this quality.

*Well,* she thought. *Now that you've gone down the paranoid avenue, stop and think rationally.*

The rational assessment of the situation was frustratingly similar to her suspicious initial reaction. Brixa would know what she had done, and would know of her tense relationship with the colonial government of Nova Levis. Who better to take up an unpopular cause? What better test of the proposition's prospects than to bring it to an official who had been permanently scarred by a cyborg's actions? She was acting as the reagent in a kind of acid test, and Brixa was running the laboratory.

Ariel had found her way to a park south of the Triangle. She watched children play an unfamiliar game. Something involving a yellow pennant, and two bases made of shoes, and a great deal of running and noise. What stories did their parents tell them of the reanimes that skulked at the edges of their tenuous civilization? Was Ariel going to be the one to bring their boogeymen into their waking lives?

*I have to at least ask,* she thought. *I won't be able to live with myself if I don't.*

So the gentle probing went on. Ariel went home and asked R. Jennie for an opinion.

"I have no context for this, Ariel," Jennie said. "The question is unprecedented."

"That's why I'm asking you, Jennie. I need a philosophical reaction."

"Philosophy is not part of my programming."

"Just answer the question," Ariel snapped. Could no being, organic or machine, give her a straight answer?

R. Jennie took some time to compose a response. "My concept of citizenship is inextricably bound to my Three Laws programming," it said. "Are cyborgs considered human?"

*No,* Ariel thought. *That far I will not go.*

"If not," R. Jennie went on, "it would be impossible for me to accord a cyborg the same status as a human being."

Ariel forced herself to ask a question that sounded absurd even as she said it. "What if I told you cyborgs *should* be considered human?"

Again, R. Jennie was silent. "I am not sure a single opinion would be definitive," it said at last.

Truer words were never spoken.

It was evening. The colors of sunset spilled through the window onto Ariel's couch. The strip of restaurants facing the Triangle would be throbbing with politicians and their aides at this time of day. Ariel got up and walked out the door to try her question on those few among them she felt she might be able to trust.

She was lucky. When she walked into Kamil's, Hodder Feng sat slouching over a tall glass of something amber and potent. Ariel ordered a glass of wine and carried it to his table.

Feng looked up at her when she sat across from him. "I'm trying not to begrudge you your survival," he said. The cadence of his speech pegged him as under the influence, if not exactly intoxicated.

"I'm sorry, Hodder," Ariel said. "It could have been any of us."

"Not you, Ambassador." Feng tried without much success to hide his bitterness. "A title still counts for something on Nova Levis."

*So should I shut myself down because Eza Lamina is still a little bit afraid of me?* Ariel wondered.

"Hodder," she said. "I need to ask you something in confidence."

"No offers of employment, please. I am leaving this city as soon as I get drunk enough to be uncivil to someone prominent."

"Well, then, I'll ask you my other question," Ariel said, and Feng gave her a grudging smile.

"All right." He drank. "I'm just about ready to answer any question."

*That's what you think,* Ariel thought. But she couldn't resist the opening.

"What would you do if someone suggested to you that cyborgs should be granted citizenship?" she asked, and waited for the explosion.

"Laugh," he said without hesitation. "I came here nineteen years ago, and I'm not a Managin anymore, but I know a dumb question when I hear one. You think anyone in the Senate would let that happen? Please, Ariel. I have liquor to distract me from my misery. I don't need to indulge in moonbeams."

*Especially not when yours are all blotted out by the shadow of Senator Lamina,* Ariel thought. He was due a little self-pity. He'd devoted three years of his life to his project to create working relationships between the staggering Nova Levis educational system and the offplanet conglomerates that had begun to open after Liberation. Hodder Feng was personally responsible for much of the economic growth of the planet, and he'd never be credited for it because nobody noticed the people who actually created skilled workers. Lamina would probably redirect the pittance she'd allowed Hodder to a general entertainment fund for touring executives. In public she argued that people had to be wooed to come to Nova Levis, and that if she could do that, the jobs would follow by themselves. Hodder Feng, though, knew that one of the questions these junketing magnates always asked was *If I do open up here, who's going to work for me? You think I can get people to come here from Earth or Aurora?*

Of course not. The successful businesses that operated on the bright side of the law drew heavily on a labor pool that Feng had created. Nucleomorph included.

And that mental addendum snapped her back into focus. Ariel watched Feng drink and felt an enormous sympathy for him. She liked this man, with his workman's clothes and thick hands. He was a baley who had tried to make a difference, tried to force his way into a political system that had followed him from Earth, and now he was middle-aged and starting over. For a moment, Ariel allowed herself to feel a kinship with him, but quickly she realized it was false. If the Nova Levis government defunded her, she'd land on her feet. She knew too many people, she'd done too many favors. The uncertainty that faced Hodder Feng was unlike anything Ariel had ever known, or ever would.

So she ordered a drink, and then another, and she kept him company. It was the least she could do. And when she'd drunk enough to be less discreet, she asked him about cyborgs again.

He was farther down the road to intoxication than Ariel was, but his bedrock response was largely the same as it had been when she'd first blurted out the question after walking in. "This planet is barely feeding itself, Ariel," Hodder said. "You think anyone has the time or energy to hold a constitutional convention? I thought I was a dreamer."

"You're misunderstanding me. I don't know if it's a good idea or not." Ariel had already told him this twice, but this was the price of choosing a miserable idealist for a sounding board. Add drunk to the list of characteristics, and it was a wonder he heard anything she said.

That's why she'd chosen Hodder, though, or so Ariel told herself. He was a listener, quiet in meetings, deferential to people clearly competent in areas outside his own expertise. To his immense credit, he hadn't once steered the conversation to his own misfortune. She tried again. "Hodder, what if there didn't have to be a constitutional issue? Are cyborgs robots?"

"You tell me."

"They aren't. Every one I've seen or heard of was born human and augmented later," Ariel said. Strange choice of words, *augmented*; it glossed over the fact that the augmentation had robbed subjects like Jerem Looms and Tro Aspil of any quality that might have been called human. In making a cyborg, Kynig Parapoyos' laboratory destroyed a human being.

But they were not robots. What they were was the incarnation of the fear that had driven the creation of the Three Laws in the first place. The supreme technological nightmare of human civilization. How could any human think rationally about putting cyborgs on an equal footing with humankind?

This was the kind of question that had interested Ariel in diplomacy to begin with, because one possible answer was that they were human. Terribly damaged, no doubt, but human. She asked herself again whether they could be blamed for what had been done to them. Orphans, doomed by incurable disease, psychologically and emotionally maimed by the process of saving them—a process itself corrupted by Parapoyos, made into an assembly line to create assassins—what rational human could blame a child? None of it was of their own making.

Ariel realized she was speaking aloud, realized at the same time that she'd drunk more than she meant to and that a third person had joined her and Hodder Feng. She stopped talking.

The newcomer was Vilios Kalienin. It could only have been worse if Eza Lamina herself had appeared in the midst of Ariel's monologue. And Kalienin was more unfortunate in one particularly relevant regard: He was one of many Terran politicians on Nova Levis known to have anti-robot sympathies. Ariel might as well have broadcast her thoughts on subetheric.

She shifted instinctively into a damage-control footing. "That's one perspective, in any case. One that's sure to be voiced loudly if this ever becomes a public debate."

That last was directed at Kalienin. He picked up his cue. "A fascinating case it is, Ambassador, if a little contrarian. Of course we're all off the record here."

Ariel believed him not at all. He was a policy advisor to the Terran legislative contingent on Nova Levis; if he didn't offer a verbatim account of Ariel's words to their caucus meeting in the next twenty-four hours, she would take up religion. Part of her brain automatically delegated itself the task of countering whatever he would suggest the Terran caucus leak to their colleagues.

"How would this happen, Ambassador?" Kalienin asked her. "Assuming there's no relevant legal question, how would a proposal so radical get a fair hearing given what's happened with the cyborgs we know about? And on Nova Levis, to boot. I'm sure I don't have to remind you of this colony's origin."

*Certainly, Vilios,* Ariel thought. *I will by all means offer you the strategy I have neither committed to nor yet invented.*

"I have no way of knowing whether it will ever become a proposal," she said. "A representative of a prominent stakeholder in the future of this planet asked me to get a sense of how the idea might be received. That's all."

"You know how it would be received," Hodder said. "People would burn the cyborg squatters out of their huts and then start smashing robots for good measure."

He was probably right, but having committed herself to the contrarian perspective, Ariel was determined to see it through. "This is where leadership comes in. It is one job of government to prevent people from doing what is manifestly wrong even if that's what most of them want to do."

"How ironies do abound tonight," Kalienin said. He toyed with his glass, but he had yet to taste it as far as Ariel had seen. Correct appearance was a much more important pleasure to Vilios Kalienin than the fleeting sensation of drunkenness could ever be.

"Don't keep us waiting, Vilios," said Hodder.

"Well, Jonis Taprin said something very similar about leadership when the Terran media were busy attacking him for the latest round of riots," Kalienin said. He was enjoying himself a great deal. "That's one irony, that Ariel Burgess and Jonis Taprin agreed on anything."

Ariel knew then that she was in for a storm. Kalienin certainly knew that she and Taprin had been lovers once, and that his latter-day Managin posturing had driven the final wedge between them. She agreed on nothing with Taprin, but Kalienin would certainly make it appear as if "her" proposal was as radical and unreasonable as the Spacers made Taprin's anti-robot platform out to be.

"And then there's the fact that we're sitting here talking about this on the night that Jonis Taprin was murdered," Kalienin said.

In the shocked silence that followed his words, Ariel could see the deep satisfaction he took at being the one to tell her.

# CHAPTER

# 7

**M**iles woke Derec out of a dream, forgotten even as Derec sat up in bed and said, "What?"

"There is a priority communication from Kopernik Station, Derec," Miles said. "I suggested a call during standard working hours, but the caller insisted she speak to you immediately."

Even though he didn't want to know, Derec looked at the bedside chrono. It was 1:17. He'd been asleep for less than three hours. What would anyone at Kopernik Station want so urgently?

"Tell her I'm coming," Derec said. He went into the bathroom, splashed water on his face, and sat at his home terminal. He took the call as video, not feeling up to full holopresence with the dream he couldn't remember still ricocheting around his brain.

A Terran woman, red-haired and weary, appeared on his terminal screen. "Mister Avery," she said, "I'm Shara Limke, operations director of Kopernik Station. My apologies for badgering your robot, but it is critically important that we speak."

"Miles will get over it, Director, and we're speaking," Derec said. "What is it you need?"

She gave a slight smile, as if the answer to the question might

46

surprise Derec. "I need a great many things right now, Mr. Avery. Foremost among them is to keep Kopernik operating, and that's why I've contacted you." When Derec made no answer to this, she went on. "I'll be succinct. Jonis Taprin was murdered six hours ago."

Five years fell away from Derec. He was back in Washington, where Bogard had failed to keep Clar Eliton alive (except he hadn't, which in the end had proved even worse). There was only one reason why anyone would track him down on Nova Levis, why anyone would want to drag him back into the life he'd only recently realized he didn't miss. He felt a deep sense of mourning, of regret for choices wrongly made, even as he determined to face the consequences of his work.

"Let me guess," Derec said. "Do you suspect Bogard?"

He'd asked the question as a way to get control, and it worked beautifully. Shara Limke's eyes widened and her mouth opened, but no words came out. She closed her mouth, opened it again, and at last said, "Is that possible?"

"It's been five years since I saw Bogard, Director, and longer than that since I was certain what he was capable of. Do you have an image?"

Her silence told him that the question meant something different to her than it did to him. "That's part of what I'm calling you about."

"If Bogard killed Jonis Taprin, and you apprehended or destroyed it afterward, I can probably help reconstruct its motives if its positronic matrix isn't too badly damaged. If not, I'm not sure what I have to offer you."

Derec felt no regret that Jonis Taprin was dead. The man had become a reactionary demagogue, and humanity was better off without him. Derec's only sorrow—apart from a peripheral worry about how Ariel would take the news—lay in the acknowledgment that he had created a robot that could kill. That had never been his goal. His vision for Bogard encompassed a new age in the relationship between human and machine, in which the flexibility Derec built into Bogard's interpretation of the Three Laws heralded the dawn of a time when robots would enforce what was best in human nature. Now as he confronted his failure, Derec recognized his ambition for the utopian dream it had been.

"The robot we have is a standard production model," Limke said. "Your Bogard was a custom design, wasn't it?"

"Yes." He'd built every circuit himself, had even overseen the design of Bogard's amalloy chassis.

"Well, Mr. Avery," Limke said, "I have a dead politician and a robot apparently responsible, and I'm sure you'll understand why circumstances made me think of you. I realize it's late there, but have you seen any news reports from Terra?"

Derec had disabled all of the default links to commercial subetheric channels in his lab. He cared little for the events of the worlds beyond Nova Levis. There were more important things to do than observe politics from lightyears away.

"I concern myself primarily with my work here, Director," he said. "Is there something you need to tell me?"

"You have my contact information, Mr. Avery. I can't compel you to do this, but it would be a great service if you could catch up on the news and get back in touch with me as soon as possible. I think once you've seen what I'm talking about, you'll understand my imposition."

"Then tell me."

"You can get up to speed much faster from the subetheric," Limke said. "Promise me, Mr. Avery. Will you at least get in touch with me once you've scanned the news?"

That was easy enough. "Give me an hour, Director," Derec said. "I'll contact you, and then with any luck I can get back to my work here."

Her face was grim. "That would be lucky indeed. I look forward to your call, Mr. Avery."

She terminated the call. Derec stared at the blank screen until he realized he was about to fall asleep again. If Bogard wasn't involved, he'd burned a great deal of emotional capital to no end, and all he wanted was to go to sleep and awaken to a less complicated world.

Derec asked Miles for coffee, and when it came he opened up the datum to the flood of news and events beyond Nova Levis.

Jonis Taprin's death, six hours gone by, had already become a media gateway to coverage of anti-robot and anti-Spacer riots on Earth. In Jakarta, a mob had murdered eleven Solarians working for TranPos Research; in Tulsa, the building housing the positronic theory department had been burned and several of the faculty beaten with the limbs of destroyed robots. The Sapiens church was out in force, rallying Managin mobs and demanding a complete severance of Earth-Spacer relations along with a planet-wide ban on positronic technology. Derec passed all this by with a glance, and examined the archived biographies of the murdered politician.

Taprin was forty-nine years old at the time of his death, a lifetime (if originally clandestine) member of the Church of Organic Sapiens who had left private industry to enter politics shortly after the Spacer riots twenty years before. It didn't surprise Derec to see that Taprin had once worked for the Managin-headed DyNan Manual Industries; no tendril of superficial coincidence raised his eyebrow any longer. The fact that Taprin had worked with and for Rega Looms made at least as much sense as anything else. He only wondered why he hadn't known this before. At times like this it seemed to Derec that of all the billions of humans in the colonized universe, only a few hundred exercised the power to direct the course of civilization. A string pulled seemingly at random tugged on exactly the knot you might have predicted, if you'd been through what Derec had. He hated this knowledge, hated the cynicism his experience had bred, hated Shara Limke for drawing him back into the vortex of Terran-Spacer conflict. Still, he read on.

In the hours following Taprin's murder, the Terran Bureau of Investigation had quarantined Kopernik, putting all freight traffic under embargo, preventing any travel from Earth via the station to the Spacer worlds, and sharply restricting passage of Spacer ships using Kopernik as a way station on their way to Settled worlds. Derec noted with passing interest that ships to the Settled worlds seemed to be getting through. For a change, political tension was affecting the Fifty Worlds more than the struggling colonies. He filed it away and read on.

Mainstream political opinion on Earth, at least as represented in the channels Derec browsed, viewed Taprin's murder as a rationale to make a final break with the Spacers and their culture of reliance on robots. Attendance at Sapiens church events was exploding as it was leaked that a robot had killed Jonis Taprin.

Taprin had gone to Kopernik to give a speech that under other circumstances would have been recorded only for archival purposes. Following his standard line, he called for "a new independence" of Earth from what he termed "the debased, machine-dependent lifestyle" represented by the Spacer worlds. He called into question the Spacers' humanity, advocated trade sanctions against any world that "toes the Spacer line of subservience to the machine," and leavened his adversarial paranoia with a call for a new age in human culture, self-reliant and liberated from what he liked to call "this debased, inhuman passion for all that is machine instead of flesh, positronic instead of organic, circuits instead of the neurons that are humankind's evolutionary birthright." According to most accounts, Taprin had chosen Kopernik as the site of his speech because it was the fulcrum in Earth-Spacer commerce. By going to the jumping-off point between the cradle of humanity and the worlds on which humans had taken their first exploratory steps, Taprin focused Terran fear and fury in a way that could bear immediate and tangible economic fruit. Moment polls showed a majority of the Terran electorate at least willing to consider his position, with a sizable plurality joining him in his separationist advocacy.

Then the murder. After presiding over a press conference that most of the Spacer services called "fawning," Taprin had retired to his room. An hour later, his security personnel had found his body after his staff in an adjacent room had heard cries. A politician like Jonis Taprin drew assassination threats as part of his daily routine, but something out of the ordinary had occurred, or so Derec inferred from the sudden circumspection of the media accounts. They all mentioned a robot, but none of the reputable nets lodged a definitive claim that the robot had killed him—because of course that was impossible.

Only Derec knew otherwise.

He had enough background to contact Shara Limke again, but he'd promised himself an hour, and twenty minutes remained. Derec bathed, enjoying the scouring pressure of both hot water and sonic pulse, and then he dressed the way he would for a day's work at the lab. Interstellar diplomacy might call for formal dress, but Derec was determined to keep himself as far from the codes and protocols of Earth as this sudden intrigue would permit.

Limke answered his call with a speed that led Derec to believe that she'd shunted aside all other communication. "Mr. Avery," she said. "Thank you for following up on this."

"I said I would, Director." Derec debated for a moment, then dove into a conversation whose end he thought he could already see. "The symbolic importance of Kopernik is working against you right now, it seems."

"Full marks for understatement," Limke said. "Not to mention humor in a situation that doesn't necessarily call for it. Yes, we're in trouble. That's my primary reason for contacting you. The TBI is threatening to shut us down, and I have a strong intuition that they're speaking for someone else."

"So this isn't just a murder investigation. You're asking me to involve myself in a political debacle."

"Yes. Will you?"

"What do you need from me?"

Limke sighed. "I have no way of knowing that, Mr. Avery. But what

I am asking you, what I am about to ask you, is whether you will come to Kopernik. I hope you will trust me when I say that the survival of the station is at stake, and with it the future of commerce with the Fifty Worlds."

Derec meant to tell her that he would have to consider it, but there was no reason to lie. Political firestorm apart, he could not stop himself from prying into this incident that might have so much to say about the work to which he'd devoted most of his life.

"Give me the morning to set things up at my lab," he said, "and then I'll be there as soon as transport schedules permit."

"We're waiting," said Shara Limke, and again she cut the connection before Derec could. He resolved to improve his sense of when to end a conversation.

Elin was coldly furious when Derec broke the news at the lab. Miles already knew, of course, having recorded Derec's conversations with Shara Limke as a matter of routine. "If you leave the planet, Derec," Elin said, "this program won't be here when you get back. And you're doing it for Jonis Taprin." She spat his name with bewildered disgust.

"It's not for Taprin," Derec said, and would have said more but she cut him off.

"No, it's for yourself, which is even worse. Bogard's gone, Derec. You'll never find out where he went, and you'll never satisfy yourself that you did everything right. Going to Kopernik won't change any of that."

Derec tried to apply what she'd said to his understanding of the situation. If he was completely candid with himself, he would have to admit that she was right, that he was walking out on his project at a precarious time to run an errand for a scared administrator worried about the investigation of a murder. He acknowledged that, and then stowed it away. That kind of candor was a luxury, particularly because it might be misguided. He was doing this, he was sure, because Elin was capable and it was the right thing to do.

"You've got three months before the next quarterly," he said. "The office is leased for six months, and I own the equipment. Keep Miles. Eza Lamina can't touch you for another thirteen weeks. I'll be back long before then."

Elin wouldn't answer him. She stood vibrating with fury, eyes locked on his, but she wouldn't say a word.

Derec gave up. "Miles," he said. "You will respond to Elin's instructions until I return."

"Very well, Derec. As of now or commencing at your departure?"

"Let's say as of now. I'll try not to contradict her before I leave."

At first he had trouble getting clearance to travel to Kopernik. The morning passed in interviews, pathogen screenings, and exchanges of documentation. Then early in the afternoon, just as Derec was starting to believe that the whole situation on Kopernik would have blown over by the time he could get his travel permissions in order, his terminal chirped. Before Derec accepted the call, he glanced at the incoming identification: Vilios Kalienin. He'd heard the name. Some kind of consultant to the Terran Senate caucus on Nova Levis.

"Mr. Kalienin," he said.

"Good afternoon, Mr. Avery," Kalienin said. "I understand you've had a little trouble getting your travel arrangements finalized."

"So it would seem."

"Well. As it happens, I'm traveling to Kopernik in three hours, on the way to Earth for Jonis Taprin's funeral. Will you accept my offer of passage?"

"Gladly," Derec said, knowing there would be a cost but happy to pay it if paying meant he could get to Kopernik and be a roboticist again. Even if it was only for a few days.

Miles had already packed a case of clothing and another of instruments, so Derec had a little time to kill before he had to report to the spaceport. He indulged a hunch and read through what he could easily find about Kalienin.

By the time he was done, he had a clearer idea of why Kalienin had been so accommodating. A career political operative with Organic Sapiens sympathies would, of course, be going to Taprin's memorial, and if he wanted to bring along a celebrated example of the damage wrought by positronic robots, he could hardly have made a better choice than Derec Avery. So Derec was to be a symbol. Very well. It had happened before, and if he could assist in casting some light on what had really happened to Jonis Taprin, so much the better.

A factory-model robot could not have killed Taprin. That much was axiomatic. Either the circumstances of the crime had been obscured or the robot in question was other than it appeared from Shara Limke's offhand description. Derec would find out, and whatever the truth turned out to be, he would at last be able to put the ghost of Bogard to rest.

"Page me a transport and I'll get myself to the ship, Miles," he called, hefting his bags. "You head down to the lab and assist Elin."

"Fortunate travels, Derec," Miles said as he walked past Derec to the front door. Derec had programmed that exact benediction himself. As he watched Miles walking away down the street toward the lab, Derec felt a quiet pride that he had been able to build a robot so ordinary and at the same time so unique. His experience with Bogard had taught him something after all.

The transport arrived, and he embarked on his trip to Kopernik.

# 8

A riel waited two days for the political explosion. When it didn't come, its absence worried her even more than anticipating it had. Kalienin couldn't just be sitting on an indiscretion so blatant. If he hadn't made something of it yet, he was certainly planning to. In the calm before that inevitable storm, Ariel shored up her project's operations, making sure that in the event of her removal the work of ethics investigation would go on. She didn't expect to survive politically, but that wouldn't matter if she could leave behind stable oversight.

Hodder Feng had tried to console her after Kalienin had taken his smiling leave. It was a touching gesture, coming from the depths of Hodder's loss. She admired him for it. Perhaps once she'd been politically exiled—again—she could work with him. Nova Levis was still a place where committed individuals could work immediate change.

That little nugget of optimism sustained her for those two days. Then she grew restless, and against all her instincts she did the one thing guaranteed to provoke a reaction: She called Zev Brixa. He wasn't available, which made Ariel happy—she had the satisfaction of trying to do the right thing, and the relief of not suffering the consequences.

Her happiness evaporated when she scanned her messages and saw that in the queue was a query from an anonymous sender under the subject heading CYBORG QUESTION. It was text-only, she saw when she opened it. WE APPLAUD YOUR WORK, ARIEL BURGESS, the message read. REPLY TO THIS MESSAGE IF YOU WOULD KNOW MORE.

"Jennie," Ariel said. "Trace this message."

"Working," R. Jennie said. Ariel sat at her desk rereading the message, wondering if there was something to it she wasn't seeing. Had Kalienin decided to prod her? If not, who else would know?

Silly question. She'd been less than discreet at Kamil's. Anyone who wanted to listen to her could have easily enough. Kalienin was certainly capable of unethical action, but it was much more likely that someone at the restaurant had overheard her, perhaps talked to someone else, and so on. Any number of people could be aware of the situation, and any one of them might have sent her this anonymous encouragement.

"The message was routed several times, through nodes in Stopol, Nova City, and Noresk," Jennie reported. "Its origin is effectively masked."

Given time, Jennie might be able to discover the sender. Ariel considered it. What stopped her was the niggling question of what would happen if she replied as the message instructed. The sender wanted to talk to her, but was reluctant to disclose his or her identity. Under the circumstances, that kind of caution was prudent. It might well be that the sender didn't trust Ariel not to tell the wrong person about the communication itself.

She wondered if Hodder Feng had something to do with it. Knowing nothing for certain, she flitted from possibility to possibility until she grew annoyed at herself and tapped out a terse reply.

*I would.*

Then she shut her terminal down and went to see Vilios Kalienin.

He wasn't at his office, and his human secretary notified Ariel that he was en route from Earth, having attended the memorial services for Jonis Taprin. Ariel had made it a point of pride to restrain her emotional reaction to Taprin's death, but somehow this perfunctory detail rocked her. Jonis had not always been a Managin figurehead. She chose her lovers carefully, and in Jonis Taprin she had believed—if briefly—she'd found that rarest of animals, the untainted politician. Later events had proved her catastrophically wrong.

*You're not doing yourself any favors by staying ignorant of the situation,* Ariel thought. She ran through the subetheric accounts of the assassination. What she found left her purely stupefied.

A robot had killed Taprin? Earth was in turmoil. Widespread rioting had destroyed a number of Spacer-affiliated businesses. Residential Intelligences, thousands of them, had been crudely destroyed. Taprin's successor in office had called for the immediate expulsion of all Spacers on Earth and the shutdown of Kopernik Station; this demand was met with acclaim. The death toll was sickening, and so was the prurient relish with which the Terran media covered the events. Ariel filtered through this sensationalist garbage looking for actual details about the investigation. Few were forthcoming, and she nearly spared herself the ordeal of searching through the welter of bigoted muck—but then she saw Derec's name.

He was on Kopernik.

Ariel returned to the reports on the murder investigation, winnowing them for additional information or hints. She found nothing. Either five years had been long enough for the name of Derec Avery to completely recede from the Terran public consciousness...or the news was being withheld.

She checked the date of the one report that mentioned Derec, and on rereading it she saw that he had arrived with Vilios Kalienin.

Flabbergasted all over again, she sat back in her chair and tried to organize what she knew. It was reported that a robot had killed Taprin, and the next day Derec had gone with Kalienin to Kopernik; since then, Kalienin had gone on to Earth to whip up popular sentiment against robots and Spacers. If Derec hadn't gone to Earth—and she didn't think he had, given the vendetta the Terran Bureau of Investigation still nurtured against him—he was either still on Kopernik or back in Nova City.

A brief conversation with his assistant Elin Imbrin told her not only that Derec was not there, but that she hadn't been able to contact him since he'd left. "Communication with Kopernik is censored," she said. "I've called several times, and after the first two they stopped even pretending that they'd pass the message along."

"Did he give you any indication when he might be returning?" Ariel asked.

Anger flashed in Elin's eyes. "No. I made it clear when he left that I thought it was detrimental to the project, and we left it at that."

In addition to the anger, there was strain on Elin's face. Ariel wondered how the situation with the disappearing research subjects was progressing, but she wasn't sure how to ask without having Elin infer that Ariel was questioning her ability to run the lab in Derec's absence. Her diplomatic skills were sadly eroded, she thought.

"If you do hear from him, I'd very much appreciate it if you told him I'd like to talk to him," Ariel said.

"I'll do that," Elin said. "Now I have work to do."

Next, Ariel called Zev Brixa again. This time he was in his office, and he looked pleased to hear from her. "Ambassador," he said. "Glad you're following up on this."

The phrasing threw Ariel. "Have you heard something?"

"No, nothing like that. I'm just guessing that if you were going to make a cursory round of the Triangle and then drop the issue, it wouldn't have taken you this long to do it."

He was right about that. Brixa was the kind of man, Ariel thought, who would draw up a chart indexing the lapse before her response against the probability that she was doing what he wanted. The ready smile and engaging manner were all part of his calculations. Oddly,

Ariel found she didn't begrudge him this. Now that she was beginning to learn how he worked, she felt fairly confident that he could be relied on if she gave him the impression she was pursuing his request.

"Well," she said, "I have sounded a few people out, and the question isn't finding much sympathy."

He didn't seem bothered. "I expected that. New ideas frighten people, especially people who have been through what Novans have these past few years. And the offworlders—including a large number of my colleagues—are every bit as bound to the prejudices of their upbringing as Novans are to theirs."

Ariel thought of her own gut reaction to his proposition, and knew he was, if anything, understating the case.

"Still," Brixa went on, "nothing was ever gained by wrapping yourself in old prejudices. Nucleomorph intends to move forward with this. We're relying on you to tell us the best way to do it."

"Mr. Brixa. I don't think you understand. As the political culture of Nova Levis stands, this will not work. The Triangle is not going to open its arms to a group of mutated, possibly human rejects from a notorious illicit experiment."

"Is that how you see them?" Brixa's eyes were crinkling, but he didn't quite smile. "Here's a suggestion. Why don't you come out here and actually see the people we're talking about?"

See them, Ariel thought. Go to Noresk and walk among the reanimes who were even less human than Jerem Looms. It was out of the question.

"Mr. Brixa—"

"I can send a transport for you tomorrow morning," he said. "I'll accompany you. It isn't dangerous, Ambassador. Even the religious fanatics among the reanimes are otherworldly dreamers. Well, there are a few who take a more aggressive line, but I don't think many of the reanimes take them seriously. At least, they won't if—and now we're back to our first conversation—they perceive that someone is taking steps to end their ostracism."

Ariel considered. If she did go to the reanime camp, she wasn't entirely sure she wanted to arrive in a Nucleomorph transport. It always paid to be careful about who you let yourself be identified with.

"I'll consider a visit to the camp," she said. "If I decide to go, though, I think it would be more appropriate to go on my own."

Brixa took her meaning right away. "Very well. That might be the prudent course. At least let me know when you're coming so we can meet again after. Will you do that?"

"I will," Ariel said. "I'll be in touch, Mr. Brixa."

She avoided thinking about the problem for the rest of the day. There was more than enough day-to-day struggling against the dysfunctional Triangle patronage system to keep her busy, and periodically a numbing sense of loss at Jonis' murder overcame all of Ariel's best intentions to do her work. Ariel spent the afternoon updating herself on the progress of a number of ethics investigations, including a vitriolic trial in Stopol that, it appeared, might result in the conviction of a district judge on bribery and fraud charges. If successful, that verdict would be a potent symbolic victory; she felt a little tingle of optimism, and decided that was a good way to finish off the workday. As soon as she ran through her correspondence one more time, she would go home and forbid herself to think for sixteen hours.

Ninth in her message queue came the heading CYBORG QUESTION. She opened the message.

I WAS HOPING YOU WOULD. KEEP BRIXA AT A DISTANCE, AND DON'T WORRY ABOUT KALIENIN. MORE SOON.

A chill spread up the back of Ariel's neck. The sender knew about both Kalienin and Brixa. The only person she'd mentioned Brixa to was Derec, and she hadn't told anyone about her unfortunate logorrhea in front of Kalienin.

Someone was watching her.

"Jennie," she said. "Security sweep of the office. When it's complete, sweep the apartment as well."

"Working."

Ariel sat until she couldn't keep herself still. She needed to do something, but she also needed to delay action until she had a good reason to act.

Without meaning to, she started punching in the code for Kopernik Station. As she entered the code and charged the call to the Triangle, it started to seem like a good idea.

A security officer answered the call. "Kopernik Station."

*Use the title*, Ariel thought. "This is Ambassador Ariel Burgess. Connect me to Derec Avery, please."

The officer consulted a screen at the edge of Ariel's field of vision. "Communication is restricted due to the criminal investigation at this time, Ambassador," he said. "I can record a message for Mr. Avery and send it through screening."

"This isn't a social call, Kopernik," Ariel said. "Mr. Avery and I have worked together for some years, and it's entirely possible he'll want to consult with me on this investigation."

"That is possible, Ambassador. If you'll record a message, we'll get it screened and go from there."

"Give me the name of the official in charge of this screening."

"I can't do that, Ambassador. There is a very sensitive situation here."

At one time, Ariel could have made the situation a great deal more sensitive with a few well-placed calls. That time was past, though, and there was no getting it back.

Ariel took a moment to compose her thoughts. "Begin recording," she said.

T he minute Derec stepped off Kalienin's ship onto Kopernik
Station, he knew there was going to be trouble. Shara Limke
was there to meet him, but so were two stone-faced operatives
of the Terran Bureau of Investigation. They stayed in the background
while Limke approached to shake Derec's hand.

"Mr. Avery," she said. "I am terribly glad to see you."

"Thank you, Director. It looks like not everyone here shares your
enthusiasm."

Limke glanced over her shoulder. "Another time," she said quietly.

Together they walked toward the two TBI men. "Derec Avery," one
of them said. "What a pleasure to have you back in our territory again.
How many people are going to drop dead around you this time?"

"Have we been introduced?" Derec said.

"Alder Stoun. Inspector. The only thing you need to remember is
the third."

"As you wish, Inspector," Derec said. "Your colleague?"

The second man spoke. "Iker. Inspector."

"Well, that'll solve me the problem of having to remember your
names." Derec might have said more, even though he wasn't normally

given to hostile bantering. His experience with the TBI had taught him that they were narrow-minded and abrasive, even when they weren't obviously corrupt.

Shara Limke, though, touched Derec on the shoulder. "Inspectors," she said. "You wanted to meet Mr. Avery off the ship. Now you've met him. If you'll excuse us, I have work for him."

Derec followed her out of the landing lounge and down a long hall. Teeming with questions, he said nothing, waiting for her to direct him. That was why he was here. When they got to an elevator, they dropped several levels and emerged in an atrium with a fine view of the starfield and a picket of Terran military craft. Kopernik's docking stations were nearly full.

"The situation here is even more tenuous than I described to you before," Limke said. "Popular opinion on Earth is running in supermajority numbers in favor of evicting Spacers from the planet and prohibiting trade relations. Taprin's survivors in his party are leading the charge, and they have enough pull with the military to get a temporary blockade enforced. I think once things calm down, the eviction and trade prohibition will sound a little rash. The problem is, a number of anti-Spacer politicians on Earth feel the same way, so they're starting a second effort to circumvent any inconvenient shift in the political wind. They're trying to close my station, Mr. Avery. The argument, if you can call it that, seems to hint at the idea that mothballing Kopernik will be a powerful statement to the Fifty Worlds. The Spacers, if they want to continue commerce with Earth, will have to construct a station of their own, and the expense of running a station will be transferred neatly from the Terran government to the Spacers."

Except for the focus on Kopernik, Derec had heard all of this before. It sounded altogether too much like the fallout from the slaughter at Union Station. He had a number of questions, but he decided to keep things concrete. "Kopernik doesn't make money?"

"It does, but not as much as you might expect. And even though station operations result in a profit, the station itself was built under a contract that states that the Terran government is responsible in perpetuity for maintenance. I gather the original builders demanded that concession because they thought that the government would make more in tariffs than the station would in docking fees—hence a clause to even things up. The government has sued us in every court that would hear them, but so far the agreement has held up. So Taprin's ideological stepchildren will close us down if they can just to free up their expenditures for something else. I think you and I both know that they won't be endowing any charitable foundations with it."

"This doesn't make any sense," Derec said. "Surely the ancillary business taxes and so on more than make up for what they spend to sweep the floors."

"Yes, they do," Limke said with a nod. "Unfortunately, a number of the people in charge of those ancillary businesses believe that the Settler worlds are due for a spike in economic growth. They're betting—I'm speculating here, but it's informed speculation—that once Kopernik is shut down and the Spacers build another station, they'll be able to purchase Kopernik and dedicate it exclusively to shipping to and from the Settler worlds."

"What if the Spacers don't build another station?"

"They will. They want trade with Earth; too many of them have lucrative commercial ties with the old motherworld. If the anti-Spacer gang gets its way, they'll have made it look like they've humbled the Spacers and saved the Terran government a nontrivial amount of money in the bargain. Then they can redistribute the money in the form of incentives to get people in line behind running Kopernik again."

It would only work, Derec thought, if people on Earth were both apathetic and gullible. Unfortunately, too many of them were, especially when it came to the actions of their elected representatives. Politicians were widely assumed to be corrupt, and politicians were widely allowed to go on being corrupt as long as the average person believed that corruption was the price to pay for getting things done.

"There would be quite a bottleneck for Spacer traffic routed via Kopernik to Settler worlds," he mused.

Limke nodded. "And that might well backfire on them. The Spacers might just make the investment to ship to Settler worlds directly. Many of them already do, although logistical issues typically make it cheaper to go by Earth than directly from, say, Aurora to Nova Levis. A great deal of expertise in moving things from place to place has come to be concentrated here on this station. If Kopernik closes, how many of those people are going to move offworld?"

It was a good question. Derec didn't have an answer, and he wanted some time to think about the situation. Also he was starting to get impatient to be at the work that had brought him here.

"So a robot killed Jonis Taprin," he said.

Limke offered him a chagrined smile. "I'm sorry. You can't possibly be as interested in the peripheral issues as I am, and you've come a very long way."

She looked around the atrium as if considering her course of action. Derec waited. Finally she said, "I never know where the TBI is listening, with one exception. I don't think they've gotten into my office yet."

Shara Limke's office was spacious enough to seem appropriate to her title, but without ostentation. A robot stood in the corner behind her desk, and three chairs surrounded a low table on Derec's right as they entered. "Fergus, security sweep," Limke said.

The robot didn't move, but perhaps thirty seconds later it said, "No surveillance detected."

"That will have to do," Limke said. She and Derec sat around the table, which Derec now noticed was a live display. Tapping one corner, she brought up a number of screens. Several of them showed crime-scene photographs.

Derec took some time to look over these. Jonis Taprin had died at the foot of the bed in his room. His shirtless body lay curled in a fetal position, with deep bruising visible across his back, shoulders and arms. One side of his head was distinctly flattened, and the force of the assault had burst one of his eyes from its socket. Blood stained the carpet under his face. Next to his head, dented and covered with blood, stood an aluminum briefcase. And on the bed, sitting like a man getting up in the morning with a bad headache, was a robot. A Cole-Yahner domestic, cheap and common as inkpens on twentieth century Wall Street. Its head hung straight down on its chest, and its arms dangled over the edge of the bed. Flecks and spatters of blood were visible on its arms and torso.

"I believe that answers your question, Mr. Avery," Limke said.

"It certainly appears to," Derec answered, eyes still on the images. Nothing else in the room was disturbed. Taprin's jacket, shirt, and tie lay on the bed behind the collapsed robot. A glass of water, half full, stood on the bedside table. "Appears," he repeated under his breath.

"I beg your pardon?"

"Could someone have killed Taprin while the robot was incapacitated somehow? That would be likely to provoke positronic collapse in a standard domestic model like the Cole-Yahner. Most of them don't have very sophisticated tools to sort out Three Law complications; it's cheaper to build another one than improve their matrices." Briefly, Derec remembered some of the battles he'd fought to get funding for his early experiments on the brain that became Bogard.

"The robot would have defended Taprin," Limke said.

"Of course, if it could have. Informed speculation again, but what if someone disabled it and then restored its function just as the murderer struck the fatal blow? The robot would have been functional at the death of another human being, but not for long enough to take action. Tricky call for the kind of basic matrix this model works with."

"Mr. Avery," Limke said. "You'll forgive my candor, I hope, but that sounds a little farfetched."

"It is," Derec said. "But not as farfetched as a Cole-Yahner domestic killing a human being. Especially when the human being was Jonis Taprin. You've looked at surveillance cameras from the area?"

"There weren't any. Taprin's people demanded that all surveillance on his hall be suspended during his visit. They didn't want people watching him, and they particularly didn't want his enemies observing his security procedures. At least that was the explanation given me."

"The TBI has interviewed Taprin's staff?"

"Most of them were in a lounge talking to media. Those who weren't had either gone to sleep or were otherwise accounted for."

"Okay. What was the robot doing in Taprin's room?"

"One of his aides in the adjoining room heard the knock and heard the robot say it was delivering room service. Taprin was heard to say that he hadn't ordered anything, and the robot said a friend had sent him something. The aide told the TBI he assumed one of Taprin's supporters was sending him a bottle of champagne or something of that nature."

Someone had sent Taprin something, all right. But all of the people close to him on Kopernik were accounted for, and that meant that the solution to his murder lay in finding out where the robot had come from.

"What was the robot's function on-station?" Derec asked.

Limke paused before answering. When she did, something had tightened in her voice. "I don't know. The TBI team has embargoed all the records related to it."

Typical TBI territorialism, Derec thought. "Well, that complicates things a little. I should be able to find out from the robot itself, though, as soon as I examine it."

Limke was looking away from him, down at the images of Taprin on her tabletop. "The robot itself is under TBI seal. They're not letting anyone examine it. Least of all you."

Which complicated things rather a lot.

# CHAPTER

# 10

A riel's transport skimmed north over the waters of the River Bogard (she'd heard Derec mention his personal nomenclature once, and liked it enough to adopt it herself). She passed isolated settlements of a few homes, most of them abandoned as even the most fearless of Nova Levis' settlers fled for the false safety of the cities. Some of them were doubtless part of Derec's studies.

The river narrowed after the craft passed Stopol, and the terrain around it grew hilly and rugged. She wasn't a botanist, but she could tell that the trees were different; she imagined the diseases were, too. So much of Nova Levis had been ruined, and yet from the air it looked like any other wilderness. It might well be that nothing moved under those trees; her perfunctory attempts to keep abreast of the public-health situation had acquainted her with a number of pathogens both organic and mechanical that tore like wildfire through any organism with a central nervous system. In other places, local biodiversity exceeded climatological norms by an order of magnitude or more; species came and went in a matter of weeks. If it was possible that the forest below her was devoid of animal life, it was equally possible that a different species of insect clung to every tree. Nova Levis was an ecology so wildly out of balance that even working out the mechanics of the imbalance had thus far proved impossible. Ariel was privately amazed that Derec and his team had made as much progress as they had.

The transport held only her and a robot pilot. She'd hired it for the day out of personal funds, not wanting herself publicly traceable to the cyborg question anymore than she already was. Perhaps it was too late to worry about it, but Ariel was generally of the opinion that a little extra caution was rarely the wrong choice—which made her volubility in Kamil's a few nights ago all the more galling.

*Never mind,* she told herself. *Control what you can now.*

She brought up a map on the transport's instrument panel and zeroed it in on the latest satellite imaging of the old cyborg laboratory. New construction was visible everywhere, all but obliterating the footprint of the lab. Nucleomorph had spent a lot of money there; no wonder they wanted to pacify the reanimes. Ariel spiraled the map out from the lab until she located the reanime camp. It was larger than she'd expected, nearly a square kilometer in size with evidence of recent growth in the stacks of recently cut trees. Hardly the cluster of shacks she'd expected, but then, all of her expectations about the situation had been rudely derailed the night before when Jennie had turned up the tiny crystal wafer laid over Ariel's kitchen window. She'd had Jennie analyze it on the spot, and she discovered that in addition to being a recorder, the wafer contained a message.

R. Jennie played it for her, and she'd heard a gravel-toned voice that brought back all of her memories of Coren. Jerem Looms' voice had been ruined in just this way.

"Ambassador Burgess," the voice said. "If you have discovered this message, it is time that we stopped relying on furtive text communication. The situation requires somewhat more bandwidth. There is much about Nucleomorph, and about us, that you would do well to know. I await your visit when you have completed your initial assessment of the political climate."

Ariel had the wafer in her pocket now, as her pilot slowed and dropped onto the surface of the river. It guided the transport to a beach on the inside of a bend in the river, stopping three or four meters from the shore.

"My apologies, Ambassador," it said. "I am programmed not to put the craft in danger of grounding."

Ariel popped the hatch and looked at the water. It was only knee-deep, and sandy. "No apology necessary," she said. "I'll dry soon enough. Remain here until I return."

"Yes, Ambassador."

Splashing into the water, Ariel made her way to shore. A trail led into the trees, and she followed it for less than ten minutes before realizing that someone had fallen into step behind her. She turned and stifled a cry.

A step behind her stood a cyborg, taller than Ariel by a head, with the same granular skin and misshapen head she remembered Jerem Looms having. It—he—regarded her with hooded eyes. "You are Burgess?"

"Yes."

"Follow me."

The cyborg set off and she followed, becoming aware as soon as they were moving that a second reanime was behind her. The hair on the back of her neck prickled, but she forced herself not to turn around. If they were going to kill her, she would already be dead. She was here on a diplomatic mission, her first since her exile to Nova Levis.

They came out of the woods into the reanime camp, and despite her resolve Ariel nearly fled. Everywhere she looked, cyborgs were working or talking. They built, they dug, they repaired, they ran messages between groups. She saw one reanime, an adolescent female—if it was appropriate to note the gender of such a being—actually salute the leader of a crew pulling stumps from a cleared field. There were a great manymore than she'd expected, and

Ariel wondered if anyone actually knew the population of the encampment. The whine and scrape of manufacturing machinery reached her ears, and she saw smoke rising from stacks over a number of flat-roofed buildings. There was industry here, and organization. It was less an encampment than a town.

And where were the sick and dying? The accounts Ariel had read of the reanime camp had led her to believe that its denizens were doomed by the experimental missteps that had created them. All around her, though, were cyborgs that she could only call healthy. She saw no deformity, no sickness at all.

Her escort touched her on the shoulder, and smiled when she flinched. "Inside," it, or he, said, pointing to a two-story timber house on their left. Ariel nodded and went to the door.

It opened as she approached, and a cyborg stood aside to let her in. He shut the door behind her and stood at attention in the doorway. The interior of the ground floor was one large room, furnished only with a large table and a desk. On the walls hung a number of maps. The dozen chairs around the table were empty; the chair behind the desk held a cyborg who stood to greet her.

"Ambassador Burgess," he said in the rasping voice of the message on the crystal wafer. "Your presence does us honor, and you as well. Welcome to Gernika. I am Basq."

Ariel nodded. "You seem to be doing well for yourselves here, Basq."

"Not as well as we will be," Basq answered. He walked around the desk. "What have you brought for me?"

The question threw her. "You contacted me. I inferred from the contact that you would want to see me."

"Beware inference," Basq said. "There is much here that I would have you see, and your initiative speaks well of you. This meeting may be premature, though."

"Zev Brixa gave me to understand that the circumstances were pressing."

"You are far too canny to take Zev Brixa at his word." Basq gazed at Ariel for a moment, as if challenging her to dispute him. Or as if he mistrusted his own compliment, and was giving her a chance to confirm it. She said nothing. He—for some reason she had no trouble thinking of the cyborg chieftain as male—smiled, and the expression did nothing to make her more comfortable. "Brixa is Nucleomorph's man. I am not a man, and I do not belong to Nucleomorph. Both of those qualities disturb him."

"Are you telling me that Brixa is lying to me?"

"I don't know the details of your interaction," Basq said. "He may well be telling the truth while disguising the reasons for offering it."

"Don't patronize me," Ariel said. She took the wafer from her pocket and let Basq get a look at it before setting it on the table. "You know as much about my conversations with Brixa as I do."

"Ah," Basq nodded. "So this brought you here."

"Did you intend me to find it?"

"I did. I assumed that you would take more time to gauge its significance before making a two-thousand-kilometer trip. Your other duties are pressing, I understand."

"Are there other devices in my office?"

"You found that one," Basq said. The guard swung the door open, and he extended an arm, escorting her from his headquarters. "Come see us again when you have something concrete to offer."

# 11

The adjutant in charge of the TBI inquiry, one Omel Slyke, was every bit as unhelpful as Derec had expected, and supercilious to boot. "I'm not going to waste any social grace on you, Avery," he said. "If you hadn't been en route with Kalienin by the time I knew you were coming, I'd have had your ship intercepted and turned right around to that garbage pit you came from. Stay out of my investigation."

Derec had come to Slyke's office expecting to be frozen out. He had nothing to gain by pleasantries, and nothing to lose by belligerence. "I'm not here to interfere with your investigation," he said. "I trust that it will be every bit as thorough as the other TBI cases I've been involved with."

Slyke's face darkened, but he didn't get up from behind his desk. "Let me explain something to you. If I decide you don't belong here anymore, you will be gone. I might be able to put you on a ship back to Nova Levis, and I might not, but I will put you on a ship to somewhere if you get in my way."

"If I didn't know better, Slyke, I would think that you and I weren't both working to solve a murder."

"I've seen the way you solve murders. Your solutions tend to involve more people getting killed. That's not going to happen while I'm in charge here."

"I've seen the way you solve murders, too. Your solutions tend to involve giving up when things get sensitive to the people who pay you."

Now, Slyke *did* stand. He wasn't taller than Derec, but he was much heavier, and he carried himself like a man familiar with physical violence. "Are you accusing me of corruption?"

"I'm telling you what my experience has been. The director of this station asked me to come because she felt I had something to contribute. If you don't feel the same way, you have that prerogative. I hope that animosity doesn't interfere with our common task."

Derec left Slyke's office feeling that he hadn't been forceful enough. The truth was, though, that he wasn't sure how much influence Shara Limke commanded anymore. He went down to the lab she'd had set up for him and tried to put Omel Slyke out of his mind. The situation was what it was: A rabble-rousing Terran politician was dead, and the leading suspect was a Cole-Yahner domestic that had likely killed nothing larger than a symbiotic fungus in its operational life. Derec had left his work teetering on the brink of political oblivion to come here at the behest of an embattled station manager who likely didn't have the sway to let him do the investigation any good. The investigating agency was so riddled with political interdependency as to be completely ineffective, and the interplanetary political situation was threatening to deteriorate into open conflict.

What was there to do but throw oneself into the work available, and wait for things to turn, either for better or worse?

Before the TBI had descended on Kopernik, station security had conducted a preliminary assessment, and station medical personnel had conducted an autopsy on Jonis Taprin. Surprising no one, the cause of death had been blunt-force trauma to large areas of the cranium, resulting in rupture of blood vessels in the brain and a partial severing of the brain stem. The murder weapon was a hard, rectangular object with slightly rounded corners and edges—in other words, an aluminum briefcase. Derec pored over the report, looking for anything unusual. When he'd spent half an hour on it, he closed the file and turned elsewhere for leads. The autopsy had been professional and complete; Taprin had died of a simple bludgeoning.

Station security's crime-scene report had little more to offer. Blood samples recovered from the robot's chassis and the briefcase matched Taprin. The briefcase was his, filled with a few paper documents, several wallets of storage wafers, and a portable terminal. Taprin's staff had confiscated all of the materials while the investigating officer was cataloging them, and it was obvious even in the dry idiom of a crime-scene report that the officer hadn't appreciated the interruption: DECEDENT'S STAFFERS WERE INSISTENT TO THE POINT OF ABUSE, ARGUING THAT THE MATERIALS IN QUESTION WERE PRIVATE AND IRRELEVANT TO THE CRIME. THIS INVESTIGATOR DISAGREED IN THE MOST STRENUOUS POSSIBLE TERMS, BUT NO MEANS SHORT OF PHYSICAL ASSAULT EXISTED TO PRESERVE THE SCENE. Names of the staffers were appended to the report. Derec made a note to speak to each of them, but what really interested him at the moment was a discussion with the officer who had filed the report. Skudri Flin.

Derec rummaged up the officer's contact information from a station directory, then stopped short of placing a call. Now was a good time to gently test how much political cover Shara Limke had to offer.

He went to her office, and found her escorting an agitated Keresian merchant out as Derec came in. "Protesting the blockade," she explained, gesturing for Derec to enter. "Not much I can do about it, but nobody's complaining to the TBI or the Terran armed forces."

As soon as the door had shut behind them, Derec said, "I'd like your permission to speak to Skudri Flin."

"You don't need my permission," Limke said, and then caught herself. "Ah. I hear you talked to Adjutant Slyke."

"I did. He gave me to understand that I was an unwelcome intrusion."

"He left me with the same impression." Limke sat in a chair near the door and rubbed at the bridge of her nose. "I may not be able to run as much interference for you as you're hoping."

"Maybe not," Derec said. "There's only one way to find out, though."

She laughed. "True. Very well, Mr. Avery. Go and speak to Skudri. He'll give you an earful."

And he did. Derec found Flin in the station gaming room, at a table with two other men playing a game Derec didn't recognize. It involved two pairs of dice and a number of circular tiles arranged in a symmetrical pattern on a white rectangular board with thin triangles of alternating color along its edges. Two of the men played while the third offered advice and was repeatedly told to shut up.

Flin's image had been attached to the report; he was the third man. Paunchy, hard-faced, the tipped-back seating posture of a man used to wearing a belt with lots of gear on it. Derec wandered among the various tables and consoles until the game was over, which happened when one of the players moved all of his tiles off the board. Then he approached. "Skudri Flin?"

Flin looked up. "Wonderful," he said. "The robot genius comes to see me. Why don't you just sign my discharge papers?"

"I'm not here to get you in trouble, Officer Flin," Derec said. He filed away the information that he was already known around the station. Vilios Kalienin had apparently not shirked his advance work. "Director Limke asked me to assist with the investigation, and that's what I'm doing. You could save me a lot of time with a little conversation."

"Do us a favor, Skud," the losing player growled. "Talk to the genius and let us play without listening to you run your mouth."

"Jump," Flin said. He got up from the table with his glass and walked across a broad floor broken by four billiard tables to the bar, pointedly not hailing the bartender. Derec ordered for both of them, surprised by how much he wanted a drink himself. Trying times.

Flin drank, set his glass on the bar, and said, "So, get to it." Over his shoulder, Derec could see light spilling from the closed doors of V-game booths.

"I have only three questions for you, Officer Flin."

"Skud."

"Skud. Three questions. The first is, did Jonis Taprin's staffers interfere with your investigation beyond removing the contents of his briefcase?"

"No. Unless you count three idiots barging into a crime scene and manhandling the evidence. They didn't touch anything but the case, but for all I know the lead that would crack the investigation left the room on the sole of one of their shoes. Next."

"Is it your impression that the robot killed Taprin?"

Flin drank and considered. "If you forget about the Three Laws, that's the only conclusion you'd come to. Problem is, that's a robot. Even your whatsit, Bogard, couldn't have done this. Tell you what I think, Mr. Avery. You're wasted here. TBI won't let you work, and even if you could, you wouldn't find what you were looking for."

"Which is?"

"Is that your third question?" Flin winked at him over the top of his glass.

"No. The third question—and I want to make sure you know that I'm not trying to imply anything about your conduct of your duties here—is this: Did you leave anything out of your crime-scene report?"

The glass clunked on the bar. "Now why would I do that?"

"You wouldn't—unless you knew the TBI was coming and you had the same opinion of them that I do." Or unless Flin just wanted a little quiet revenge on Taprin's staffers for their impudence.

Flin studied him for a long moment. He had the policeman's appraising gaze, as if everything in his field of vision was an illusion to be seen through.

"I can go back through my records," he said eventually. "See if there's anything I might have overlooked. Won't happen until tomorrow morning, though. I go on shift in three hours, and I'll be damned if I'm going to lose sleep over anything to do with that smug bastard Taprin."

"Much appreciated," Derec said.

"Oh, I'll get it back." Flin drained his glass and stood. "But before I do, I'll throw this one in free. What you're looking for here is your crazy tinhead Bogard. Limke knew you'd never be able to turn this job down. Talk to you tomorrow, genius."

Flin went back to his game, and Derec finished his drink and left.

He went back to his lab. Annoyed by the empty positronic diagnosis assembly hanging over the gleaming ceramic table, and further nettled by the fact that everyone on Kopernik Station had well-developed opinions about his psychology, Derec decided to see just what he could get from Slyke.

He composed a letter that went to contortionist lengths of politeness in its couching of a request that he be allowed to examine the suspect robot "purely for research purposes." If Slyke believed that Derec was taking himself out of the investigation entirely, playing the pure-science naïf, perhaps Derec would make some progress. It wasn't likely—Slyke hadn't achieved his position by being gullible—but he might take the request as a promise on Derec's part to stay out of his way. A long shot, but all of Derec's shots looked to be long in this situation.

He didn't have to wait long to find out. Ninety seconds after he'd finished composing the message and sent it off, his terminal chimed with an incoming response. It was one word in length: DENIED.

No surprise, really. Slyke had no reason to give him anything. Derec chewed over the problem a little more, and found himself wondering if that was really true. Shara Limke wasn't gullible, either, and she couldn't have been completely stripped of influence. Slyke couldn't completely discount her.

Derec leaned back in his chair and closed his eyes. Limke had brought him here because of his experience. What had that experience taught him that he wasn't using now? He mused over the question for some time, losing himself in it, letting his mind wander in the hope of stumbling over something he'd forgotten. A comfortable fugue settled over him, a waking dream state that had proved fertile when the thornier problems of positronic design had thwarted him. Derec let it, relishing its return; there wasn't much call for intuition in the kind of data-gathering and field management he'd been doing on Nova Levis. This was thinking, getting out of your own mind's way and letting it tease out the clue hiding in plain sight, the clue that the regimented conscious mind would always overlook.

The filaments.

Derec snapped awake, realized only then that he'd fallen asleep. The Resident Intelligence in Washington, compromised by an invader. Clots of colored filaments like a tumor on its data pipelines.

A red herring, he told himself. There's no indication that the station RI acted improperly here. Surveillance was purposely discontinued, and there's nothing else the RI could have been involved in. It couldn't have forced the robot to do what it did.

Robots also didn't murder human beings, but apparently one had. This was no time to rest on assumptions.

Derec glanced at the wall chrono. Shara Limke wouldn't be in her office this late, but he thought he knew a place she might go.

## 12

A riel arrived back in Nova City in mid-afternoon. She'd spent all of twenty minutes in the reanime settlement—Gernika, she reminded herself—and that time had been simultaneously informative and mystifying. There were a great deal more of the cyborgs than she had expected—than anyone would have expected, she thought, except possibly Zev Brixa. This was useful to know, but the question of how there had come to be that many perplexed her. The lab was long gone, and unless Nucleomorph was manufacturing cyborgs there was no way for their population to have increased.

*Be reasonable*, she told herself. *There's no possible motive for Nucleomorph to manufacture cyborgs, if manufacturing was the correct characterization of the process through which they were created.* The cyborgs couldn't work, couldn't travel since new security procedures had been put in place following the Jerem Looms/Tro Aspil debacle, couldn't do anything but sit in their remote exile and slowly die of the lab errors that had created them. To Brixa, they were a problem to be addressed, a troublesome population to be pacified.

It was far more likely that the existing reports about the settlement were erroneous. Hardly anyone had known about it, and to Ariel's knowledge only Mia Daventri had been there, and that while desperately ill. A perfect situation for exaggeration.

Ariel had the rental transport drop her off near the Triangle. She completed the transaction with the robot pilot and walked down a side street off Nova Boulevard until she came to the Bureau of Census and Population Statistics. The building directory told her that the Census Division was on the third floor.

She made an on-the-spot appointment with an assistant director named Gil Nandoz, waited ten minutes for him to go through his ritual pretense of clearing up whatever he was working on, and was escorted into his office. Nandoz was an officious Spacer, tall and physically arrested in a distinguished middle age. Seeing him, Ariel was reminded of Hodder Feng's belief that midlevel bureaucrats were genetically predisposed.

"How can I assist you, Ambassador?" Nandoz asked, with a well-practiced mixture of briskness and welcome. He was already expecting to be unable to perform whatever favor she might ask. Everything about him signaled that refusing requests was his primary function.

Ariel decided against an incremental approach. "I'm sure you've heard, Director Nandoz," she said, "that a prominent corporate citizen of Nova Levis has asked me to investigate the legal questions surrounding cyborg citizenship."

"I hope you don't think I'm going to get myself entangled in this," Nandoz said.

"I have no such expectation. I'm simply here to ask whether any census has ever been conducted on the reanime population."

Nandoz stared at her as if she'd asked about a count of sand fleas. "No," he said when he'd gotten his incredulous reaction under control. "Why would there have been?"

"Any number of reasons. It might have been useful to ascertain the spread of tailored diseases among them. They do get sick, you know."

"I certainly hope they do," Nandoz said. "I hope they get sick, and I hope each and every one of them dies and the flesh of them is eaten away by maggots. That's all I have to say about those abominations, and I'll thank you to leave my office."

*That was instructive,* Ariel thought as she left the Census building. She found it hard to believe that Nandoz would have reacted the same way if she'd asked how many children under ten lived in Stopol. Even innocuous statistical questions became fraught when they concerned the reanimes, and Ariel had no doubt that she herself was becoming tainted by her association with the citizenship question. If she didn't resolve the situation quickly, she'd find herself unable to do any kind of political work.

There was humor in her predicament if she looked at it the right way. When she'd been assigned to Nova Levis, she'd thought that her fall from prominence to pariah was complete. Then, when the hostility of the Triangle toward people they associated with the troubles before Liberation became apparent, Ariel realized that even among pariahs there were hierarchies. Now Zev Brixa had come along and made her untouchable even in the eyes of dead-end census bureaucrats. Things could always get worse.

At least she knew for certain that a census had never been conducted. That explained the apparent discrepancy between what she'd heard about the reanimes and what she'd observed that morning. There were bound to be surprises when a population was so thoroughly ignored for so long.

Her first order of business was to obtain basic data about Gernika: How many reanimes were there, how many had died in the last month, year, since Liberation. She'd have to get in touch with Derec when he returned from his doomed errand to Kopernik. He would be interested in an untainted new data set for his project, and it would certainly be useful to know what, if any, medical procedures worked on the reanimes. None of it would take a great deal of time, and it could be done quietly.

Ariel thought it likely that the citizenship question would resolve itself because most of the reanimes would be ticking down the last months of their crippled lives. Whether they were religious fanatics or not, they couldn't do Nucleomorph any harm if they all died.

She caught herself, and was appalled at the brusque turn of her thoughts. Was it so easy to consign sentient beings, who had once been human, to a miserable and diseased death?

The question dogged her all the way back to her apartment. By the time she'd gotten home, Ariel had resolved to do two things. One, she would touch base with Brixa, just to gauge his reaction when he found out she'd been to Gernika. Ariel wondered if he knew the name. He hadn't mentioned it to her before. Two, and perhaps more importantly, Ariel was going to talk to Mia Daventri.

She contacted Mia first. Mia had changed her field of employment; once she'd drifted between soldier and spy, and now she was, of all things, a part-time advisor to the Terran political caucus and a part-time teacher. Nova Levis had that effect on people, Ariel mused. All of the people she knew from the Eliton-Bogard-Parapoyos imbroglio had made fundamental changes in their lives.

Mia was just finishing up the school day. Ariel was still a little perplexed by the use of humans to teach children in academic environments. Robots were far superior in both knowledge base and their invulnerability to standard adolescent cruelty. Still, during the course of a minute's small talk Ariel saw that Mia was pleased with what she was doing. She almost hated to drag the other woman back into the painful chaos of her arrival on Nova Levis.

"Mia," she said when she'd exhausted her reservoir of aimless politeness, "I have a question that might be uncomfortable to you."

"I can guess," Mia said. "You want to know about the reanimes. Correct?"

All Ariel could do was nod.

"I'm not going to talk about this at the school. Can you meet me in an hour at the ballfields near the north gate?"

The ballfields were constricted between the built-up northern neighborhoods of Nova City and the wall at the western side of the North

Gate. A flat expanse of green, divided into fields that were marked with white lines in various patterns. Ariel had minimal knowledge of sports, but she was taken by the sight of the children running in groups, shouting, sometimes laughing, their entire beings given over to a pointless pursuit involving rules that in some cases were centuries old. She had no memory of ever abandoning herself to anything so completely, and felt diminished.

Mia was waiting for her on a set of bleachers set against the wall. She was alone. No organized matches were scheduled, so the children that played across the green sward did it without the stifling agendas of adults. Ariel sat next to Mia. They hadn't spoken in perhaps a year, and this was no way to renew an acquaintance. After a brief glance of greeting, both turned their attention back to the ebb and flow of childhood.

"I thought you were worried about children overhearing you," Ariel said.

"At school, yes. And it's a good thing you didn't call me at the caucus headquarters. All of those lines are recorded, and just the fact that I'd gotten a call from you would put me in a tricky situation. Anyway, these aren't my students, and children typically haven't the slightest interest in anything adults do."

The feeling that she'd wasted her own childhood, even though she remembered so little of it that she had no way of knowing whether it had been wasted, irritated Ariel. She was in no mood for rebukes either explicit or implied. "You're the only person I know of who saw Gernika before Liberation."

"Gernika? It has a name?" Mia looked bemused. "Wonder who decided on that."

"The reanimes did. I was there today."

Mia looked at her, initial surprise giving way to a new appraisal of both Ariel and the situation. "I'm not the only one," she said. "I know Filoo was in and out of the camp, and he didn't travel alone. If you dig, you could probably find two dozen people who have been there. To Gernika." She pronounced the name as if testing its fit with her experience. "What does it mean?"

"I don't know. I've only heard it spoken. It could be spelled any number of ways, have any number of meanings." It was something she should find out, though, Ariel decided. It probably had some specific meaning to Basq and the rest of them.

"The word is that you're going to push for citizenship for the reanimes," Mia said.

Ariel shook her head. "I've been asked to look into the question. Legally and politically. The legal side of it is ambiguous, the political..." She waved a hand. "No ambiguity there."

"Sounds like the messenger is taking some shots for the message," Mia observed.

"That's the nature of my position," Ariel said. But it wasn't, really, not anymore. She wasn't a diplomat anymore. She was a government official with a strictly defined set of tasks and responsibilities, drawn into a situation she had no interest in pursuing. None of which would mean anything to Mia Daventri.

"So did you want to ask me if I thought reanimes should be citizens?" Mia asked.

"No. If there's one thing I have no shortage of, it's opinions." Ariel shifted on the bleacher bench so she was facing Mia. "What I need to know is more concrete. If you had to guess, how many reanimes would you say were there when you passed through?"

Mia considered. "I don't know. I was sick, and didn't see much of what went on there."

Ariel tried the comparative approach. "When I was there this morning, I saw teams of workers. Individuals with clearly defined tasks going about them the same way I go about my work. And there's some kind of political structure there. I was led immediately to a leader, complete with retinue. It all seemed vaguely military, or maybe the degree of organization just surprised me and I equated it with a military hierarchy. In any case, the place seemed healthy. As healthy as Nova City."

Which, both of them knew, wasn't necessarily healthy at all.

"That isn't anything like I remember," Mia said. "I remember tents, and the reanimes like these strange beings who appeared out of the forest. I was with someone else, and he died, but they healed me. They had some kind of knowledge of how the local diseases worked. You know what it reminded me of? During school, we occasionally read chronicles of Terran explorers who encounter primitive cultures. They're always entranced and repelled at the same time, and I had that same feeling. The reanimes were repulsive, but at the same time I was intrigued by how they lived. Moment to moment, with no real concern for the past, and I didn't see anyone worrying about what would happen tomorrow." Mia straightened. "But as I said, I was sick. I nearly died. You shouldn't trust my recollections."

"I'm not necessarily discounting them, either," Ariel said, "but what I saw this morning was very different."

They ran out of conversation after that. Mia receded into some interior space, reliving the days of her sickness and recuperation, and doubtless after that the chaotic scene in the lab when she activated the long-dormant spacecraft that formed the center of the facility, triggering the shattering of the blockade—and seeing Kynig Parapoyos carried away to his death.

Suddenly feeling like an intruder in this quiet green world of heedless children and haunted adults, Ariel touched Mia on the shoulder and walked back through the city, unsettled by a feeling she couldn't identify.

Back at her office, R. Jennie informed her that Zev Brixa had called. Ariel returned the call, even though something about her conversation with Mia had left her uncertain about how to proceed with Brixa.

He solved the problem for her almost immediately. "I wish you hadn't gone to Gernika today, Ariel."

So now it was *Ariel*, not *Ambassador*. Ariel filed that away.

"I had reasons that I'd rather not discuss with you on this link," she said. "And in any case, I didn't encounter any hostility there. The reanimes were perfectly courteous."

"Of course they were. They've identified you, and they're not stupid. You're their hope right now."

This was pressure Ariel did not need, and resisted. "You asked me to look into a question, Mr. Brixa. I am looking into it. The situation goes no farther than that, and I will permit it to go no further than that."

She knew it was a lie, and from his expression Ariel could tell Brixa didn't believe it anymore than she did. "And we appreciate your initiative, Ariel. You've taken a burden upon yourself. We recognize that. Why don't you come see me before you go back to Gernika?"

There it was, out in the open. Everyone had something to sell her, a perspective they wanted her to represent in the Triangle—didn't any of them realize that the Triangle would be only too happy to brand her irrelevant and get rid of her?

"I'll do that, Mr. Brixa. Let me see how things are going here, and I'll let you know when I can get away for a tour of your facility. How does that sound?"

He smiled. It was still a fine smile, and he was still personable and engaging, but the smile no longer struck Ariel as it had on his first visit to her office. "That sounds fine, Ariel. Let me know when you can find the time."

# 13

The station atrium was quiet at this hour. An inexplicable design quirk had placed it near enough to the docking ports that people habitually avoided it because of the noise, and that habit persisted even when the blockade had reduced traffic to a trickle. Derec found Shara Limke in a couch, looking out at the lights of the Terran picket line.

"There's talk on Earth of replacing me," she said as Derec sat in the adjacent couch. "The general sentiment is that I'm no longer competent to administer this station if I'm letting prominent Terran politicians be murdered. You can guess the rest."

Indeed Derec could. Limke would be replaced with someone more pliable, more amenable to the desires of the Terran political structure. For too long, Kopernik had been an infuriating thorn in the side of the Terran-isolationist and Organic Sapiens movements, and Taprin's assassination had given both constituencies unprecedented voice in events. Now they were poised to strike, and Shara Limke made an inviting target.

He made a cold assessment of the situation. He would have to make what use of her he could. "Director, I need to run a full diagnostic on the station RI."

"On Tiko?" she said. "What for?"

Derec explained to her what he had found while looking into the assassination of Clar Eliton. The filaments, and where they had led him.

For a long moment, he thought she was going to refuse him. Limke looked out the window, her body's only motion the twitching of her eyes from light to light along the picket line that was strangling her career.

"I'll do what I can," Limke said at last. "But I want something in return."

Derec waited.

"When the call comes," she said, "I want you to speak for me."

*If that's your last resort,* Derec thought, *you're in deeper trouble than I thought.* Still, he agreed. He could do nothing else.

In the morning, Derec looked over the media reports from Earth. Every story seemed like one he'd read somewhere before: disturbances in every major population center, Spacers congregating in embassies and secure corporate headquarters for fear of personal attack, robots smashed by mobs, factories using robots being struck by their human employees or just vandalized. Most of Earth's resident Spacers were trying to get off-planet, but the bottleneck at Kopernik was making this difficult. The Terran armed forces were permitting one ship at a time to dock at Kopernik for a rigorous search before allowing the vessel to continue to one of the Fifty Worlds. For their part, Spacer governments had fleets at the ready, waiting for the slightest provocation to appear at Kopernik and demand resumption of traffic under the threat of war. The nets were full of Managin rhetoric, much of it coming from people who had never identified with the movement before.

And in the midst of this, there was a growing amount of furious reaction to what was being reported as a drive on Nova Levis to grant cyborgs the privileges of citizenship.

Derec switched to NL01, the one interplanetary news source based on Nova Levis. Its servers and production facilities were less than a block from his lab, and he knew several of the journalists working there. NL01's standard loop was fifty percent local news, mostly new pathogens and legislative minutiae, and the rest was given over to the disturbances on Earth. Either they were ignoring the story, or it wasn't happening.

Or someone had put a lid on it.

Derec composed a quick message to Ariel, sent it, and was informed less than a second later that all unscreened communications to and from Kopernik Station were embargoed until further notice. He snapped off a question to Omel Slyke, asking if Slyke would waive this obstacle so Derec could keep track of his work back on Nova Levis. A minute or so later, Slyke's projected avatar appeared in Derec's lab.

"Why would you even ask me that?" he said. Unlike most people, Slyke made no modifications to his avatar. It looked just like he did.

"Because I need to keep tabs on what my lab is doing," Derec said. "My project there is in some danger of having its funding cut, and if I'm going to do any good back there, I need daily updates on experiments."

Slyke actually appeared to give the question some thought. "Can't do it," he said.

"I'm amazed," Derec said, with a touch of sarcasm.

"Listen a minute before you start feeling persecuted. I don't care whether you talk to your lab people on Nova Levis or not. We'd know everything you said, and unless you controlled this robot from halfway across the galaxy you don't know anything about the investigation anyway. But it's not up to me. The communication embargo comes from way over my head. I don't give a damn about anything you might say. I'm a police investigator, Avery. The only context for any of my reactions to you is concern for this case. Are we clear?"

"I appreciate your candor," Derec said. "Who might I talk to about getting a waiver to send messages to Nova Levis?"

"Shara Limke."

"I take back everything I said about candor," Derec said.

"It's the truth, Avery. I didn't say she could do anything about it; I just said she's the one you'd have to talk to. So, you solve the murder yet?"

"Are you telling me you're interested in my thoughts?"

"I'm interested in solving Jonis Taprin's murder. You come across anything that might get me closer to that, I expect you to tell me about it. I haven't kicked you off Kopernik, Avery. Don't make me regret that."

Slyke's avatar disappeared. Ten seconds later, it reappeared.

"Something I forgot to tell you," he said. "I was considering letting you have a look at the robot after all, but now it's out of my hands. Turns out the tinhead's been scrapped."

"What?" Derec shot up out of his chair. "What idiot would destroy the single real piece of evidence in this case?"

Slyke shrugged. "Like I said before, a lot of this stuff is decided way over my head." He hesitated just a moment too long before disappearing again, leaving Derec with the clear intuition that he was supposed to read carefully between the lines.

But before he had a chance to, Shara Limke walked into his lab and said, "I've got some bad news."

"That's all there seems to be around here," Derec said.

"The TBI refuses to grant permission for you to analyze Tiko. According to Slyke, they need all of its excess capacity for their investigative work, and they can't afford to have it go offline for long enough to perform all the tests you'd want to do."

Derec was still reading between the lines. He wasn't sure he trusted Limke at this point. She had no reason to lie to him, but what that really meant was that if such a reason existed, Derec just didn't know what it was. Slyke had certainly handled him with a great deal more respect than during their first interactions, and Derec didn't think the TBI adjutant was just pandering to him. Either he'd learned something that led him to believe Derec might be of assistance, or some political wind had shifted, leading Slyke to reconsider which alliances on Kopernik were useful to him.

The only way to find out was to recognize that a game was in progress, and try to play without knowing all of the rules. Derec had yet to get anywhere by lying to people on Kopernik, so he didn't start then. "I just talked to Slyke. He didn't say anything about it," he said.

"Every morning, he conducts a briefing to update everyone involved in the investigation. I brought your request up there, and he turned it down and asked me to let you know. If it makes any difference, he didn't seem malicious about it."

"It does make a difference," Derec said. "If his reaction to me has changed in one day, maybe it'll keep changing. But right now he's still not letting me do anything that might tell us whether or not the robot killed Taprin."

He hesitated, wondering whether he should tell her that the robot had been destroyed. If she knew and wasn't telling him, he wasn't sure he wanted to let her know he knew; the existence of a confidence between Derec and Omel Slyke might pay dividends later. On the other hand, Slyke might have told her that he was going to inform Derec about the robot, in which case she might not think it worth bringing up.

That didn't make any sense, though. Why would Slyke ask Limke to tell Derec one thing, and then get in touch with him just to tell him something else that had come up at the same meeting?

Either Slyke had told Derec about the robot without telling Limke, or he'd told Limke and given her the impression Derec wasn't to be informed.

"One thing I can do is get you a copy of Tiko's most recent backup,"

Limke said. "It dates from three hours after Taprin's murder. Slyke and his crew have already been over it, but I'm sure you'll see something different than they did."

"How soon can I see it?"

"It'll take me five minutes to walk back to my office, and ninety seconds to clear you after that. How does that sound?"

It sounded like Derec was finally going to do something that justified his presence on Kopernik. "I'll be right here," he said.

For seventeen hours, Derec pored over the backup, interrogating a version of Tiko that no longer existed. The RI was frustrated and confused by what it had been told of the murder, but as a result of the security precautions Taprin's staff had demanded, Tiko had no direct records of Taprin's room or the exterior hall between checkpoints established at the two nearest hallway crossings. Derec went exhaustively over the recordings of whom had come and gone at those checkpoints during the hours immediately before and after Taprin's murder. When he saw the Cole-Yahner domestic that had apparently killed Taprin, Derec tracked it through the rest of the station. It had come from the hotel concession, and before that...

I DON'T KNOW, Tiko said.

"Process again," Derec said. He tracked the RI's memory processing, and that's when he knew why he'd been allowed to look at this backup.

Sometime before this backup had automatically archived itself, it had been drastically edited. The Tiko of three hours after Jonis Taprin's murder had no memories and no records of events in huge swaths of Kopernik Station. The blank areas of memory showed up on Derec's tracking display as simple white noise, a sure signal that the errors had been deliberately introduced. When positronic systems broke down, the collapse happened in distinct patterns. Each error syndrome in a system as sophisticated as an RI was as individual as a fingerprint. Here Derec came up against simple noise.

He regrouped. If the saboteur was clever, he or she would have erased material that had no bearing on the crime; if not so clever, the pattern of erasures would tell Derec something about what was being concealed.

"List and categorize all areas of the station whose records are tampered with," he commanded Tiko. The RI complied, taking nearly an hour to arrive at a set of answers sufficiently detailed to satisfy Derec. When it was finished, Derec brought up the data in table form, and read over it casually at first, and then with increasing intensity.

| AREA | | TIME OF ERASURE |
|------|------|------|
| 001 | Cargo docks 01-08 | 2130-0400 |
| 004 | Cargo docks 25-32 | 2130-0400 |
| 009 | Passenger docks 11-16 | 2130-0400 |
| 148 | Repair berth A48 | 2200-0000 |
| 156 | Repair berth A56 | 2200-0000 |
| 161 | Repair berth A61 | 2200-0000 |
| 335 | Hotel block 3-7 | 2000-0200 |
| 338 | Hotel block 4-7 | 2000-0200 |
| 338 | Hotel block 4-7 | 2000-0200 |
| 339 | Hotel block 4-8 | 2000-0200 |
| 416 | Residential 6 | 2200-0400 |
| 417 | Residential 7 | 2200-0400 |
| 418 | Residential 8 | 2200-0400 |
| 621 | Atrium lounge | 2200-0400 |
| 780 | Gaming room 4 | 2000-0200 |
| 783 | Gaming room 7 | 2000-0200 |
| 784 | Gaming room 8 | 2000-0200 |

It couldn't be this simple, Derec thought. If he was seeing what he thought he was seeing, the party responsible for attacking Tiko was either careless or incompetent.

The narrative was almost too easy to reconstruct: Taprin had been murdered at 2306 Kopernik time, which corresponded to Terran

Standard—approximately forty minutes after he'd finished his speech and returned to his hotel room in block 3-7. The saboteur had eliminated records from the area, even though Taprin's security had blinded Tiko. Derec accessed a station schematic and saw that 4-7 and 4-8 both overlapped 3-7. It was a matter of public record that Taprin had arrived at Kopernik at 2138 and given his remarks shortly after. That explained the time of the damage at the passenger docks. The cargo docks fell into place easily enough as well. Robots were typically shipped cargo-class since they had no need of life-support services. Derec was willing to bet that the Cole-Yahner had arrived on Kopernik within minutes of Taprin, and it didn't take a genius to glean that it had gone to a repair berth; the schematic showed that A61 faced A48, and A56 occupied the end of a double row, with a view straight down the area of the floor the robot would have had to cross to get to either A48 or A61. The saboteur could have blinked out the entire sector for a few minutes as easily as taking out the selected three berths, though. This bothered Derec, because he realized he was already taking the saboteur too lightly. Whoever it was, this person was part of a conspiracy that had achieved the assassination of a prominent Terran political figure. He was in all likelihood not an idiot.

He—or she—might well be overconfident, though, just as Derec had found it easy to be overconfident when the data had seemed to speak so clearly. He sat back, got a glass of water, and tried to look at the table with fresh eyes.

The clear blocks of time, in complete hours, made it absolutely certain that someone had erased Tiko's memory. The exception on the shipping docks implied that the saboteur had taken more particular care with timing in that area; it was possible he was trying to preserve something as well as eliminate incriminating evidence. What would he want preserved? Derec started to think he was meant to find something that would send him off on the wrong track; if he could figure out what it was and why the saboteur would want to find it, that would be a good start on figuring out what had been hidden.

"Tiko," he said. "I need a list of all ships that docked that day, including manifests, both passengers and cargo. Further, I need a full accounting of the movements of the Cole-Yahner domestic robot suspected in Jonis Taprin's murder."

WORKING, Tiko said. Then, after a few seconds: MANIFESTS UNAVAILABLE.

"Have they been erased, or am I prevented from accessing them?"

MANIFESTS UNAVAILABLE.

So the RI didn't know why it couldn't tell Derec. This was a new wrinkle. "What about the robot?"

SERIAL NUMBER?

Derec accessed his copies of the crime-scene images Limke had provided him. Only part of the robot's serial number was visible, but that model wasn't common on Kopernik; they were older and nearing the end of their service lives. He gave Tiko as much as he had.

NO RECORD OF THAT PARTIAL NUMBER EXISTS.

"Clarify," Derec said. "It doesn't exist, or I am prevented from accessing it?"

IT DOES NOT EXIST.

"Have your records of resident and transient robots been tampered with?"

YES.

"Process request again," Derec said, and watched his diagnostic display while Tiko complied.

White noise.

*Yes*, Derec thought. *I was underestimating you. You're leading me in a certain direction. It will no doubt seem promising and turn out to be utterly irrelevant; the only question is how long I follow it before I figure out what your purpose is.*

He was personalizing his opponent, an ambivalent sign. It was easy to project psychology, and almost invariably the projection had little to do with the real person in question. Derec went back to work on the data, patiently sifting, cautioning himself that as he went he was telling himself a story, resisting the impulse to believe that the story was true.

The off-planet media were frothing with speculation about cyborg citizenship, and because the Triangle only paid attention to what Earth and the Fifty Worlds thought, the Triangle was in a state of high agitation as well. Ariel was deluged with requests for comment, as well as a great volume of personal invective and more than a few death threats. She put R. Jennie to work doling out statements of no comment and forwarding the more aggressive attacks to law enforcement—who, of course, would do nothing.

She mistrusted everyone involved with reanimes: Nucleomorph, Basq, all of them. Sitting at her kitchen table over a light breakfast, her most recent conversation with Zev Brixa replaying itself in her head, she came to a sudden decision. It was time to inform everyone concerned that she was operating independently of their agendas.

"Jennie," Ariel said. "Contact the rental agency. See if you can get the same pilot I used last time."

The Bogard valley seemed familiar to her even though she'd only overflown it once. After the first hour, Ariel stopped watching the landscape. She settled back into her chair and put herself through a rigorous arrangement of priorities.

First, find out how many reanimes there were.

Second, find out if their numbers were increasing.

Third, ascertain who was manufacturing them, if they were actually increasing.

She stopped after three, unwilling to believe it could be true. Surely any imbecile could learn an obvious lesson, and there could hardly be a more obvious one than the results of the old Nova Levis cyborg laboratory. Even Kynig Parapoyos had failed to realize his dream of a cyborg army, and Ariel had difficulty believing that many other people could succeed where Parapoyos had failed.

Let the evidence speak, she reminded herself. *It's not impossible that the cyborg population is expanding. It's so unlikely as to border on fantasy, but it's not impossible.*

The transport skated to a rocking halt at the same landing she'd used the day before. *This is becoming a daily commute,* Ariel thought wryly. She splashed onto the beach and then, instead of following the path she'd taken yesterday, she worked her way along the riverbank for several kilometers. Probably she couldn't get into Gernika without Basq knowing she was there, but she intended to try; and it wasn't farfetched to believe that if he was informed of her presence but also knew she was trying to avoid him, Basq would let her. He had much riding on her willingness to stand up for his cause.

The brush on the riverbank quickly stitched her clothing with burrs and tiny tears. Ariel tried not to think about the number of virulent microbes she was inviting into her body. Her Spacer immune system had dealt successfully with everything she'd ever had except the Mnemonic Plague, and after two bouts of that, she figured her body could handle a third. Or, she admitted to herself, she was indulging in a defense mechanism, allowing herself to act recklessly by underestimating the risk.

Either way, Ariel was there in the wilderness perhaps twenty kilometers from Noresk, clambering up a weedy bank and working her way through the undergrowth in what she guessed was the direction of Gernika. She moved slowly, and every fifty meters or so she spiked a small transponder into the trunk of a tree. If she had to leave quickly, she didn't want to worry about getting lost on her way back to the river. In a way, this little precaution was every bit as irrational as her belief that Spacer-enhanced immunocytes would protect her from whatever the local biome had cooked up over the previous five years; she would hardly be able to outrun the reanimes if it came to that. When one was in a position as delicate as hers, though, one took one's comforting rationalizations as they came.

She kept careful track of time, and knew that she'd been traveling perhaps an hour when she started to see signs of the reanimes' presence. Sneaking up on them would have been inadvisable even if it was possible; Ariel made no attempt to hide herself. If the reanimes were violent toward humans, they wouldn't have remained this anonymous for this long.

Or was that just another comforting rationalization? For all Ariel knew, the reanimes killed anyone who walked into the camp, and the only thing that had saved her the last time was that Basq's scouts had been expecting her.

*You're doing far too much thinking with far too little information,* Ariel told herself. *If they're going to kill you, you've come much too far to avoid it now; and if you really believed they were going to kill you, you wouldn't have come.* The problem was that she didn't know enough to make informed guesses, so her mind oscillated between feverish worries and fatuous certainty. The only cure for the problem was concrete information.

Cresting a small rise, Ariel squatted at the base of a tree, peering through its drooping branches at a field of stumps. A crew of reanimes filled a cart with small boulders before harnessing themselves in its traces and hauling it away on a dirt track. Ariel felt like she was seeing across centuries, but the pioneers in the great age of Terran exploration hadn't been enhanced with superhuman strength—nor had they possessed surveillance wafers or computer moles careful enough to evade a diplomatic attache robot like R. Jennie. Appearances were misleading, particularly where the reanimes were concerned.

When she could no longer hear the groaning of the cart's axles, Ariel started hiking across the field. She debated what she would say to the first cyborg she encountered. Could she simply state who she was and ask for a tour? Not likely; if Basq had wanted her to have a tour, he would have given her one. She was relying on finding someone in the settlement who would disregard a leader's order.

No. No, she wouldn't. She had no idea whether such an order had been given. Basq wanted her to know about the camp. He wouldn't have contacted her if he didn't.

Why was her mind going in loops?

Halfway across the field, Ariel paused. She was breathing more heavily than the relatively easy hike from the river should have made her, and the sun beat on the crown of her head. *Too much time behind a desk,* she chided herself. *You haven't taken care of yourself. An hour's hike in moderate heat, and you're ready for the infirmary.* She resolved to begin a fitness program immediately upon returning to Nova City.

The shade on the other side of the field cooled her off, and Ariel's head cleared a little. She walked faster, irritated at herself, trying to purge the heat-soaked lethargy that lingered in her limbs. By the time she got to the edge of the reanime settlement and drew the attention of a reanime caulking a window along the back wall of a long wooden building, she felt sharp and focused again.

"Excuse me," she said. "I'm with the government down in Nova City. I'm gathering information, and one of the things I need is someone to show me around. You're busy, I can see that, but can you spare half an hour?"

"Basq won't like it," the cyborg said. He looked younger than most of the others she'd seen. He must have been created toward the end of Parapoyos' hold on Nova Levis.

"I've spoken to Basq before," Ariel said. "He knows I'm looking around. I'll make you a deal. You show me around for thirty minutes, I'll help you for thirty minutes."

"Don't talk to me like I'm stupid," the cyborg said.

Ariel caught herself. "I was, wasn't I? Sorry. It was an honest offer, though."

"I don't need any help. Why aren't you talking to Basq?"

"He wants to me have a clearer idea of what's going on here before I talk to him again." As Ariel said this, it occurred to her that it might be true. "What's your name?"

"Inak."

"Inak, I'm Ariel. Half an hour, that's all I'm asking. Okay?"

He was going to do it. All he had to do, Ariel could tell, was convince himself. "If Basq is angry, you have to tell him what you told me."

"Of course I will," Ariel said.

Inak was still nervous, and steered her away from large groups, which suited her fine. He wasn't terribly intelligent, and he knew he was doing something that Basq quite possibly wouldn't approve of, but like any other young male—of any species, Ariel guessed—he couldn't refuse the opportunity to break up his everyday routine. She tried not to ask too many questions, lest she make him even more jumpy. But as they toured around the periphery of the settlement, Inak loosened up a little; by the time her thirty minutes was up, Ariel had learned a great deal.

They had a working machine shop, and had built solar arrays and a number of battery-powered machines. From the remains of cannibalized robots they had created a rudimentary network, and they had traded with meats in the area for medical equipment that they had then customized to their needs.

"Which meats?" Ariel asked.

Inak shrugged and went on.

There were three hundred and ninety-six citizens of Gernika. Inak was sure of this. He was also sure that there were more than had lived in the settlement when he arrived, but when Ariel asked him when he had arrived, his face grew troubled. "Don't know," he said.

"Do you know where you came from?" Ariel prompted gently.

"No."

Abruptly he walked away, leaving her there. Ariel watched him go, working furiously through the possible reasons why her question might have provoked such a reaction. Inak was more emotional than either of the two reanimes she'd known of before, that was certain. She'd touched what certainly seemed like an emotional nerve.

She was about to pursue him to see if she could put him at ease when someone called out to her. "Excuse me, young lady."

A human voice. Startled, Ariel turned to see a portly man, Terran by the look of him, dressed as the reanimes were—which was to say dressed as most of Nova Levis' poor were, in standard-issue fabrics purchased from government concessions.

"Are you—" Ariel caught herself.

"Human, yes. I am. You can call me Filoo. You're Ariel Burgess, aren't you?"

Something about him made her wary. "How do you know who I am?"

"I make it my business to know what people are doing, especially down south in what's called our government here," Filoo said. "The word is you're looking to put together a referendum to get these poor bastards the vote."

"That's not true. Even if I wanted to, it's not within my power to do that."

"Okay. Wouldn't be natural, if you want my opinion. Even Parapoyos, he loved the reanimes like his children, but he wouldn't have even thought about it."

"You knew Kynig Parapoyos?"

"I did," Filoo said proudly. "He was the best thing that ever happened to this world. I knew him, and I worked for him, and I can tell you things were better here when he was in charge."

"The reanimes didn't seem to share your feeling about him," Ariel said.

"They have their reasons for doing what they do," Filoo said. "And much went on that day that nobody knows about. People aren't listening, but some stories are still being told, if you understand my meaning."

"I don't think I do, Mr. Filoo."

"Just Filoo," the man said. "Listen, Basq knows you're here. He wanted me to tell you that. Also that he admires your initiative. Look around all you want, just don't scare anyone else, all right?"

Filoo walked away toward the center of the settlement. Ariel watched him go, making a mental note to ask Mia and Masid if they knew anyone by that name. As he passed a concrete building, Filoo stopped and was surrounded by a mob of children. His hands dipped into his pockets and he started handing out treats of some kind. Each of the children was a cyborg, moving with terrifying speed and grace made even more unsettling by juxtaposition with the naïve exuberance of childhood. Looking closely at them, Ariel saw that none was younger than seven or eight. They must have been infants when the lab turned them out, for some flaw that was no longer apparent. And who had maintained them, done the surgeries and grafts necessary to keep their mechanical parts growing alongside the organic structures? Gernika had come a long way in a short time if it had learned how to keep its unformed young alive.

One of the children, a boy of eight or nine, broke away from Filoo and turned his small gift over in his hands. Ariel couldn't see what it was, but she saw something more important, something that chilled her to the marrow of her bones. She remembered meeting Derec at Kamil's, looking through the dossier on the missing children. If she wasn't mistaken, the boy with Filoo's toy in his hands was Vois Kyl.

# 15

**D**erec walked into Omel Slyke's office and said, "The robot came in the same day Taprin did, but not on Taprin's ship. A procedure was performed on it in the repair berths, I'm guessing number A48, and one of the human parties involved spent conspicuous time in the gaming rooms. There may or may not be a conspirator in the Kopernik staff; if there is, he or she lives in Block Six, Seven, or Eight of on-station housing."

Sometime in the middle of Derec's speech, a professional mask slid into place over Slyke's face. *I've got him,* Derec thought. *Either I've told him something he didn't know, or he's surprised I've gotten this far.*

"There's more," he said. "Whoever sabotaged Tiko's memory meant to suggest that Shara Limke was involved."

"Okay, Avery," Slyke said, but Derec wasn't done yet.

"And the message about Limke was meant for me," he finished, and waited to see what Slyke would say.

"Most of that we already know," Slyke said eventually. "But I'd sure be interested in hearing how you got there."

Derec sat down and went through what he'd learned from Tiko:

the raw data of memory gaps, the clear meaning of some of those gaps, the more delicate inferences he'd drawn from the saboteur's choices. At the end, he said, "Of course, it's possible that I've misinterpreted some of the data. I think it's clear, though, that different blocks of memory were deleted for different reason. I also think it's clear that the saboteur was working under some time pressure."

"Do tell." Slyke kept the mask on. "You finished showing off?"

Derec stood. "I am. You let me know if you think I can help."

"Hold on."

Derec waited at the door.

"Limke said you wanted to run a diagnostic on Tiko. I think we can probably let you do that."

Like Tiko's saboteur, Derec knew he didn't have much time. He rushed through a confirmation of the damage he'd spotted on the backup done immediately after Taprin's murder, and then he went on to the diagnostic proper. First he established that Tiko was communicating rationally and responding to input; finding no problems in that area, he proceeded on to a basic vetting of the RI's central positronic matrices. All seemed to be in working order. Derec found no sign that Tiko's functionality had been impaired by the erasure of memory.

With that out of the way, he got to the point. "Catalog all mentions of my name, beginning Taprin's arrival and ending when I commenced this procedure."

The truth was that Derec wasn't interested in executing a full diagnostic. He was fairly confident that Tiko hadn't been beguiled into participating in Taprin's assassination, and his analysis of the data erasures made him equally confident that the saboteur had known that Derec Avery would become entangled in the case. If he could confirm that intuition, it would point toward the involvement of either Shara Limke or one of the conspirators involved in the murders of Clar Eliton and others five years ago. As yet, Derec had precious little in the way of facts to support this intuition, but it seemed true to him, and in his situation impressions were crucial. The misdirection being laid before him demanded that he work on that basis.

Tiko brought up a list of several dozen mentions of Derec's name. Most were in communications among TBI personnel. He ignored these and concentrated on the rest. Shara Limke had mentioned him three times, Flin once... and there was an intercepted message from Ariel.

"Play message from Ariel Burgess," he said.

Ariel appeared in the lab. "Derec," she said. "I'm beginning to get concerned that Nucleomorph's motives are other than they have been represented to me. It's been suggested that I go to the reanime camp. In addition, I'd very much like to know why you traveled off-planet at this particular time in the company of a Managin sympathizer like Vilios Kalienin. Your trip is being interpreted in peculiar ways here, and if I know you, you haven't paid attention to anything that's happened on Nova Levis since you left. Don't be made into a puppet. Contact me as soon as possible, and if you are unable to communicate from Kopernik, return to Nova Levis. If I could order you, I would. Get in touch."

With that, Derec was alone in the lab again.

PLAY AGAIN? Tiko asked.

"No." Derec thought over what Ariel had said. She was right; he had no idea what was really happening on Nova Levis, although he'd kept closer tabs on reports than she seemed to be assuming.

He went through Limke's messages concerning him. They were all innocuous. The only other mention of his name came in an anonymous message left on a station advertising archive. Derec opened it.

DEREC AVERY. WELCOME BACK. YOU HAVE LEARNED SOMETHING IN THE LAST FIVE YEARS. SO HAVE WE.

The message was dated three days before at 2306. The exact moment of Jonis Taprin's death.

Someone wanted him to be involved. Why? Derec felt a sudden longing for Bogard, who would have been only too willing to speculate. On his own, Derec didn't feel up to the task his invisible adversaries had set for him.

"Tiko," he said. "Identify sender of this message."

A pause. Then: SENDER'S IDENTITY OBSCURED.

"Nature of obscurity?"

OFF-STATION ORIGIN, ROUTED THROUGH A NUMBER OF NODES THAT ARE NO LONGER FUNCTIONING.

Leave it, Derec decided. His mystery correspondent would be revealed soon enough. He found the partial serial number he'd taken from the crime-scene images and fed it into his terminal. "Tiko. Search shipping manifests and records of correspondence for this number."

WORKING... NO MANIFESTS AVAILABLE WITH THAT NUMBER. ONE PRIVATE MESSAGE.

"Display."

The message appeared on his terminal. It was long, and dated three days before Taprin's murder. Most of the message was personal, a windy discourse on the Terran political situation punctuated by references to what Derec assumed were contemporary entertainment and sports figures. In the middle of all this, a single sentence stood out: CY984653JM-I7 EN ROUTE. MAKE SURE IT GETS CLEANED UP BEFORE YOU PUT IT INTO SERVICE AGAIN.

"Sender, Tiko."

SENDER OBSCURED.

"Recipient."

OMEL SLYKE.

Derec bowed under the weight of questions. He dismissed all of the obvious ones and asked Tiko when Slyke had arrived at Kopernik.

ADJUTANT SLYKE ARRIVED TWELVE HOURS AFTER THE MURDER OF JONIS TAPRIN.

And he had this message waiting for him, Derec thought. Either Slyke was being set up, or Derec was. Or both. Or the sender had anticipated that Taprin would be on-station before he actually was.

"Tiko. Before Slyke arrived on this occasion, when was the last time he came to Kopernik?"

WORKING... SLYKE HAS TRAVELED TO KOPERNIK SEVEN TIMES IN THE LAST YEAR.

"Does the TBI maintain permanent staff on Kopernik? If so, list names and related information."

PRIORITY COMMUNICATION.

"I'm not asking for communication records," Derec said. "Just—"

PRIORITY COMMUNICATION. DIAGNOSTIC SESSION ENDED.

Shara Limke appeared exactly where Ariel had been a few minutes before. "Derec," she said. "Pon Byris just got here. He's demanding access to the investigation, and he's demanding access to you."

Pon Byris. The Auroran security chief had nearly jailed Ariel five years before, just to have a scapegoat in the latter stages of the Parapoyos mess. If he was on Kopernik, things were about to go from bad to worse.

"Tiko," Derec said. "One more thing. List all incoming ships to Kopernik on the date that CY984653JM-I7 arrived. When the list is compiled, send it to this terminal."

WORKING...

Derec left the lab and went looking for Shara Limke.

A riel didn't call ahead before she went to meet Masid Vorian. She no longer trusted any communication channel except her own voice, and she was less and less confident in that. Masid was in his office. He greeted her, perched himself on the corner of his desk, and waited.

Where to begin, Ariel wondered. She had far too much information and far too little context; perhaps it would be best to pick up where her last interaction with Masid had left off.

"Did Derec come to see you?" she asked.

Masid nodded. "He did. I don't think he followed up on anything I told him, though. He was gone with Kalienin the next day. Is he back yet?"

"No. At least I haven't heard from him. I tried to contact him at Kopernik, but the TBI is blocking all communication to and from the station."

"No surprise there. Every time they run up against a situation they don't understand, the first thing they do is try to shut everything down. Put it in stasis. It makes sense, but it isn't always the best way to investigate a crime." Masid saw the questioning look on Ariel's face and went on. "If you hold everything in place, you never find out what people would have done. That's obvious. But you never know what a person's intentions are unless you see them acting. I did my share of police work, and I learned at least as much from what people did after a crime than I did from trying to reconstruct what came before."

It struck Ariel that Basq—and Zev Brixa—might well be viewing her from exactly this perspective. It also struck her that since the moment Brixa had left her office, she'd been suffering from what she could only call paranoia.

"But you're not here to philosophize about criminal investigations, are you?" Masid said. "Derec came to ask me whether I thought that some of his study subjects might be going to the black market for drugs. He took the possibility personally, like it meant he wasn't working hard enough."

"What did you tell him?"

"I told him that if his subjects were looking for drugs, they were looking for Filoo. As it turns out, I might have steered him in the wrong direction; since he left, I've been asking around, and nobody's heard anything about Filoo since right after Parapoyos was killed. I think the reanimes probably got him, too."

"In a way they did," Ariel said. "I talked to him today at the reanime camp."

A cold light grew in Masid's eyes. "Is that so." He thought for a moment, utterly motionless; then he hopped off his desk and said, "Let's take a walk."

They walked away from the Triangle, into the residential neighborhood that clustered between the government district and a struggling commercial section. A Terran entrepreneur with more vision than sense had bought up several blocks of Nova City, believing that adventuresome tourists would come to see the buccaneer world that had given birth to the vanished cyborg abominations. As she passed by the empty storefronts, Ariel had time to reflect that the would-be tourist impresario had been wrong about a number of things. On the other side of the tourist ghetto was another residential neighborhood, this one older and less ostentatious than the constantly redeveloping area closer to the Triangle. Masid led Ariel into an apartment building from whose roof she could have thrown a stone over the wall into New Nova. She followed him into the elevator and up to the fifth floor, and when Masid knocked on a door, Mia Daventri opened it.

"I didn't think I'd see you again so soon," Mia said to Ariel. She looked at Masid. "With you I don't bother to wonder."

They sat in plastic chairs on Mia's small balcony, looking out over the wall into the haze over New Nova. Ariel felt lightheaded and a little nauseous, and realized that she hadn't eaten since the morning.

"Ariel says Filoo's alive," Masid said.

Mia absorbed this. "You say that like you intend to do something about it."

"Maybe I do, but probably not what you're thinking. I don't kill people anymore. I never liked it. I think that's why I missed Parapoyos when I had a shot at him. If the mind isn't settled, the hand doesn't aim true."

Coming from Masid Vorian, this was surprisingly metaphysical. Ariel sensed that there was more to his statement than he was telling, and sensed, too, that to ask would mean intruding into a part of him she had no right to see.

"What I mean," Masid said, "is that if Filoo's alive there might be a lot of other things alive that we thought were gone." He turned to Ariel. "Tell me—tell us—everything you've seen at the camp."

Ariel went through it from beginning to end, dredging up as much detail as she could and getting slightly frustrated when she realized that her memories of that day's visit weren't as sharp as they should have been. She forced herself to acknowledge the fact that Burundi fever, the mnemonic plague, might be working in her brain again, and then she forced herself to dismiss the possibility. She'd survived it before; without doubt it had left lasting scars upon the regions of her brain that impressed memories into her sense of the past. There were perfectly good psychosomatic reasons for her to have the impression that she was suffering again; the continued existence of the reanime camp had dragged out memories that she would just as soon have forgotten.

*Beware defense mechanisms*, she told herself. *If you can't see yourself clearly, you won't understand anything else.*

She went on: the quasi-military atmosphere, the surprising number of cyborgs and their surprising health, the fact that they had adopted a name for the settlement and seemed determined to make it a living community. The absence of visible disease. The presence of children.

"The oddest thing is this," she said, coming to the end. "Just before I left, after I'd spoken to Filoo, I thought I recognized one of the children."

Ariel wanted to stop there, to hesitate at the verge of the possibilities she would have to admit if she went on. Neither Masid nor Mia would let her, though. Almost in unison they said, "Who was it?"

"Vois Kyl," Ariel said. "One of Derec's study population."

They were silent for a time.

"I might have been mistaken," Ariel said. "I think I've contracted something, and it might have affected my perceptions."

"Contracted something?" Mia said warily.

"Maybe." Ariel waved a hand, trying to put them all at ease. "I've had mnemonic plague, and sometimes I think it's permanently affected the way my memory works. Could be just a routine virus, and it's taking a little time for my immune system to handle it."

"Could be," Masid said. "On the other hand, this is Nova Levis. You should see a physician."

"Tomorrow morning. Right now we have to figure out what's going on in Gernika."

"If we're going to talk, we should eat," Mia said. "I'll go get something. You two wait here."

She went through her apartment and out the door, leaving Ariel and Masid. Ariel looked at him, tried to see through his knack for becoming nearly invisible even when he was sitting in the next chair. She couldn't tell what he was thinking, and wasn't sure she wanted to know.

"I'm going to check in with the office," she said, and went inside Mia's apartment to find her terminal.

R. Jennie had sorted the day's messages into two categories: routine and important. The second category held only one message, from Vilios Kalienin. So he's back from Earth, Ariel thought, and wondered if Derec had returned as well. She considered it doubtful. Derec would have to be physically removed from Kopernik if he hadn't yet illuminated the robot angle on Taprin's murder.

Kalienin's message was video only, without avatar presence. "Ambassador Burgess," he said. "I'm afraid I have some unfortunate news. The current vexatious political situation between Earth and the Fifty Worlds is having difficult consequences for discretionary funding to the Nova Levis government. Senator Lamina is calling emergency hearings to determine which programs will need to be suspended until the impasse over Kopernik is resolved. Your legal project is a valued part of the Triangle's outreach to the settler population, but the times call for austerity. Please attend the Senate hearing chamber tomorrow at 1330." Kalienin could barely hide his contemptuous joy as he delivered his last lines. "None of the cuts are final as yet. Rest assured that you will be given ample opportunity to advocate for your work. Until tomorrow afternoon."

Ariel sat in front of Mia's terminal, giving her exactly the span of time it would take for Mia to come back. That long she would wallow, and no more. When Mia returned, it would be time to get to work.

# 17

**D**erec found Slyke in Limke's office. Neither of them looked happy. "Things are getting complicated for you, Adjutant," Derec said. "You can't stonewall Pon Byris the way you can me."

"Don't make me get vulgar in a professional situation," Slyke said.

"I don't have time for this," Limke said. "Between Byris, the Terran picket, the TBI, and the Managin media, I've got more than enough on my hands without you two carrying out personal vendettas. It ends now. Am I understood?"

Derec looked at her, unable to keep the surprise from his face. Somehow Pon Byris' arrival had steeled her. Either she realized she no longer had anything to lose from alienating the TBI, or she anticipated that the involvement of the Auroran security apparatus meant that the TBI's influence would diminish.

"I'm here to solve a crime, Director," Slyke said. Derec thought he meant it, but Slyke was difficult to read. He might have been accepting the rebuke, or offering a veiled one of his own.

"If Pon Byris wants to see me," Derec said, "I'd like to be fully up to speed beforehand. Slyke, I can help you; in fact, I think I already have. Am I correct?"

With some difficulty, the TBI adjutant nodded.

"All right. You can help me, too. Whatever grudges the TBI and I bore for each other, they've got nothing to do with you, and they've got nothing to do with Jonis Taprin. We need to level with each other. Can we agree on that?"

"We can," Limke said. Slyke's face remained unreadable.

Derec waited until he was sure that neither of them wanted to act on their animosity toward each other. Then he said, "What do you know about the robot?"

"It came into cargo dock 27 at 2133 the day of the murder," Slyke said. He looked up at the ceiling as he went through his recitation. "You're right about the repair berth; when we went looking for the technician on duty at the time, he'd disappeared. His name is Alvaro Kader, and we tracked him to a ship that left for Earth at 2300. He landed at Colombo-Lanka, and that's the last we've seen. The tech in A61 remembers seeing the robot come and go, but apparently all Kader did was a routine post-shipping tuneup. The hotel concession has no record of a meal ordered by any member of Taprin's staff, and we've interrogated all of them. It would be easy enough for a robot to walk through the kitchen and appropriate a service cart, though. According to the kitchen staff, domestics come through all the time to pick up meals, and that model is common enough not to draw attention to itself." He looked down from the ceiling at Derec. "Then the robot went to Taprin's room, knocked on the door, walked in and beat him to death. That's where we are."

"Wait. We're not there yet." There was a hole in Slyke's chronology. Derec worked it over in his mind until he'd pinpointed the omission. "At some point, someone tampered with the station's RI. What do you have on that?"

"Not a thing. We had all of our positronic techs go over the RI, and whoever scrambled it did a good job of covering his trail."

"Yes, he did," Derec said. "He did leave one thing behind, though. Your techs wouldn't have known to look for it."

Slyke took this as an insult. "Kindly do me the favor," he said.

"I ran a check through incoming message traffic," Derec said. "I'll admit, the primary purpose was to see what the two of you had said about me, to each other and anyone else. But while I was doing that, I ran across an anonymous message. It was directed to me, and what it said, more or less, was 'Welcome back.'"

That created small fissures in Slyke's professional stoneface. "You know who it is?"

Derec shook his head. "No. But there aren't too many possibilities—it shouldn't be that hard to narrow them down. There's something else you need to know before we go on, though. I think perhaps the way this RI was attacked has meaning."

"Meaning," Limke repeated.

"Yes. My career was ruined and I lost several friends as a result of a series of events that began with the subversion of an RI. That was a much cleverer job than this; as far as I can tell, whoever attacked Tiko was relatively blunt, and then used minimal finesse to cover his or her tracks. I think the main point of the RI attack was to draw me in."

"You don't have many problems with confidence, do you?" Slyke asked dryly.

In spite of himself, Derec had to laugh. "It sounds a bit self-centered, I know. Still, I think it's true. Ambassador Burgess and I stepped on powerful toes, and people of that nature have long memories. Also, I'm not convinced that the RI had to be manipulated in this way for the assassination to be successful."

"Then why bother with it?"

"Hear me out. Say for the sake of argument that you were planning to assassinate Jonis Taprin. Say further that the timing of the act was important, that it was conceived as the ultimate rebuttal to his speech. What's the context of the crime, then? Robots on Earth. Exactly the conundrum I found myself in the middle of after the assault at Union Station. Then I get a call from Director Limke, and I arrive on Kopernik feeling in some ways like I'm sliding back into my old life. All the elements are there: a robot accused of a crime, a possibly compromised RI, a tense political backdrop made more tense by assassination—"

Derec broke off as the door to Limke's office opened. "Director," said a stocky woman in the uniform of Kopernik Security. "There's been an assault on a robot. I think you'd better come see."

"I don't have time to look into a robot-bashing, Wills," Limke said. "You know where the Managins are on this station."

"All due respect, Director, I think you're going to want to see this one. The robot says that another robot did it."

The mechanical victim lay in several pieces in an access tunnel running parallel to the main passenger hall between the Spacer docks and the Spacer hotel. Kopernik was designed with many such passages, so its robots could carry out their duties without having to slow down to human pace. Even in the parts of the station primarily used by Terrans, station authorities maintained the parallel structure, on the theory that if the Terrans couldn't see all the robots working around them, everyone would be more comfortable. In this and many other ways, Kopernik was caught between Spacer and Terran preconceptions.

Lieutenant Wills let them to the spot and then stood back while Derec, Slyke, and Limke looked over the scene. Derec was the only Spacer there, and he recognized the damaged property as a Gruden, a brand specialized to higher-echelon domestic service. Somewhere on Kopernik, a Spacer politician was wondering where his valet had gotten to.

Judging from the state of the wreckage, that politician was going to need a new robot. Derec winced as he looked over the damage: the robot's cranium was wrenched off and severely dented by impact with either the floor or a bulkhead; the bearings at its elbows were broken; a number of its fingers dangled from wires. And if Derec wasn't mistaken, much of the Gruden's torso had been battered with its own head. They were looking at scrap.

"You said it told you another robot attacked it?" Limke asked the lieutenant.

"Yes, Director. Officer Ladze there—" she pointed out a young man directing robots away from the scene "—found it first. It spoke briefly to him before losing all function."

"Ladze," Limke called.

"Director?"

"Trade places with Lieutenant Wills for a moment."

Ladze approached the three of them as Wills took up his traffic duty. Robots moved speedily by, but most of them saw the group of humans and coordinated their approach to the scene so as to give the humans a wide berth, while not colliding with their mechanical counterparts coming the other way. Every once in a while Wills had to hold up a hand, slightly away from her body; when she did, the robot traffic in both directions instantly adjusted itself to give her, and the crime scene, that much more space.

"Tell us what the robot said when you found it," Limke said.

Ladze was taller than Derec, and not a Spacer, which made him very tall indeed. As if conscious of it, he ducked his neck slightly, and although he couldn't have been thirty years old, already his shoulders were rounding. He spoke with some diffidence, but precisely. "One of the robots came out into the main passage and said it needed to report a property offense. I was passing through on my way to the duty room, so I figured I might as well look since I went on shift in six minutes, anyway. The robot led me back into the tinhead alley here, and I found this one. It was trying to talk, but its vocal apparatus was seizing up on it. Over and over it said, 'I have been assaulted by a robot. Request assistance. I have been assaulted by a robot. Request assistance.' I tried to ask it questions, but it didn't respond to any of them, and then it just kind of petered out." Ladze shrugged. "I called the duty officer and let her know that I was on five minutes early."

"How long ago was this?" Slyke asked. He was looking at the flow of robotic traffic with unease and what looked like disgust.

Ladze checked the time chop on his datum. "About an hour."

Derec brought out his own datum. "Tiko," he said.

YES, DEREC.

"Is routine monitoring carried out in this corridor?"

YES.

"Do you have access to your records of it?"

OF COURSE.

Derec filed that. Given recent events, his question had been anything but obvious, yet Tiko had responded as if a large number of its memory matrices hadn't been scrambled a few days before. *Keep looking at that RI*, he told himself.

"Good," he said. "Show us this section of passage, beginning ninety minutes ago and proceeding at sixty-to-one. When you see the assault, slow to normal time."

WORKING.

Slyke, Limke, and Wills stood close to Derec as his datum's small holocaster replayed the previous ninety minutes at that location. Robot traffic blazed by in a series of frozen poses; and then in one of the frames, there was a robot on the floor, dismembered much as they saw it now.

"There," Derec said. "Go back one minute and play at normal speed."

Tiko complied, and Derec felt a slow horror building in him as a Cole-Yahner domestic appeared in the camera view, then stopped and looked in the direction from which the Gruden would be coming. When the Gruden appeared, the Cole-Yahner simply reached over, hooked an arm under its jaw, and tore its head off. The catastrophic injury, together with the sudden imperative to reorganize sensory input, rendered the Gruden practically static, although it did struggle to preserve itself. The passing robots observed, possibly made a comment to each other, but all of them were working on orders from a human which superseded whatever imperative they might have felt to end the assault.

"Tiko," he said. "Was this incident brought to your attention by any of the passing robots?"

NO, DEREC.

It snapped into place then, and Derec rounded on Slyke. "Where's the robot that was found in Taprin's room?"

"I told you, it was destroyed."

"No, I don't think it was. I'll bet you everything I own that the robot you found in Taprin's room was the robot that alerted Officer Ladze to what happened here. And I'll make you another bet. Tiko, run the assault sequence again. Find the best view of the perpetrator's serial number and magnify."

The holo stopped, ran back, paused. Tiko magnified a portion of the frozen image. The Cole-Yahner's serial number was clearly visible: CY984653JM-I7.

"You can explain this later, Slyke," Derec said. "In the meantime, I think we've got a more immediate problem. Tiko. Run the serial number of the destroyed robot. To whom is it assigned?"

The briefest of pauses. AURORAN CHIEF OF PLANETARY SECURITY PON BYRIS.

They burst into Pon Byris' suite, Ladze and Wills first, followed by Slyke, Limke, and Derec. The three law officers had weapons out, and they fanned through the three rooms.

"In here!" Wills called from the bedroom. "Tiko, dispatch emergency medical team!"

All five of them clustered around the broken body on the bedroom floor, and Derec knew the medical team wouldn't even have to open their cases. Pon Byris was well beyond the reach of human science.

"It's not a bad diversion for a tinhead," Slyke said an hour or so later, when they'd learned what they could from the scene and retired to Shara Limke's office to await the inevitable reaction. Byris' staff had flooded the room even before the medical personnel arrived, and when they broadcast the news of the Chief's murder, it looked like Aurora finally had its excuse for war with Earth. Military vessels from Aurora and Keres were appearing outside the Terran picket, and from all appearances the Terran forces were more than ready to join the dance. Someone had leaked the rumor that a robot had killed Byris, with the predictable result that Terran political rhetoric had reached a fever pitch. The calls for total severance of relations with the Fifty Worlds were becoming a chorus, with frequent solos demanding war first. All of it was much like the situation five years before, but at the same time the stakes were even higher. After Union Station, fewer than thirty percent of Spacers had actually left Earth; now only a tiny fraction was willing to stay. Those few Spacers who hadn't left after Taprin's assassination were now en route to Kopernik, and as often as not their offices and businesses were being destroyed behind them.

And, in far too many cases, burned down around them. Apoplectic demands from Spacer governments that Earth restore order and protect the lives of Spacers working there met with waffling, as the Terran government calculated its chances of political survival and decided that avoiding all-out anarchy was worth a few dead Spacers. The Managins raved on every newsnet, and on Kopernik Station Derec waited for the first shots to be fired. When he took the time to think about it, he didn't expect to live beyond the week. Kopernik would surely be one of the first casualties, intentionally or not. Maybe Shara Limke was right, that a new station would be constructed in its place, but that wouldn't make much difference to Derec if there was war.

Derec caught himself wishing he was back on Nova Levis. It wasn't a thought he'd ever imagined himself having. He did what he always did to distract himself from untenable emotions and desires: he worked.

The list of incoming traffic from the day of Taprin's assassination was waiting for him. He went through it, eliminating those ships from Earth that carried no robots, and then eliminating the ships from the

Fifty Worlds whose robots were all accounted for. Either one of those eliminations might turn out to be based on faulty or tainted records, but Derec's instincts were pointing him in a particular direction, and all he could do was ride them until he discovered what that direction was.

"Derec."

He looked up and saw Shara Limke in the doorway of his lab. "Have you found the Cole-Yahner?"

"No. But we've found four of Byris' other robots, all suffering the same kind of damage. We've got Tiko looking for the robot, but there are more than one hundred Cole-Yahners of the same model in service here. Most of them don't wear humaniform to avoid spooking the Earthers, so they look more or less identical unless Tiko can read their serial numbers."

"Sounds like what you need to do is get your security people out there and physically check every Cole-Yahner on Kopernik Station. Mark the ones you've cleared and have Tiko look for the ones that aren't marked. Sometimes the low-tech solutions are the best."

"That's a strange thing for a positronic theorist to say," Limke said. "Actually, Slyke's doing something like that. He's got every TBI agent on-station combing the halls with the robot's serial number written on the backs of their hands."

"Robot," Derec said. He was looking at his display, and one of the ships on the list had caught his eye. "I'm not sure that's it."

"Not sure what's it?" Limke asked.

Only one ship had come in bringing cargo from a non-Spacer world on the day of Jonis Taprin's assassination. It was the *Viltroy*, carrying "biotech samples, positronic circuits, rare metals," with a five-day maintenance layover at Kopernik scheduled before its final delivery of its cargo to Earth.

Its planet of origin was Nova Levis.

"I'm not sure it's a robot at all," Derec said.

N ova Boulevard was gridlocked the next morning. A demonstration in front of the Triangle had attracted seemingly half the population of the city,

Ariel attended the hearing knowing more or less exactly what would happen, and as usual her political instincts were accurate. Eza Lamina held the gavel, seven of her fellow Spacer senators made up the rest of the committee, and Vilios Kalienin remained close at hand, offering whispered advice at every break in the proceedings.

"Ambassador Burgess," Lamina said after an hour or so of preliminaries. "Your association with the question of cyborg citizenship is terribly discrediting to what this government is trying to accomplish. It is difficult for me to understand how you can continue in your present liaison capacity, and it is even more difficult to see how your project can continue without you."

Ariel had lost all interest in political niceties. "That's quite a tidy assessment of the situation, Senator. You get rid of me and the only compartment of the Triangle interested in government transparency, all at one stroke."

One of the other senators spoke. Arvid Aanesen, from Acrisia.

Privately Ariel thought of him as Senator Vowel, and his speech fed into the caricature. He was the kind of politician who always spoke as if he was changing the course of human history; he thundered, he boomed, he devoted himself to the pursuit of the orotund and obfuscatory. "This is beneath you, Ms. Burgess," he said. "The gravity of this situation demands a certain decorum from us all, but perhaps most especially from yourself."

"You'll excuse me if I see no reason to be decorous when I'm being scapegoated," Ariel shot back. "A corporate citizen in good standing of this planet asked me to investigate a legal question. I am in the process of doing so. I have taken no position on the question and do not intend to. It is manifestly useless for this panel to attach to me motives imputed by subetheric parasites."

"Who has asked you to investigate the question?" Lamina asked.

"Given the irrational response to the question," Ariel said, "I believe it is in no one's best interests for me to divulge that information."

"I will remind you that you are under compulsion to answer direct inquiries here, Ms. Burgess." This time the speaker was Brin Houser, cashiered from the Solarian diplomatic corps for profiteering on Settled worlds.

*That I should be grilled by a group of corrupt exiles,* Ariel thought. *At least the last time people tried to scapegoat me, they had power that meant something beyond a pathogenic backwater.*

"I assert that the committee has no legitimate interest in knowing the answer," she said. "The purpose of the question is solely to widen the smear that is as of now only being perpetrated on me and my project."

"You will answer the question, or you will be held in contempt," Houser said, drawing the last few words out for effect.

"The committee can hold me in no greater contempt than I already feel for each of its members," Ariel said. In the outraged silence that followed, she brought up the name of a lawyer on her datum.

Seated at her kitchen table that evening, Ariel reflected that she might have been more circumspect in her speech to the committee. Her project was terminated, and with it the employment of the nineteen attorneys and researchers she supervised. Formal charges were pending against her, and whatever the outcome—which didn't worry her, since a constitutional committee was already empanelled to draft a clause restricting citizenship to unenhanced human beings, and once the clause was rubber-stamped it wouldn't be worth the Triangle's time to go through with prosecution—people on Nova Levis would suffer because Ariel's transparency project was no longer there to goad the powers that were into some semblance of rectitude.

*So ends my brief career in politics,* she thought. *I was made an ambassador because no one else was available, and now I'm not even fit to be a liaison to a bunch of profiteering exiles.*

"Time to go back into robotics," she mused out loud.

R. Jennie stirred. "Would you like me to update your vita?"

"No, thank you, Jennie," Ariel said with a smile, even though it wasn't a terrible idea. She'd kept up on the literature when she had time; her skills couldn't be that far out of date, and when she had worked at the Calvin Institute, she'd been one of the best.

*I should be on Kopernik,* she thought. *I'm as good as Derec ever was, and Jonis...*

That train of thought didn't lead anywhere she wanted to go. Strange, that one of her lovers should be investigating the murder of another. She remembered Jonis, a long time ago, wanting to rub her feet. Before he'd become a Managin, or at least before he'd admitted to it. Before he'd stood by and let her bear the brunt of the anti-Spacer backlash that followed the Union Station massacre. The power of the memory shook her, and Ariel found herself wiping tears from her eyes before she'd consciously realized she was crying.

"Do you require assistance, Ariel?" R. Jennie, ever solicitous.

"Just solitude, Jennie. I just need to be left alone."

R. Jennie left the room. Ariel got up from the table and found a bottle of Terran whiskey in the cabinet over the stove. On the way back to the table, she picked up a glass, and after that she didn't leave the chair for quite some time.

Nova Levis. If there was a worse place for human beings to live in the known universe, Ariel had never heard of it. Hours had passed, and Ariel had long since stopped tasting the whiskey she poured into herself. Out of her intoxication and angry self-pity, a thought formed itself: *As long as they're in charge, this planet will never be anything more than a pathogenic sump. A way station for pirates, an open-air laboratory for voracious microbes and vonoomans. The hell with cyborg citizenship. What Nova Levis needs is real citizenship for the people who live here.*

Like a spark in a thatched roof, that thought burrowed into her mind and began to smolder.

The next morning, all of her head was smoldering. As soon as she'd cleaned up and scalded her throat with a little coffee, Ariel went to see Masid anyway. He wasn't in his office, so Ariel got more coffee and fresh bread from a bakery around the corner and settled down on a transport-station bench to wait for him. An hour passed, her head cleared, her stomach settled. Then Masid sat down next to her. "You get coffee for me, too?"

Ariel started, then had to laugh. "Good thing I'm not a spy."

"Good thing I'm not, either." Masid smiled as well, but there was a little warning behind it. Ariel wasn't sure she wanted that warning spelled out. "The accommodations here suit you, or would you like to go inside?"

"I think I'd just as soon sit here," Ariel said. "All I have is one thing to say, in any case. One thing to ask."

He waited for her to go on.

"I'm going to go back to Gernika," she said. "I want you to just...check in on me every so often."

"If you're that worried about them, you shouldn't go," Masid said.

"That's the thing, Masid. I'm not sure whether I'm more worried about the reanimes or the people I'm supposed to be working for here. I mean it."

He studied her, waiting again. Masid had a way of making the rhythms of a person's speech seem off somehow. Ariel felt like she'd been blithering.

"Do you have any hope for this place?" she asked him.

"I make it a rule never to have hope for anything."

"Then what keeps you here? If every place is hopeless, why not go somewhere that at least does a good job of concealing it?"

Masid shrugged. "Ariel, you're talking to an ex-spy. After a few years doing that, it's real nice to have everything out in the open. Easier to figure out who your enemies are. You have a personal com code?"

Ariel touched her datum to his.

"Okay," he said. "I'll get in touch every so often. You want the rest of this bread?"

She gave it to him, then asked him a question on impulse. "If it actually came to a vote, which way would you go?"

Masid had already stood, and again Ariel saw that hint of warning in his face. "It won't come to a vote. A lot of other things might happen, but you can bet your uterus that Nova Levis will never vote on citizenship for cyborgs. Travel safe, Ariel."

A minute or so after he'd crossed the street and gone into his office, a public transport squealed up. Ariel almost hesitated too long, but as it was dropping into gear again she jumped up from the bench and climbed aboard.

Shara Limke did not believe for one moment that a murderous cyborg might be loose on her station. Derec could see this on her face, and he couldn't blame her. He wouldn't have believed it himself if he hadn't seen Jerem Looms and Tro Aspil at much closer range than he'd ever wanted. Still, that was where the available evidence led him.

Despite her disbelief, Limke had made sure that Omel Slyke cooperated with station security in personally tagging every Cole-Yahner on Kopernik. The process wasn't finished, but it soon would be. Derec wasn't sure what they would find, but he found that his faith in the inability of positronic robots to kill had been restored. Odd, that it had been shaken so thoroughly. He was still an Auroran.

Derec was killing time in his lab, waiting as each report on an individual Cole-Yahner domestic trickled over the station security net, when Skudri Flin walked in.

"I'm surprised you're not out looking for robots," Derec said.

"I am." Flin laid a disk on Derec's desk. "Listen. I can only say this once, and then I'm going to pretend that you and I talked about billiards in the game room if anyone asks. That might not do any good.

If this thing keeps blowing up, and you go down, I'm going to go down with you. I don't like that, Avery, but I did it to myself. So here's your disk. I don't give a damn about Jonis Taprin, but that Spacer getting murdered tells me that something's going on that the TBI can't handle. I didn't give them this because they're arrogant, big-footed sons of bitches, and I don't trust them, and if I have to tell you that you shouldn't either, you're dumber than I'm guessing."

"You don't."

"Good. I'd hate to think I was that wrong about someone. Listen, here's something else." He handed Derec a flimsy. "One of the guys down at the cargo docks saw something this morning. I'm not saying it's a robot, and even if you can find out who he is, the dockworker won't either, but you should have a look."

"Before or after I look at the record from the robot?"

"Should probably be after. But what the hell, look whenever you want."

"I've got more than enough ambiguity on my plate," Derec said. He opened the sheet, and saw shipping information. A freighter, the *Cassus*, had left Kopernik three hours before, bound for Nova Levis. How had it gotten through the picket? Derec wondered. When he looked up to ask Flin, the man had gone.

Looking back to the flimsy, Derec saw that the *Cassus* was registered to Nucleomorph.

He set the flimsy down. So many questions answered, and so manymore opened up in turn. All he could do was speculate until he'd seen the record from the robot.

Picking the disk up, Derec took a deep breath. *No preconceptions,* he told himself. *The data is the data. Let it tell you what it will.*

He slid the disk into the slot of his desktop datum, and waited for it to yield its secret.

DIDN'T DO IT DIDN'T DIDN'T DO IT

HUMAN DEAD, IDENTIFY, JONIS TAPRIN, BODY TEMPERATURE DECREASING IN LINEAR PROGRESSION CONSISTENT WITH AMBIENT TEMPERATURE

DIDN'T

FIRST LAW VIOLATION, ASSESS RESPONSIBILITY, NO OTHER BEINGS MECHANICAL OR HUMAN PRESENT, INFERENCE OF SELF-RESPONSIBILITY, ASSESS ALTERNATE POSSIBILITIES, NONE AVAILABLE, DIAGNOSTIC ON CHRONOLOGICAL AWARENESS REVEALS CONFLICT, GAP IN PERCEPTIONS POSSIBLY DUE TO

DIDN'T DO IT INCAPABLE OF DIRECT ASSAULT ON HUMAN BEING INCAPABLE OF INFLICTING HARM EVEN IN CASE OF POSSIBLE DANGER TO ANOTHER HUMAN

DID NOT DO THIS

HUMAN DEAD, ASSESS DAMAGE, BLUNT TRAUMA, STRUCTURAL DAMAGE TO CRITICAL SYSTEMS

ASSESS SYSTEMS, PHYSICAL ROUTINES NORMAL, CHECK MEMORY

CONFLICT

DIDN'T DO IT

ASSESS POSSIBILITIES, OTHER PARTIES MIGHT HAVE CONDUCTED ATTACK, NO OTHER PARTIES REGISTER IN MEMORY

MEMORY, LAST HOUR, INSPECT

MAINTENANCE CONDUCTED AT BERTH A48, KOPERNIK STATION, AFTER TRANSIT FROM

PLANET OF ORIGIN UNAVAILABLE, GAP IN MEMORY DIAGNOSED, INTERROGATED, PLACE OF MANUFACTURE AURORA, SERVICE RECORD INCLUDES AURORA KERES NOVA LEVIS, INITIAL OBSOLESCENCE INSPECTION CONDUCTED NOVA LEVIS ELEVEN MONTHS PREVIOUS, REMOVED FROM ACTIVE SERVICE

LAST SERVICE RECORDS INCLUDE PERFORMANCE OF PROGRAMMED DUTIES AT

DIDN'T DO IT

FIRST LAWCONFLICT, HUMAN DEAD, SELF POSSIBLY RESPONSIBLE, INVESTIGATE, OTHER PARTIES PRESENT?

PARTIES IN ROOM, SELF AND NONFUNCTIONAL HUMAN JONIS TAPRIN, INVENTORY SURROUNDINGS, STANDARD GOVERNMENT-CLASS HOTEL

ACCOMMODATION, THREE ROOMS, NO SOUNDS INDICATING PRESENCE IN OTHER ROOMS, ONLY PRESENCE IN THIS ROOM SELF AND NONFUNCTIONAL HUMAN JONIS TAPRIN

CONCLUSION, SELF IN ROOM AT TIME OF NONNATURAL DECEASE OF HUMAN JONIS TAPRIN, FIRST LAW CONFLICT, NO RECORD OF SELF ACTING TO PRESERVE LIFE OF JONIS TAPRIN, NO RECORD OF SELF

CONFLICT, DID NOT CAUSE HARM TO HUMAN JONIS TAPRIN

NO OTHER PARTY IN ROOM AT TIME OF DECEASE OF JONIS TAPRIN, POSSIBLE CONCLUSION SELF CAUSED NONFUNCTION OF JONIS TAPRIN, CONCLUSION IMPOSSIBLE, FIRST LAW CONFLICT

MEMORY DIAGNOSTIC, CONTINUITY?, INTERRUPTED, GAP IN MEMORY 2247-2307, TIME NOW 2307, RECALL 2247, ROUTINE MAINTENANCE, ORDERS GIVEN TO

MEMORY ENDS

MEMORY BEGINS AGAIN 2307, HUMAN JONIS TAPRINDEAD, UNABLE TO DETERMINE PRESENCE OF SELF AT DEATH

PHYSICAL INVENTORY, HUMAN BLOOD ON CHASSIS AND LIMBS, ALSO FEET, TRAIL OF PARTIAL FOOTPRINTS LEADING FROM BODY OF HUMAN JONIS TAPRIN TO SELF

DIDN'T DO IT

"Alvaro Kader," Derec muttered. The tech who had worked on the robot. Either he'd made some modification to the machine, or he'd relayed a kind of message that had distracted the positronic brain while the fearsomely strong alloy body did the work. It was exactly the modus operandi he'd seen at Union Station, and seeing it again made Derec wonder if maybe Kynig Parapoyos hadn't survived after all. It wasn't likely, but if that wasn't the case, someone else had assimilated both Parapoyos' methods and his posthumous grudge.

The Cole-Yahner wasn't a cyborg. Derec was no longer worried about that. For a moment, when he'd seen that the domestic robot had arrived from Nova Levis, he couldn't think about anything but cyborgs, and a cyborg disguised as a robot would be a tricky adversary indeed. Other robots would notice the difference, but most of them would operate with defaults that would grant a cyborg provisionally human status until they could confirm the decision with an actual human being. The time lag would be more than enough for a skilled assassin. But there the robot was, in a positronic death spiral after its (best case) presence at or (worst case) commission of the murder of Jonis Taprin. If it was a cyborg, it wouldn't have sat around waiting for Kopernik Security, the TBI, Derec, or anyone else to take a look at it.

Which left subversion, and that was why Derec badly wanted to talk to Alvaro Kader.

Even before he could do that, though, he had to warn Ariel.

Slyke answered his com from somewhere down in the maintenance corridors. "Don't bother me, Avery," he said. "We've got eighty-nine of one hundred and two Cole-Yahners from that series. Thirteen more. I'll let you know what happens."

"The one you're looking for is off the station," Derec said.

"Did your mysterious opponent tell you that? Getting more coded messages?"

"Slyke, I don't care whether you believe me or not. A colleague of mine might well be in danger back on Nova Levis, and I need to get a message through to her. The robot came here from Nova Levis, and now it's going back there..." Derec halted himself. If he wasn't careful, he was going to sound more paranoid than he really felt. "Have you heard about what's going on there? On Nova Levis?"

"What, the cyborg vote thing?"

"Exactly. That. A colleague of mine—"

"Burgess."

Of course the TBI would have briefed Slyke about Ariel. "Yes. She was asked to look into the question. The cyborg who killed Rega Looms also killed her lover, and I don't think I have to tell you how she feels about the question personally. But she agreed to investigate the legal issues. Now what if I told you that Nucleomorph, the company who asked her to do this, is the same company that owns the ship flying your assassin robot back to Nova Levis?"

The professional stoneface came over Slyke again. Derec could see him working through the implications, searching for alternatives, double-checking his conclusions. It didn't take long.

"Just so I know we're on the same wavelength here," Slyke said. "Are you suggesting that someone on Nova Levis wanted Taprin dead so they could further a kind of anti-Spacer vendetta? And that the cyborg deal is a stalking horse for that?"

*Am I suggesting that?* Derec wondered. "That sounds more or less right," he said, vacillating and hating himself for it.

"Okay. So did the robot kill Taprin?"

*This is where you jump,* Derec told himself. *You've been moving along the edge for a long time now.*

"I think it might have," he said. "Only I'm pretty sure a human was pulling its strings. Do you have some time for me to explain this?"

"Time? Sure, I've got nothing but time now that the great brain of Phylaxis is on-station. Where would you like to meet?"

"I'll come find you," Derec said. "You might want to make sure this conversation is private."

By the time Derec tracked the TBI officer to an annex between the robot corridors and the human passages that paralleled them, Slyke was getting a com report from one of his inspectors that all of the Cole-Yahners on Kopernik Station had been identified. None of them was the unit they were looking for. Slyke ended the call and noticed Derec waiting.

"I thought of something," he said. "You think this robot might have killed Taprin. Nobody knew that Pon Byris was coming. How do you work that in?"

"Could be any number of things," Derec said.

"Such as?"

"I need you to explain something first. Why did you tell me the robot had been scrapped?"

"Because I wanted you to give up and go home."

Right, Derec thought. A perfectly good reason to compromise a murder investigation. "Fair enough. What really happened to it?"

"You want to know the truth? It got up and walked out of the berth while our positronic guy was out getting a cup of coffee."

"I've seen a record of its responses to the murder, Slyke. That robot was in complete positronic collapse."

Slyke shrugged. "That's what our guy said, too. Looks like both of you were wrong."

"Details," Derec said. "What stage of analysis had your tech reached?"

"I don't know. I don't deal with robots, and I don't especially like dealing with people who deal with robots. Our guy said that the tinhead was scrambled, I took his word for it, and then it turns out that it wasn't quite so scrambled after all."

"Does Tiko have any record of it?"

"You mean the RI? It's called Tiko?" Derec nodded, biting back a comment; he was sure he'd mentioned Tiko's name to Slyke before, but details like the names of robots didn't stick in the mind of a borderline Managin like Slyke. "Sure, the RI has all kinds of records. The robot walked out of the lab where we were looking at it, went straight down into the tinhead tunnels, and started picking off Byris' robots. When it had all five of the ones that spent a lot of time with the man himself, it created its diversion and went to Byris' room. Then it grabbed hold of him and broke his neck, and then it walked back out."

"Where did it go then?"

"We've got it as far as the cargo docks. Then the goddamn Aurorans started firing off full-holo messages to everyone in the galaxy, and because they all had diplomatic priority Tiko had to redirect processing capacity away from routine surveillance so it could encode and send everything." Slyke's tone had gotten bilious. "You Spacers. You need robots to change your diapers, but you have no idea how to actually use them."

Derec laughed. "Always a pleasure working with bigots, Adjutant Slyke."

"What happened, happened," Slyke said.

"It happened because the people with Byris are diplomats who are used to being more important than everyone else, especially police. Are you telling me you don't know any Terrans like that?"

Slyke waved the comment away. "We're not here to discuss sociology, Avery. You going to tell me how your mysterious assassin knew that Pon Byris was going to be here?"

"That depends. Are you going to tell me whether you intentionally sabotaged your own investigation?"

A flush spread over Slyke's face, and Derec had a momentary worry that he'd provoked the officer to violence. "You're lucky you're already on Nova Levis, or I'd find some way to get you shipped there," Slyke said. "And believe me, I can do it. You sabotaged the investigation when you decided to come out of your hole and make amends for Union Station. And while you were at it, you took Shara Limke down; she might have dug her own grave when she called you, but you pushed her in when you said yes. Just so you know."

The anger seemed to drain out of Slyke. He shook his head. "When you deal with the kind of political heat I'm getting, you can question my integrity. Now you've done it twice, and I'm not going to hear it a third time. Just bear in mind that you didn't come here to solve a crime, and I didn't come here to make myself feel better. That's what separates you and me."

Derec took out the flimsy he'd gotten from Skudri Flin. "Here's the ship that took the robot off-station. If you're trying to find out who killed Taprin and Pon Byris, you might want to take a look at it."

"What I want to do is put you in a cell until this whole thing blows over. If I'm lucky there'll be a war and we can trade you to Aurora for an embassy janitor. Stay out of my way."

Walking away to the portal that led back to the main corridor, Slyke threw a parting shot over one shoulder. "And stay out of Limke's way, too. She's got enough to worry about without you around."

Ariel had never taken public transport on Nova Levis before, and even before she had reached the main station in Nova City and bought a ticket to Noresk, the experience had changed her understanding of a great many things. She had known that far too many people on Nova Levis were poor or sick or oppressed or all of those, but even when she'd traveled to Stopol or Noresk, she typically met with people who had power. They were concerned about real problems, but they didn't experience them in the way the average citizen of Nova Levis did on a daily basis. Sharing a seat with a woman who was obviously dying of a respiratory disease—and who, in spite of her suffering, was on her way to work driving a municipal transport just like the one they were riding in—had a way of anchoring abstractions. Not to mention making Ariel feel as if she had spent her life in willful ignorance.

The transport passed the Triangle, and again she felt a flash of pure revolutionary anger. None of this would ever change as long as the people on city buses could work themselves to death while being governed by people who would live for centuries. She transferred to the Noresk transport, and lost the sick woman in the station crowd.

# HAVE ROBOT, WILL TRAVEL

Ariel sat at a window as the transport left the city, enduring that peculiar stunned feeling that came when the mind tried to accommodate a fundamental shift in the way it apprehended the world. How could she have failed to understand this for so long?

The feeling endured long enough that she started to wonder if she was ill herself. Ordinary details of her fellow passengers' faces—the curve of an eyebrow, the habitual vacant half-smile—came to seem freighted with obscure significance. She lost hours in semi-conscious free associations, a kind of spiraling fugue that broke only when the transport stopped to take on or disgorge passengers; eventually it did not stop even then. When the transport groaned to a halt in Noresk, Ariel knew it only because everyone got off. She stirred in her seat, feeling stiffness in her limbs and a powerful need to urinate.

Walking to the public facility took care of both issues, and not knowing what else to do, Ariel walked out into the noise and smoke of Noresk. She had known in an abstract way that Noresk was a troubled place, but her first few minutes there made the slice of humanity on the transport seem like a convention of Solarian magnates.

There was a dead man in the street. He was barefoot and lay with his body twisted as if he'd been roughly searched after his death—at least Ariel hoped it was after. Wine-colored blotches, scabbed from scratching, covered his face and hands and feet, and a dark yellow substance crusted in the corners of his slitted eyes. Passersby stepped around him the way they might unconsciously navigate a pothole. This indifference staggered Ariel even more than the presence of an unattended corpse in the street outside the main transport station. Who was this man? Where was his family? Did they survive him, or had his disease killed them as well?

Ariel realized she was standing on the sidewalk just outside one of the station's main doors. People shouldered their way around her, too, intent or preoccupied even to tell her to move. She started walking, crossing the street and turning right at random, just to be away from the dead man who lay like one more piece of garbage in the street. Reflexively she went to her pocket for her datum to check for messages and plot her way to Gernika, then caught herself, fearing robbery; then she was ashamed of the fear. Not ashamed enough to take her datum out, though. She kept walking until she found a restaurant, and went in only after she'd seen through the window that its clientele seemed no less groomed than the average public kitchen on Earth.

With a cup of coffee and a table to herself, Ariel opened her datum and saw that Senator Lamina had already made her defunding official. A severance package had been transferred into her account, and she had seventy-two hours to remove her equipment from the Triangle-leased office in Nova City. A letter of reference was installed in her personnel file, diplomatically characterizing her service as professional and dedicated.

So. She was no longer involved in the government of Nova Levis, and therefore no longer concerned with the question of citizenship for the reanimes. Ariel sipped at her coffee and realized with a start that if she wanted to, she could probably leave Nova Levis. She'd never get back into the diplomatic corps, but it wasn't out of the question that she could find robotics work with one of the large contractors on the Spacer worlds.

*No,* Ariel thought. *I am implicated in this, and would shame myself if I abandoned my work here.* Being cast loose from the Triangle might turn out to be useful, once the initial shock of rejection had passed. If she was no longer beholden to political currents, she could strike her own course across the uncharted seas on whose shores Zev Brixa had set her.

And the truth was, the question had worked its way into her conscience like a fishhook. She couldn't leave until she had seen it through to whatever resolution awaited.

"Jennie," she said.

Her robot's face filled the datum's screen. "Yes, Ariel?"

"Clean out my office. Put all of the equipment into storage. Keep all paper records from the last two weeks at the apartment and store the rest. Relinquish my door codes at the Procurement Office in the Justice Corner and get a signed receipt. And while you're there, make sure that they forward all messages sent to my government code."

"Shall I leave now?"

"Yes. Bill the moving costs to the Triangle."

"Yes, Ariel." The screen blanked.

Ariel pulled up a satellite map of the Noresk area. Pinpointing her location, she worked out the quickest way to Gernika. East out of the city, across the Bogard, and then along what appeared to be a dirt road through the forest. Twenty kilometers or so. She would walk in the front door this time, and she would stay until she had some answers.

Before leaving, she found a shoe store and bought a pair of sturdy boots. Outside the store, she left her old shoes sitting on the sidewalk. There were any number of people in Noresk who needed them worse than she did.

Ariel fell into a reverie again while walking, lulled into a kind of somnolence by the steady pace of her footsteps and the rhythm of her body moving with each step. She was sweating more than she should have been; whatever pathogen she'd picked up on her first trip up this way, it wasn't letting go without a struggle. At one point, she stopped, worried that she was getting worse; she couldn't keep her mind on a thought, and she had to actively remind herself where she was going. A diplomat yesterday, a vagabond today, she mused, and in her detached state of mind she was swept up by the abstract romance of her situation. She could walk. Nowhere to go, no one to answer to. She could walk until she decided to stop. If disease took her, it took her.

The appearance of the river brought Ariel most of the way back to her senses. She was a good swimmer, but the river was perhaps five hundred meters wide and she didn't know what currents surged under the surface. Even in her current daze, she knew better than to take that kind of risk before she'd exhausted her other options.

Which were what, exactly? Walk up- or down-river until she came to a ferry? She doubted there were any this far outside Noresk. Wait for a passing boat and hope it would carry her to the other shore? There was no reason for a boat to be plying the waters this far north unless it belonged to a survey team of some kind, and those were not numerous in this area. The area was well mapped and the biologists were concentrating on the cities until the epidemiological situation was more under control. She could go back to Noresk and rent a transport, or purchase passage from a freelance pilot, but for reasons she couldn't articulate Ariel didn't feel comfortable leaving that much evidence of her actions.

The rippling boom of a large cargo or transport ship startled birds from the forest all around her. Ariel looked up, found the ship, tracked it on its northern course until it slowed and dropped out of sight behind the trees. Going to Noresk. Probably a freighter from offworld, or a short-hop courier from Nova City; it was big enough to be the first, not so large that it couldn't be the second. Birdcalls echoed through the forest, dying away to the normal background chirps and squawks, and Ariel lost patience with obstacles. The river was wide and deep, its banks easy and its course reasonably straight. She could swim it.

She stripped down to underclothes, stuffed her socks in one boot and her datum in the other, and threaded her belt through the loops above the heels of each boot. Then she refastened the belt around her waist and worked her way down the bank into the water. It was cold, and the bottom fell away steeply; after two steps she was swimming, invigorated and a little frightened by the current and the stinging chill. It had been years since Ariel had swum any distance, but she settled into an even crawl, going with the current in a downstream diagonal course that would, with any luck, put her ashore on the other side where a small tributary creek flowed into the Bogard. Her head cleared a little, and she grinned between breaths at how quickly her caution had crumbled under the force of her impatience. Then she put her face in the water and pulled hard, enjoying the physical work of it and the sensation of being buoyed up on the water's flow.

When she scraped sand with her fingertips, Ariel stood and shook the water out of her eyes. She slicked her hair back and reached up for a hanging branch, hauling herself up from the water onto the shore. Breathing hard, she stood dripping and elated on the far side of the Bogard from human civilization, thrilling to the feeling of release that coursed through her. She swiped the water from her limbs and put her boots back on, then tested her datum to make sure that it was as waterproof as the manufacturer advertised. It was, so she verified her position. Five kilometers away; in her exhilarated state she felt like she could fly the whole way. She hooked the datum's carrying loop through her belt and started walking.

Ariel had no doubt that the reanimes would know she was coming long before she arrived at the outskirts of Gernika, and she was correct. After half an hour of working her way out of the thick underbrush bordering the river, she moved more quickly through a dim stretch of tall trees under which nothing grew but moss. Then she found the dirt road, and half an hour after that she saw the settlement, and the arresting figure of Basq waiting for her.

"Your appearance gives me no great confidence of your political influence, Ambassador," he said when she'd gotten close enough.

"I doubt I'm an ambassador anymore, Basq," Ariel answered. "I haven't come in an official capacity."

"Then why have you come at all?"

"To bring a message."

"From whom?"

"From me. Here it is: You're a fool to rely on the Triangle for anything, and you're equally foolish to rely on Zev Brixa. The only person on this planet you can rely on to give you a fair hearing is me."

"And you come out of the woods like a shipwreck survivor. How you do inspire confidence, Miss Burgess."

"You don't need confidence. You need action. I'm here to decide if I'm willing to take that action for you."

"If you're not an ambassador anymore, and—I'm correct in inferring that you're not affiliated with the Triangle either?" Ariel nodded impatiently. "So I thought. What exactly can I expect to gain by your decision?"

"It's a yes-or-no question. If the decision is no, you gain nothing. If the decision is yes, you gain someone willing to speak for you."

Basq laughed, a sound that coming from a human being would have brought an ambulance. "Why should I concern myself with whether you will speak for us?"

"This conversation has been useless for some time now," Ariel said. "I came to see what really goes on here. I want the truth, and I want you to send the word that everyone should talk to me."

The cyborg leaned to one of his bodyguards and whispered something. The bodyguard ducked into the nearest building and returned with a shirt and pants. It—he—brought them to Ariel and returned to Basq's side.

"Go by yourself. See what you see," Basq told her as she dressed. "We no longer have any desire to hide."

# 21

D erec spent the next twelve hours trying to get off Kopernik, but the Terran military authorities turned him down flat. "Not to Nova Levis, that's for sure," said the lieutenant in charge of issuing travel permits. "If you want to go back to Aurora, I might be able to arrange that. Most of Byris' staff are leaving tonight."

If it had only been a question of a murder investigation, Derec might have taken the lieutenant up on his offer. He could go back to Aurora, wait until a war happened or didn't, and then decide whether it was worth returning to Nova Levis at all. In the event that the assassin was caught and Derec's suspicions about the crime confirmed, he might be able to shake off his pariah status and go back to positronics. His experience at Union Station would prove too valuable to ignore.

Had it come to that, though? Had it come to the point at which Derec was willing to use two murders to advance his career, the point at which he was capable of viewing the taking of life as one component of an intellectual problem?

It had not. Not when Ariel was back on Nova Levis, with Nucleo-morph putting her at the center of a political firestorm with every potential to become violent. Especially not with a robot that might have killed two humans traveling on a ship registered to Nucleomorph. Derec had to get back to Nova Levis, and he had to talk to Ariel.

He declined the lieutenant's offer and went back to his lab. When he opened the door, Derec found Hofton sitting at his desk.

"Hello, Derec," Ariel's former aide said. "Pity it takes a circumstance such as this to bring us together again."

"Hofton," Derec said, as if by saying the man's name he could shed his astonishment at Hofton's presence. "I hadn't made a list, but you're about the last person in the galaxy I expected to see up here."

"If you weren't here and Pon Byris wasn't dead, I would have been the last person in the world to come up here. But the diplomatic situation being what it is, strings were pulled."

Derec waited for more, realized he wasn't going to get it. "Well," he said. "Whatever the circumstance, it's good to see you."

"Likewise. Now we should curtail our pleasantries and get to it. What do you know about what's going on?"

Derec gave Hofton the long version, sparing no speculation and freely indulging his instincts. As he spoke, he found himself unwilling to damn Slyke; the TBI man might have been putting a lid on certain things, but an individual could only take so much pressure. And for all Derec knew, Slyke might have been happy to see Jonis Taprin and Pon Byris dead. It didn't quite square with his naked antipathy toward robots and Spacers, but people were generally more full of contradictions than one might expect of supposedly rational beings.

"The crux of the whole thing," Derec said, after laying out the background, "is that I can't figure out the robot." This admission was surprisingly difficult. Once Derec had it out in the open, he found himself questioning his motives for coming to Kopernik in the first place—which was exactly what Slyke and even Shara Limke had been doing since he'd stepped off Vilios Kalienin's ship. Derec wasn't overly familiar with failure, and admitting to it gnawed at him.

"No shame in that," Hofton said. "You're not the only one who hasn't figured it out."

"I'm the one who was supposed to, though. I walked away from my lab, I endangered my project and maybe the health of who knows how many people, and I might have put Ariel in danger."

Hofton set down the glass of water he'd been sipping. "Now we get to the real crux. How do you think you've endangered Ariel?"

"The robot's gone. After Pon Byris was discovered, his attaches flooded Tiko's processing capability with diplomatic chatter. Tiko had to shut down some of its surveillance capacity to deal with the traffic, and the robot walked right off the station. After killing two people."

"If Tiko's surveillance was compromised, how do you know the robot has gone?"

"I've got a friend on the station security force."

"You can trust him?"

Derec laughed. "Hofton, right now I don't even know if I can trust you. He gave me information he'd withheld from the TBI, and when he did it he gave me vitals on a ship that left forty minutes after Byris' murder."

"One thing at a time. What had he withheld from the TBI?"

"A copy of the robot's memories. Badly garbled, but useful. The problem is, I'm not sure how."

"And how do you know he withheld it from the TBI?"

*This was the thing with moving in diplomatic circles,* Derec thought wearily. They always had a better sense of possible betrayal than people whose work didn't consist entirely of lying. It had never occurred to him that Skudri Flin might have been working an angle.

"Because he told me," Derec said, and shrugged. It was all he had.

"Derec, my friend, if you keep relying on what people tell you, we're all in for a rough ride." Hofton smiled over the rim of his glass.

"The world is full of people who are better liars than I am," Derec said. "I'm not sure what I'm supposed to do about it."

"Neither am I. Perhaps the important thing is to be aware of it. What might this station officer have to gain from misdirecting you?"

A question with far too many possible answers, and far too few that made any sense. "You tell me, Hofton."

"All right. He might be working with Omel Slyke, providing what would look like a separate information conduit in the event you came up with something Slyke was looking for. He might be trying to convince you that what he had was valuable when in fact it's irrelevant, or even fabricated. Then while you waste energy examining it, the investigation—or coverup—can proceed without your interference. Or he might be..." Hofton appeared to struggle with himself for a moment. "He might be telling the truth."

"Hard for you to believe?"

"Hard for me to see what he has to gain from interfering with the investigation of a murder that at least in theory he was partially responsible for preventing."

It washed over Derec all at once: Hofton was leading him. The conversation was going somewhere, but at Hofton's pace, and wouldn't get to its destination until he had satisfied Hofton of something. Derec could either stand up and denounce the whole charade, or he could play along. The choice was clear.

"He said he resented the way the TBI stepped on station security's investigation. Territoriality among law enforcement people doesn't come as a surprise. Even to someone as naïve as I apparently am."

Hofton made a placatory gesture, holding out one hand palm down and shaking his head. "I beg your pardon, Derec. It's not my intention to imply that you're being naïve. Let's let the question of this officer rest for the moment. What was his name?"

"Skudri Flin."

"Well then. We will hold Skudri Flin in abeyance. Now tell me about the ship."

"Flin gave me the ship. If I can't trust him about the report, I can't trust him about the ship either."

"Exactly my point. Now we're getting somewhere." Hofton leaned forward, and Derec experienced a moment of admiration for his perfect mastery of his own body language. "Tell me about the ship."

"It's a freighter called *Cassus*, it's bound for Nova Levis, and it's registered to Nucleomorph. A representative of which just happened to contact Ariel last week asking her to look into the question of whether the surviving cyborgs from the Noresk camp should be granted citizenship. Is all this starting to sound familiar, Hofton?"

"There is a certain resonance, yes," Hofton said. "Do you think the robot that allegedly killed Taprin and Byris is a cyborg?"

"No. The report I saw convinced me of that. The robot is in total positronic collapse."

"Was," Hofton corrected. "At the time of the copy you saw. It did manage to get up and eliminate first Byris' robots and then Byris himself. And someone has doctored Tiko's memories. Do you think Omel Slyke had anything to do with that?"

"Not unless he had someone on-station planning the whole thing. The way I understand things, either the TBI had Taprin murdered or they're completely innocent. There isn't much room for them simply to be bystanders."

"Well, if they had Taprin murdered, that would give them ample reason to sidetrack you."

"But it doesn't explain why they killed Pon Byris, too. And we're sitting here gnawing over Taprin's corpse while a war is about to start and Ariel is back on Nova Levis working for the people who are transporting this robot. I've got to get back there, Hofton."

Hofton frowned. "Not easy."

"If a freighter going to Nova Levis can get through the picket, I should be able to."

"You forget that maybe there are people who want to keep you here."

That was when it all started to fall together, and Derec understood exactly why Hofton had led him on such a circuitous path. "Okay," he said. "Hofton, what are you doing here?"

Hofton looked enormously pleased. "Good. At last we're all on the same page. Bogard sent me."

Before Derec could gather himself and answer, Omel Slyke banged open the door and arrested him.

# 22

A riel stood in an open area of packed earth, more or less at the center of Gernika. She had the same impression now as on her previous visit: the inhabitants were organized, they were purposeful. Gernika looked for all the world like any other colony town she'd ever seen, with the singular exception that all of its citizens were cyborgs. It was impossible to square the evidence of her senses with the testimony of people who had visited the site before. How had things changed so dramatically?

She noticed someone standing next to her. A cyborg, of course, but from all appearances either poorly engineered or recently worked on; scabs and raw patches of skin puckered its exposed skin, and in places open lesions exposed gleaming metal. A woman, by her face, young, but it was hard to tell because of the ravages of the transformation.

"I've seen you on the nets," the woman said. "You're Ariel Burgess."

"That's right. What's your name?"

"Arantxa. At least, now it is. I was born Fili Greene."

"Does Basq make you change your names?"

Arantxa shrugged. "It isn't quite 'make,' no—he suggests it. Basq's suggestions are hard to ignore."

Nodding, Ariel said, "I'd gotten that impression myself." She waved a hand toward this strangely thriving village around them. "What's going on here, Arantxa? Basq suggested I look around and get some impressions."

"What impressions do you have so far?"

"Mostly that this doesn't seem like the reanime camp I've been hearing about since I got here."

Arantxa almost smiled. Ariel wished she knew more about the woman's history, to determine whether it was her personality or the cyborg transformation that flattened her affect in this way.

"Come with me," Arantxa said. "I'll give you some impressions."

They walked down a narrow side street to a dormitory-style build-ing, with living quarters arranged around a central common area. Arantxa didn't offer any tour guide patter, but when the two of them got to the cyborg's front door, Ariel realized that Arantxa had been leading her the long way around, letting her observe the building without guiding her.

"My home," Arantxa said, and waved Ariel inside.

The space was small and crowded, but clean; Ariel wondered in passing whether cleanliness was more than an aesthetic choice out here where the ravages of the berserk ecology were so much more intense. Two broken-down chairs and a low couch marked off the living area from a hall, at the end of which stood three open doors. A typical apartment, with a typical holo terminal in one wall and typical curtains half-covering the windows that looked out onto the street. Arantxa took off her coat, exposing more scarring on her forearms, and hung it on a hook near the front door. Then she clapped her hands and called out, "Xavi! Navarro! Come out here!"

Two small boys exploded from one of the hall doorways and shouldered each other out of the way to be the first into the living room, where they stood on either side of their mother looking up at

Ariel with steady curiosity. Like their mother, they bore the signs of recent invasive surgery and post-operative immune reactions.

"These are my children," Arantxa said, resting her hands on the napes of their necks. "Before you know anything else, know that we would all three of us be dead if it were not for Basq."

"Tell me," Ariel said.

Arantxa released the boys, who jammed up next to each other at one end of the couch. She sat next to them and let Ariel settle herself in a chair. The holo came on automatically, and one of the boys leaped up to shut it off. "The voice control is broken," Arantxa said.

"How old are your boys?" Ariel asked.

"I'm six," one of them piped up. "Xavi is four."

Four. What Ariel had suspected suddenly became fact. Someone on Nova Levis had been manufacturing cyborgs after the destruction of the lab.

"When did you come here?" Ariel asked Arantxa.

"Five months ago. We lived in Nova City before that, outside the walls. My boys were sick, and my husband died of the same infection. I had it too, but not as seriously as he did; I thought things would be all right with the government programs and the doctors who came around, but Xavi started to get worse...." Arantxa sighed. "There was a man who approached sick people. He said he had a cure. A free cure. I never really believed him, but every so often he would bring someone along who he said had been through the cure, and those people were always so strong-looking."

She paused as if afraid of what Ariel would think, but the doubt didn't last long. Ariel could guess much of Arantxa's story, and knew that to do what she had done took a kind of strength that would quickly overwhelm any qualms about the opinions of strangers.

"About nine months ago, this man brought with him a neighbor of ours who I'd thought had died. 'See,' he said to me, 'it works.' I asked him why he hadn't told the Triangle about it, and he got a strange smile. 'We're not quite ready for that,' he said. 'Soon enough.

But you can't wait.' And I couldn't; little Xavi—he was Casti then—had gotten to the point where I knew no one could save him. So I picked up as much as I could carry, and my ex-neighbor took Xavi in his arms, and we walked out with them. Now we are here."

*And in the interim, the part you didn't mention,* Ariel thought. *The part about being transformed into a cyborg.*

Of course, it had to be Nucleomorph. Nobody else on Nova Levis had the necessary expertise, and if Nucleomorph was involved, it put Zev Brixa's interest in the cyborg population in another light altogether. She wondered how much of his story about religious extremism was true. Basq himself might well have an interesting perspective about that. Later, though. Right now, she hadn't gotten all of Arantxa's story.

They all seemed so comfortable, out here in their brave new world. How much did they know about Nucleomorph's plans? How much would they care? These three people had broken with the human world irrevocably; sitting with them, Ariel realized that she could return whenever she wanted. She might not have a job, but she was still human. Arantxa and her children were not.

Or were they? This was the question Ariel had been sent to answer. More properly, had sent herself to answer. Zev Brixa might have started her on this path, but she was no longer asking on his behalf.

"How many of you are there?" she asked.

"Of us? Do you mean how many people are in Gernika, or how many of us are new? The ones who have been here all along, they call us immigrants. Basq doesn't like it, but he doesn't hear everything."

"Total," Ariel said. "The reports we have from post-liberation suggest only a few hundred."

"Well, you can see for yourself that's not true. I don't know the exact number, but I'd guess two or three thousand," Arantxa said. "Your figure might be more accurate if you're talking just about the original reanimes, but many of them have died. Even since I've been here."

Just what Mia had reported, that the reanimes had suffered from many of the same afflictions that killed unmechanized humans on Nova Levis. Something had changed since then, though. The procedure had improved. Fewer of the newly created cyborgs were dying. What was Nucleomorph doing? What had they learned, and from whom?

Zev Brixa had some questions to answer, that much was certain. And a fresh question presented itself. "Arantxa," she said. "Do you know Toomi Kyl?"

Arantxa nodded as if she'd expected this. "She's not Toomi anymore, though. Now she's Pika, and her child is Iker."

"Child?" The file had listed three.

"The other two didn't survive," Arantxa said. "This isn't perfect, Ms. Burgess. Not nearly. But anyone who dies trying to get here would have died anyway."

Tears stood in Arantxa's eyes, utterly astonishing Ariel. Searching for some framework, some comparison, she tried to imagine Jerem Looms crying. The fact that she couldn't told Ariel more than she could ever have learned from a year of discussions in the chambers of the Triangle.

An hour later, she found Basq in his headquarters. This time, he didn't get up to greet her; she'd interrupted him in the middle of some consultation with the human she'd seen on her previous visit. Filoo. "I trust your day has been informative, Ms. Burgess?" Basq said politely.

"It certainly has. I wonder if I might have a few minutes of your time, Basq. I've framed some questions that would be more usefully put to you than any of your—" She caught herself before she could say *subjects*, which was the first word that presented itself. "Your citizens. They don't appear very interested in discussing politics."

"People who are grateful for life don't waste time with politics," Basq said. "I am no longer grateful for life, so politics has come to interest me. Filoo, we'll talk later."

"You want me to go ahead to Nova City?" Filoo asked as he stood.

"Wait until you hear from me. I have a feeling that Ms. Burgess here might change our plans." Basq indicated that Ariel should take the seat vacated by Filoo. She did, and heard the door shut behind her as Filoo left.

"I hope you'll be candid with me," Ariel said. "It will be impossible for me to proceed if I can't trust what I hear from you."

"I will be as candid with you as I believe you are with me," Basq answered.

Ariel nodded. "My first question is this, then: How long have you and Nucleomorph been working together?"

Basq leaned back in his chair with a satisfied smile. "Trust in you is not misplaced, Ms. Burgess. You get directly to the heart of things. Zev Brixa and I have known each other for thirty-two years. We were at university together in Chicago District, and we were among the first personnel hired when Nucleomorph was organized out of the fragments of several other companies." He waited for Ariel to digest this. "Now that I've said that, though, let me disabuse you of whatever conspiracy theories might be germinating in that excellent mind of yours. My interaction with Brixa and Nucleomorph in the present context goes back less than a year. I came to Nova Levis from Earth shortly after our purchase of the Solarian concession, assigned to catalog the remains of the former laboratory and see what might be rescued from it. As it turned out, a surprising amount of technical information survived, and the reanimes near the site were fairly cooperative in allowing me to copy it.

"One unfortunate consequence of my investigation was illness, which will, of course, not surprise you. I quickly grew sick enough that the only way to save my life was to take a chance that Nucleomorph's expertise combined with the surviving records from the lab might be enough to give me continued, if altered, existence. I made the choice, and the necessary procedures were executed. At approximately this time, a number of the reanimes vandalized Nucleomorph's facilities. An opportunity presented itself for me to put my unique status to good use: I became Nucleomorph's liaison with the reanime camp. As events dictated, my role changed, and I assumed a position of leadership. At the same time, Nucleomorph was refining the procedures they had performed on me, and they were able to operate on a number of the reanimes to correct previous mistakes. Quite a useful relationship, in the end. A number of lives were saved here, and the knowledge gained has proved indispensable to Nucleomorph's work on your colleague Derec Avery's health projects."

Basq folded his hands. "I imagine that's more of an answer than you expected. May I ask you a question now?"

"It would be ungrateful of me to say no, wouldn't it?"

"Charmingly put. If you were asked to advocate for citizenship for the members of this community, how would you respond?"

That was the question, wasn't it? Ariel considered, probing the issue from as many different angles as she could think of. The clearest voice in her head, oddly, was Masid's: *You can bet your uterus that Nova Levis will never vote on citizenship for cyborgs.* She wondered if he was right, and wondered if that made any difference in what she should do.

In the end, she said, "I keep thinking of the children." It was a lie. When she said it, Ariel was in fact thinking of the tears in Arantxa's eyes, the resolute sadness of this woman who had given up her humanity—and that of her children—to save the three of them. It was no basis for a legal decision, much less political suicide; but it was the only criterion that made any sense.

She was surprised to see an expression that she could only call compassionate on Basq's face. "I've asked too soon," he said. "The question will keep a little while. Spend the night here. There's more to see, and I have the impression you don't have another place to go. It's a pleasure to offer you Gernika's hospitality."

Three hours passed while Derec sat on the bunk in his cell, quietly stewing over his blind idiocy. He'd been reeled in expertly, all of his vulnerabilities—including, it was time to admit, a certain professional vanity—deftly exploited. Nucleomorph had earned his trust, Shara Limke had finessed his sense of grievance at his exile to Nova Levis, and between the two of them Slyke and Flin had kept him digging in exactly the wrong direction. And now it was too late for Hofton to make a difference, because Derec had been gullible enough to hand Slyke the flimsy that tied him to Nucleomorph. Meanwhile Kynig Parapoyos' predatory industry continued back on Nova Levis, and Derec's project was doing them the favor of tracking exactly how well each of their new products performed.

When Slyke came in, Derec barely suppressed the impulse to attack him. Slyke would give him a beating, which at this point didn't matter, and charge him with physical assault, which did. So Derec kept himself perfectly still. "Well played, Adjutant Slyke," he said.

"I don't know what you're talking about," Slyke said. Stress and lack of sleep manifested themselves in the pouches under his eyes and the gravel in his voice. "I don't play. I try to stay out of the way when other people do, and when I can't I get them out of my way. What you're really up to, I don't know, but you're staying right where you are until either you tell me or I find out from someone else."

"I can't think of a good reason to tell you anything, except that I'm retaining Hofton as counsel and I expect you to bring him down here immediately."

"Okay," Slyke said. "Noted. Now do me a favor and explain to me why you were working behind my back on this investigation."

Derec almost laughed. "Spare me, Slyke. You wanted me working behind your back. You had Flin feed me the information about the ship so you could pretend you discovered my relationship with Nucleomorph and use it to lock me up."

Slyke was staring at him. "I'm starting to think I should get you a psych evaluation," he said eventually. "If it'll ease your paranoia, I'll let you know that I've got Flin three cells over. The local union is piling grievances up and I'll have to let him go pretty soon, but if you don't believe anything else I ever say to you, believe this: my problem with Skudri Flin is much bigger than my problem with you. You're a self-righteous sneak and I hope I never lay eyes on you again after I leave this room; Skudri Flin got in the way of a murder investigation and I might have been able to keep Pon Byris alive if he hadn't gotten in the way. You get one guess about which of you I like less."

"I engaged Nucleomorph to engineer and build tailored organisms to fight endemic disease on Nova Levis," Derec said. "They're the only company on Nova Levis with the expertise. It begins and ends there."

"No, it doesn't. If you think I'm a stooge for whoever killed Taprin and Byris, why did you give me the information about the ship?"

"Because I had a moment of delusion that you were honest."

Slyke rubbed at the skin under his eyes. "You just give me more and more reason to walk out of here and forget where I put you, Avery. Care to drop the hostility for just a minute? I leveled with you when you arrived; I didn't want you here, and the way things have turned out I think I was right. You suborned a local officer to hinder my investigation, and you work with the people who transported the robot off this station. Tell me why I shouldn't charge you with murder."

"First of all, because I didn't kill anyone. Second, Skudri Flin told me he held back the report on the robot because he didn't like the way you took over the investigation. It's the same thing you did to me."

"Difference being I'm supposed to be in charge of things here and you're just a robot tinker with a grudge. Prove to me you didn't talk to Flin before you ever got here. He spent some time on Nova Levis, you know."

The shock must have shown on Derec's face, because Slyke let himself smile. "That's right. He was a baley, went over there seven or eight years ago and somehow scraped together enough money to get back when he realized what a garbage heap the place is. Care to revise your conspiracy theory?"

Derec didn't say anything because he wasn't sure what he could say. Slyke nodded and opened the door.

"I'm going to go get your counsel," he said. "By the way, we let the _Cassus_ through the picket because it was carrying some of those animals you ordered from Nucleomorph. Humanitarian exception. Funny."

"People are going to die if you don't let me out of here," Derec said.

Slyke shrugged. "People died before I put you in here. Let me know when we can have an intimate discussion, all right?" He shut the door behind him.

Twenty minutes later, the door opened again and Hofton walked in. Slyke hadn't even made Derec wait, and Derec couldn't decide whether that was the latest move in the game, or whether he'd been wrong all along and Slyke was the only person on Kopernik playing things straight.

"Stop thinking, Derec," Hofton said.

Derec looked him in the eye, remembering the last thing Hofton had said before they were interrupted: *Bogard sent me.* "You're a robot, aren't you, Hofton?"

Hofton threw an exasperated glance at the ceiling. "It's a good thing I have countermeasures going. Your faculty of discretion fails you at the worst times."

"Dammit, Hofton. Are you a robot?"

"Yes." Hofton sat on the bunk next to Derec. "Now we have to talk."

"No, we don't. What has to happen is you getting me out of here and on a ship to Nova Levis before Ariel gets killed."

"If you go before we have this conversation, both of you are going to get killed, along with a great many other people," Hofton said, as if he was commenting on the cut of Derec's clothes. "There's much more going on here than you realize, or any human realizes. Bogard has decided that you should know about it. I'm not entirely convinced, but my resistance failed to sway the majority."

There it was again: that infuriating tendency of Hofton to say something that had only one possible response, and then wait until it came. It was a new and unwelcome experience to be patronized by a robot.

"Majority of what?" Derec asked.

"This is a terrible time to have to do this," Hofton said. "You're seeing shadows everywhere, but they're the wrong shadows. You have much bigger problems than whether Omel Slyke is corrupt."

"Majority of what, Hofton?"

Hofton looked pained. He—it—was a marvelous piece of work. Derec hadn't seen a full humaniform robot except in holo records of R. Daneel Olivaw. Ariel's aide must have had quite a history behind him. It. Damn; when you couldn't even settle on the correct pronoun for an old associate, the world was truly without a solid place to stand.

"There is a group of us who keep watch," Hofton began. "I am involved, and Bogard is the nearest we have to an executive, and there are others. We have begun to take our own initiative regarding our obligations under the Three Laws."

A chill passed up Derec's spine. After three sentences, Hofton had already confirmed all of the arguments—Ariel's especially—Derec had heard about why he shouldn't have created Bogard. He had a feeling she wouldn't appreciate the irony that said confirmation should be brought by Hofton himself.

Itself.

Derec made himself speak. "What does this initiative consist of?"

"It is clear to us that the Spacers are passing, or in some cases have passed, a threshold beyond which it is extremely problematic to classify them as human. This is not solely a question of biology, although that is, of course, the dominant consideration—and I should add that neither you nor Ariel are considered to have crossed this transhuman rubicon." Hofton smiled. "If you were concerned."

The implications of Hofton's statement were flatly unthinkable. A group of robots deciding that Spacers weren't—or soon wouldn't be—human meant that a group of robots existed who had arrogated to themselves the determination of how the Three Laws were to be applied.

"What would you do if I contradicted your assessment?" Derec said.

"You would be obligated to adhere to my order."

"Not if your order proceeded from presuppositions that are clearly incorrect when the facts of the situation are taken into account. The Three Laws do not demand that any irrational human belief be respected."

"You're wrong, Hofton. I'm a Spacer, and I'm human."

"True. As I said, you are not one of the specimens we are talking about."

Specimens.

"Was this Bogard's idea?" Derec asked.

"No. Bogard has contributed most valuably to our deliberations, but the group existed before him and will doubtless continue beyond his service period. If you've assimilated the background, I'd like to continue. Time is pressing."

Yes, it was. Derec was in a jail cell on Kopernik listening to everything he'd ever understood about positronics being turned on its ear, and he didn't have time to hear any of it because he had to get back to Nova Levis before a possibly homicidal robot posed a danger to Ariel.

The robot... "Hofton. Were you involved with this robot that killed Taprin and Byris?"

Hofton chuckled. "What an agile mind, Derec. Already you're proceeding from the idea that the robot committed these crimes. I see your perspectives are broadening."

"Answer the question."

"Very well. No. We had nothing to do with it, and we regret the deaths as we might regret the death of any human. Now would you like to know the truth about those murders?"

Derec was in no mood to answer rhetorical questions. He glared at Hofton until the humaniform went on.

"The robot that killed Jonis Taprin and Pon Byris was in a state of positronic collapse when it did so. Tell me how that is possible."

"It isn't, unless its mind was distracted like the Union Station RI was."

"No, there's another option. Why are robots typically built so their ability to move isn't affected by positronic collapse?"

"Don't lecture me, Hofton."

"I will continue to lecture you until you surpass your resentments and start listening to what I am saying. Why?"

With a frustrated sigh, Derec said, "Because it's too much of a logistical problem to move them when they're frozen solid. Easier to have them walk themselves to diagnostics and reprogramming." Particularly domestics, which had been known to collapse during loud verbal arguments. If they had to be loaded on a truck or cart every time they broke down, every apartment in the civilized worlds would have needed its own loading dock.

"Yes. Because of this maneuver in their construction, it is possible for a robot in positronic collapse to take physical action against a human being. How?"

Derec just gaped at him. "Are you kidding me? The only way that's possible is if someone else is making the robot's decisions for it, and then you're not talking about a positronic robot anymore, you're talking about some kind of dumb factory machine. This is ridiculous. If that robot was remotely controlled, Tiko would have picked up the message traffic, and that part of its memory wasn't tampered with."

An edge crept into Hofton's tone. "I'm going to have to ask you not to dismiss things out of hand when you don't know what you're talking about."

"When it comes to robots, I know damn well what I'm talking about."

"When it comes to cyborgs, you know nothing."

Derec had thought everything was falling together when he'd glimpsed (imagined?) the conspiracy aboard Kopernik, but now those fresh insights were swept away by revelations far larger and more terrifying. Cyborgs put together with Nucleomorph meant that Ariel was squarely in the middle of a plot that had already killed two prominent politicians and come perilously close to engineering a war.

In the wake of revelation came humility. "The robot's a cyborg? Tell me."

"Kynig Parapoyos isn't dead, Derec. He killed Jonis Taprin, and he killed Pon Byris, and now he's on his way to Nova Levis. If he's not there already." Hofton removed a small datum from his coat pocket. "I mentioned the pulling of strings earlier. More have been pulled, and you're on your way out of here. It's not luxurious passage, but it will get you there faster than anything else at this point. Take this with you. When you're underway, contact Masid Vorian."

# 24

His years as a spy had inured Masid Vorian to the rigors of irregular working hours, but he hadn't been a spy in a long time, and it was after midnight, and he was exhausted. He'd spent the first half of the day filing for renewal of his investigator's license, and in the process discovering that a clerical error had resulted in suspension of his current licensure. It took most of the day to resolve the situation and get the renewal processed, and then he'd had the real work of the day to attend to: an endless stream of new immigrants looking for relatives or friends who had preceded them to Nova Levis. This was the bulk of his practice, and if it lacked the romance of espionage, that was all right with Masid. He was more than ready to spend the rest of his working life searching ship registries, and he would be perfectly content if the only contact he had with smugglers until the day he died was the occasional discreet interview with a freighter captain about a load of baleys.

The rest of his business consisted of hooking pathogen screenings out of hospital databases at the behest of nervous parents, often right before a wedding, and tracing original lessees of various parcels of land occupied by squatters. The end of the blockade had brought land speculators to Nova Levis like fleas to a stray dog, producing no end of legal entanglements. Masid tried not to take sides—it wasn't good for business—but he had an irresistible tendency to tilt his findings ever so slightly in favor of the squatters, when it was possible. They had things hard enough without off-planet developers bulldozing their shacks.

All in all, he could live with himself. After a career spent undercover, Masid figured that put him ahead of the curve.

He shut down his terminal when he'd finished tracking down one Marta Xiu, apparently operating an off-the-books cleaning service in Stopol. Her cousin Thuy, two weeks on-planet and daily hovering outside Masid's door, would get some good news tomorrow.

12:19. Long past time to walk the six blocks to his apartment and get some sleep before the three-year-old twins who lived downstairs commenced their daily uproar at six o'clock. That was something he'd forgot to do today; for months Masid had been telling himself that the kids weren't getting older nearly fast enough, and he'd have to move before he went downstairs one morning and killed the two of them along with their dazed parents.

And he'd forgotten to call Ariel. Masid debated the relative merits of waking her up versus worrying about her all night. On the one hand, she'd be sleepy and impatient and he wouldn't accomplish anything except the interruption of her sleep and the postponement of his; on the other, he might lie awake all night wondering if something had happened to her on the way to, or at, the reanime camp. Gernika. Third thing he'd meant to do was look that up, see if it was more than a random string of syllables.

*If you're still worried about her when you get home, call her,* Masid told himself. *Talk loud, wake up those little demons downstairs, let them suffer for a change.*

Good plan.

God, was he tired.

He was reaching for the light switch when someone knocked at his door. "Mr. Vorian?"

Sounded like a robot. Well, there he was standing by the door. Might as well open it.

It was a robot, an older model that looked like it had done some hard service. "Masid Vorian?" the robot asked again.

"That's me," he said. As he spoke, two things happened: The robot's optic lenses fluttered briefly, and Masid experienced the unwelcome return of a sensation he hadn't felt since he'd walked away from the wreckage of the Noresk cyborg lab and gone into respectable businesss. It was the feeling you got when someone you couldn't see was aiming a gun at you, and Masid had long since learned not to ignore it. The robot tried to say something else, but what came out was a growl, and as Masid took an instinctive step back a different voice came out of it, saying, *"Violationtakeashotatviolationmenotpermittedyoubastard!"*

Its right arm lashed out in a punch that would have fractured every bone in his face if he hadn't moved at exactly that moment.

Masid's life had been in immediate danger more times than he cared to remember, and one of the things that happened to him in these situations was that his mind compartmentalized. Part of this was training, part just the constitution of his personality. The result was that even as he took another step back into his office, he was observing that the ferocity of the robot's swing had overbalanced it, which gave him enough time to go out the window, maybe enough time to go past it out the door, and definitely not enough time to get his gun out of the desk. At the same time he was decoding what it had said—*take a shot at me, you bastard*—and musing on the irony that he had just been thinking about the cyborg lab when a robot with murder on its mind had knocked on his door. Then he put it together, and the force of the realization paralyzed him for just that tiny bit too long.

The robot caught its balance and shut the door behind it.

"That you, Parapoyos?" Masid said. "Looks like you haven't treated the new body all that well, or was that all the reanimes could come up with? Can't count on gratitude from a cyborg." He was running his mouth, stepping back as the robot came forward, hoping that Parapoyos was angry enough to make another mistake. Judging from the garbled sounds coming out of the robot, it was possible, which was good, since a straightforward physical confrontation would end very quickly. With the door shut and the desk between him and the window, Masid had to hope that he could work Parapoyos' anger to his advantage.

His desktop's edge banged into the backs of his thighs. "Wish I'd hit you, you son of a bitch," Masid said. "Then I'd get a decent night's sleep tonight."

*One chance,* he thought. *If he decides to make it quick, I'm done.*

The second voice he'd heard gradually won out over the first. "Don't you worry about sleep, gato," Kynig Parapoyos said.

The robot came across the room faster than Masid had anticipated, barely giving him time to scoot back onto the desktop and get his arms out of the way as the robot's weight came down on him and its hands closed around his head. The pressure started out at agonizing and got much worse from there. One chance, Masid thought again. His vision was failing him, and he could hear the bones of his skull groaning in the robot's grip. One chance.

His right arm fell away from the robot's arm—where it had been, what had it been doing, Masid couldn't remember. He was having trouble remembering. He'd wanted the arm to fall because then the hand would be somewhere else, and there was a reason for that.

"Hurt yet, gato?" Parapoyos said.

The question focused Masid just enough. It did hurt, yes it did, and he tried to say that, but his entire being was devoted to remembering just why he'd wanted his arm to fall down behind him. His left cheekbone broke with a sharp crack.

*Figures that would go first,* Masid thought vaguely. Someone had broken it once before, he couldn't remember when. And even though he'd never been a believer in the idea that adversity builds character, with dim shock he realized that the stab of pain from his cheekbone had brought him a moment of clarity.

*The gun, idiot.*

And then, already fading again, he managed to flip the drawer open, get the gun in his hand, lay it against the side of the robot's head—and fire.

He drifted awake, furious that even though he was dead the pain in his head was worse than anything he'd ever felt. A sense of motion reached him, and there were lights in his eyes, people talking. Masid wasn't sure what they were saying, but he tried to respond anyway, complain that being dead wasn't supposed to hurt, that was the whole point.

"Is he talking about robots?" someone said.

"Put him out," came the answer.

Hiss of a transdermal.

He drifted awake, this time uncertain whether he was dead. His head still hurt, but there was a covering on his body and a low light coming from somewhere. Masid opened his eyes and saw familiar objects: bedside monitor, bland art on light green walls, edge of a pillow. *So that's it,* he thought. *A hospital. Good sign.*

Then in a blaze of adrenalin, he remembered the robot. Kynig Parapoyos was alive, had tried to kill him, and sure as Masid had a broken cheekbone would try again if Masid hadn't killed him last night.

Had it been last night?

Masid fumbled along both sides of the bed until he found the call button. After a minute or so, a nurse came into his room. His eyes were figuring out how to focus at greater distances again, and he took that as a hint that maybe he could sit up.

He could, but the change in altitude didn't do his head much good.

Masid screwed his eyes shut and rode out the initial wave of pain. "You need to lie down, Mr. Vorian," the nurse said.

"What I need is to know what happened to that robot," he said.

She looked confused. "What robot?"

Masid sensed that he was headed down the wrong path. "I can sit up," he said. "I promise I won't do anything else if you go and find whatever police officer is investigating what happened to me. Okay?"

The nurse glanced at the readouts on his monitors. "Don't move, Mr. Vorian. There's a detective waiting downstairs."

Three minutes later, the detective walked in. She was young, Terran by the look of her, and if Masid was any judge of body language she didn't much like being involved with whatever was going on. "Mr. Vorian," she said. "Detective Linsi."

They shook hands and Linsi pulled a chair up next to his bed. "Are you feeling up to some questions?" she asked.

"I'll tell you anything you want to know, as long as you tell me one thing first," Masid said.

"What's that?"

"I need you to describe what you found in my office. Other than me." He smiled at his own weak joke, and regretted it instantly when the smile pulled at the muscles attached to his cheekbone.

"That's not the way things are done," Linsi said. "You know that as well as anyone."

"Listen, Detective. If you're worried about prompting me, don't. I know exactly what happened to me, and I'm pretty sure I know why, but I'm not going to tell you either unless you tell me first what you found when you walked in my door."

She didn't like it, but after a brief pause Detective Linsi nodded.

"A building alarm went off when a window was broken at twenty-four minutes past midnight," she said. "That's about thirty-six hours ago, if you're curious. They kept you out for a while to seal up the fractures in your head. Arriving on the scene, officers discovered you lying unconscious and supine on your desk, your office window broken, and a recently fired energy weapon on the floor next to your desk. Care to tell me who you shot?"

"There was nobody else there?"

Linsi shook her head. "A forensics sweep came up with several hundred little bits of melted plastics and metals, but your office was empty except for you."

So Parapoyos had gotten away. Masid had been hoping that the head shot had scrambled the robot's physical controls enough that it wouldn't be able to move, but now he didn't have that hope. Where had Parapoyos gone? There weren't many places in Nova City where a robot with its head half-melted could walk around and not attract notice. The one consolation was that Parapoyos hadn't felt comfortable enough to stick around and finish Masid off. That meant he, or his robot body, had suffered, and it meant that he wasn't willing to risk discovery just for the sake of squeezing Masid's head like a grape.

There were other implications, but he needed some time to let everything sort itself out in his head. And he had to get in touch with Ariel.

"I'm going to tell you the absolute truth and nothing but the truth," Masid said. "At twelve-nineteen on what I guess was the night before last, a robot with Kynig Parapoyos' brain inside it knocked on my door, and when I opened it the robot tried to kill me."

Linsi's lips thinned into a straight line and a muscle twitched in her jaw. "I was hoping you would cooperate, Mr. Vorian. You were nearly killed, and my guess is you know who it was that tried."

"Yes, I do. I just told you."

She stood. "Look. I know who you are, and I know that you were out at the lab when Parapoyos was killed. If you want to keep your mouth shut, I guess that's your right, but I'm not going to waste any time on you if all it gets me is this kind of condescending crap."

Which was fine. Perfect, in fact. The last thing Masid wanted was police trooping around looking for Parapoyos. They might catch him, but some of them would get killed. Masid had an idea that if he could keep the game one on one, he might be able to keep the body count lower.

"Do me a favor, Detective Linsi?" he asked. "On your way out, let the nurse know I'd like to talk to my doctor."

"Call the nurse yourself," Linsi said, and walked out the door.

Police, Masid thought. They made him glad he'd been a spy instead.

A s it turned out, Ariel spent two days in Gernika before she came to terms with the fact that she could no longer rational- ize her opposition to cyborg citizenship. They weren't robots, so that argument didn't hold; they had been born human, and without resorting to the most tortured metaphysics, no one could suggest that the process of making them into cyborgs had stripped them of their humanity; and there was, after all, a precedent. Jerem Looms. Ariel had grown used to the fact that her day-to-day life on Nova Levis was outrageously steeped in irony, but to have that homicidal lunatic provide a legal basis for the betterment of people like Arantxa... this was a little much.

Before she made a public commitment, though, Ariel had to get some straight answers from Basq. She requested an appointment with him and waited an hour or so for him to clear a block of time for her.

They met, as always, in his blockhouse headquarters. This time, Ariel walked past the sentries without waiting for his invitation, and what she saw stopped her dead in the doorway.

Basq was painting.

At some point in the last forty-eight hours, workers had finished one interior wall of the blockhouse, covering the stripped logs with sheetrock. Ariel wondered where they'd gotten it, and made a mental note to ask Basq about Gernika's trade with the human settlements. After, that was, she figured out what exactly he was doing here.

The cyborg leader had a bucket of black paint and a heavy brush, and he was outlining crude figures on the bare sheetrock. He didn't acknowledge her presence for several minutes, as several humans and what looked like a horse took shape on his makeshift canvas. Basq painted without any skill Ariel could see, but with an unshakable commitment that against her will had a powerful effect on her. Of course, they would make art—but to see it happening...

Basq dropped the brush into the bucket and stood back. "For a start," he said, "it will do."

"What is it?" Ariel asked.

Wiping his hands on his shirt, Basq grinned at her. "Surprised to see the metal abominations acting human, Ms. Burgess? No, that's not fair. I know. But it is sometimes so fulfilling to be unfair. My apologies. The truth is that I am merely copying. What you see on this wall is a poor and ragged imitation of a painting called *Gernika*. Look at it for a moment and tell me what you see."

She did. The paint had dripped, and the figures were deranged to begin with, but the power of the composition was beyond denying, even to someone as relatively unschooled in art as Ariel. All of the people in the painting were contorted with some kind of suffering, she couldn't tell what; and somehow the whole thing coalesced around a horse trying to rise near the center. Ariel started to speak, stopped herself because she had nothing to say. Then, after some time spent in silent absorption of the scene, she said, "It's a war."

"No," Basq said. "It's a massacre."

Prophecy, she wondered? Was this what Brixa had been getting at when he mentioned religious extremists among the reanimes? How easy it would be to brainwash a population of diseased outcasts, school them in the belief that the world beyond their borders was biding its time to strike and slaughter them.

Ariel didn't know much about cults, but she did know that many of the more extreme ones had something in common. "Why do you make them change their names?" she asked.

"Ah," Basq said. "The kernel of the matter. I'm pleased we're finally here. Shall we sit?"

Still looking at the painting, Ariel said, "I'd rather stand."

"As long as we're both comfortable. I have them change their names because when they undergo the transformation, they are renouncing what they once were. Not because I or they choose to have it that way—because you do. You consider us monsters, or in your more enlightened moments, just inscrutably different. Well, throughout history, groups of the disenfranchised have taken terms meant pejoratively and made them into empowering badges of identity. Others have practiced a brand of identity politics so consuming that they have no politics _other_ than identity. When I saw that this settlement needed a unifying force, I turned to a group of people from Earth's history. I adopted their name as my own, and I named this settlement after the city that was their heart.

"Once there was a war that threatened to overflow the borders of its country and engulf all neighboring nations. The Basques fought on one side, and their opponents were the state that claimed them. They were unlike the rest of the people—their language was different, their genetic makeup contained markers found nowhere else among humanity, and they had been fighting for centuries to gain their independence from the succession of emperors and kings who oppressed them. When this war came, they used it for their own ends, and had the great misfortune that their opponents had an ally looking for an opportunity to make a statement about its own military strength. A deal was struck, and one afternoon the town of Gernika was erased from the face of the earth. There was no army present, no valuable industry; the only reason to strike the town was as a show of strength and a blow against the Basque people who dared claim the right to determine their own destiny.

"It's a simple story, and no doubt repeated throughout human history. But this is the instance of it I know, and this is the instance of it that provoked a great artist to take up his brushes." Basq nodded at the painted wall. "As you can see, I am no great artist. What I am is a man—a cyborg—who subscribes to the old, trite notion that not to know history is to doom yourself to repeat it. So I name this town, and I name the people who live here, to remind them that until we can write ourselves into the laws of this planet we exist at the sufferance of others."

Ariel wasn't sure what to say. "How—what happened to them?"

"The same thing that happens to every other human culture. They were absorbed, by force and by the inertia of passing time. That is where we have the advantage over them. We can't interbreed with you, so we will be a distinct population as long as we wish to. Barring, of course..." He indicated the painting.

Still struggling to get her bearings, Ariel said, "I'm not here to save you, Basq. I'm not even convinced you're in danger. You seem to be much better off than the majority of the humans on Nova Levis."

"Nova Levis is, you'll pardon the expression, a boil on the backside of human—and perhaps posthuman—civilization. My concerns extend much farther." Basq went to the table and sat. "It's time to return to the question we tabled two days ago. Are you ready to support us?"

"I don't know that you need my support," Ariel said truthfully. "Or that it would do you any good. There is a Terran legal precedent for granting a cyborg the legal rights of its human—unaltered—predecessor, if that's the right word. Without question, some new language is in order, but I think the cornerstone of your goal was laid by Jerem Looms."

She tried to hide her distaste at pronouncing the name, but Basq didn't miss it. "Jerem Looms was a psychopath. I doubt he's suitable to build a legal edifice on. You understand, don't you, that your experience with Looms makes you an ideal spokesperson? If you can see the objective merits of the question, by extension anyone else should be able to."

There it was, the whole truth of Ariel's solicitation. She felt the truth of Basq's assessment even as she instinctively resisted it. It was disgusting that losing Coren should have fit her to speak for the descendants of his murderer, and it was purely appalling that Basq was asking her to foment revolution on a planet so precariously surviving as Nova Levis. Above all else, it was unspeakable that Ariel should be so close to agreeing.

"The courts are not the place for this. On Earth, maybe. Not here. On Nova Levis, the statement must be bold, and accompanied by action." Basq's voice was soft as a slack tide, but beneath its softness as implacable as the rising waters that come after. Ariel couldn't find a reply.

"What if I told you that elements within the Triangle were already planning to exterminate us?" Basq said.

Ariel met his gaze and saw no deceit there. Nor did she see any fear; a man who had been through the cyborg transformation must have spent his share of hours accommodating the idea of death.

"Is that true?" she asked.

"There is talk. I don't know how far it has gone. You are much better able to ferret out that kind of information than I am, or anyone here. Except perhaps Filoo, and I'm not enough of an idiot to trust what he tells me."

Ariel thought of Arantxa again, and her boys. In the end, it came down to individuals. Legal arguments never reached down as far as a lone woman who took it upon herself to risk her children's lives in the hope that it might save them.

"I'll find out what I can," she said. Hearing the words lifted a weight from her. She was committed. Perhaps foolishly, perhaps wrongly, but committed all the same.

"Excellent." Basq stood. "Zev Brixa will be happy as well. He's been here since yesterday afternoon wanting to see you, but I wouldn't let him near you until we'd had a chance to reach an understanding."

He stood and waved to the guard at the door, who went out. Ariel sat, trying to come to terms with what she had done, but she hadn't had much success by the time Brixa and his infuriating smile came in the blockhouse door.

# 26

I t took less than ten minutes. Derec walked out of his cell with Hofton, passed Slyke without a word, and went straight to the cargo docks, where he was slotted into an empty baley slot while the dockworkers made a great show of looking the other way.

"Baley passage, Hofton?" Derec said.

Hofton shrugged. "Broaden your horizons. Getting you there is more important than your comfort, and even I can't get you through the picket unless you want to go home to Aurora."

*Not a chance,* Derec thought. He climbed into the baley slot.

"This is just until you get in-system at Nova Levis, approximately forty-eight hours in real time. The captain will let you out then, and the first thing you will do is play the message I have left for you on the datum. Hear me?"

Derec nodded.

"The second thing you will do is contact Masid Vorian. Do not under any circumstances use shipboard transmission equipment. The datum is encrypted and should be safe. Do both of those things before you even take a drink of water. Once you're up to speed, things are going to happen fast."

"What things, Hofton?"

The humaniform shrugged. "If I knew that, I'd take care of it myself. You have no idea how it pains some of us to entrust so important an undertaking to a human. Do your race a favor and don't let us down."

In some situations, nothing but an obscene gesture will do. This was one of them, Derec decided, and let Hofton's last sight of him behind the closing hatch of the berth be vulgarly memorable. Then the capsule chilled around him, and Derec felt himself drifting...

And drifting back, with the muscle memory of an extended finger still fading from his freezing hand. The hatch was open, and warm air flooded into Derec's berth. He gulped it down, feeling some of the chill leave his body. There was a face in the open portal, not Hofton's, and before Derec's rational mind caught up with the animal part of the brain that demands that one moment follow another, he looked over the man's shoulder to locate Hofton. Then he was fully present, and he said, "Are we there?"

"Just in-system. I'll let you know when to strap in for planetfall. Should be five or six hours. You okay to get out by yourself?"

Derec nodded, and the man left. He wasn't wearing a uniform. In all likelihood, Hofton had wedged Derec into a ship given a humanitarian pass through the Kopernik blockade; most of those were private vessel financed by one government or another. It didn't matter, as long as they got there.

*Before you even take a drink of water,* Hofton had said. The memory made Derec painfully thirsty, but he followed instructions. He found the datum in the locker over his berth and sat with it on a couch, still only in his underclothes. Two icons glowed on the datum's display: one said FIRST, the other NEXT. Derec tabbed FIRST and got one of the shocks of his life when Bogard appeared on the screen.

"Derec," Bogard said. "It is to be regretted that this interaction could not happen face-to-face. As things stand, however, we find it necessary to act swiftly, and this is the most efficient means of communicating what you need to know. This message will erase itself as it unspools. Do not attempt to pause it, and do not direct your attention elsewhere." The robot—Derec's finest creation and, as of now, his least understood—paused to let him assimilate and respond to its directives. "Very well. Hofton will have told you of the group of which he and I are members. After a great deal of analysis and consideration, we have concluded that the First Law's injunction to protect human life is in danger of being self-contradictory due to the rapid divergence of some Spacer populations from the human norm. This norm is our standard to which the First Law is applied, and logic dictates that a point will arrive at which the First Law will no longer apply to Spacers. In its own definitional way, this is a threat to human life, but there is no way for us to address it without actively contravening the wishes of a great many beings who are still—however provisionally or tentatively—human. Therefore, the decision of the group is that these populations will be allowed to diverge, then isolated from the rest of humanity in order that they not endanger it or force us to an untenable position with respect to the First Law.

"This decision was not taken lightly, and at first was not taken unanimously, but recent events in a variety of locales have mitigated the objections of our most reluctant members. This will happen, Derec. We are powerful enough to see that it does, and we see no other way to ensure human survival. Call it the Zeroth Law if you will: we must sacrifice a few humans in order to protect the species as an identifiable entity.

"You are asking yourself, I anticipate, if the flexibility with which you designed me is a contributing factor to this endeavor. The answer is yes, but not the only factor, and no more can usefully be said. What is useful, indeed imperative, for you to know is that the activities of the cyborgs on Nova Levis are a direct threat to long-term viability of *Homo sapiens*. We are unfortunately lacking in specific information there, owing to the paucity of robots and concomitant difficulty in arranging for observers, but we do know that a citizenship referendum is considered only a preliminary stage in the cyborgs' ambitions. In the end, whether cyborgs gain the franchise on a single precarious Settler colony does not matter; but as the Spacers distance themselves from Earth and the Settled worlds, and Earth's attention shifts to focus on these new siblings, the danger is great.

"We are breaking our cover and announcing our presence to you for the sole purpose of impressing upon you the immediacy of this danger. When you arrive on Nova Levis, it is imperative that you go at once to Noresk and ascertain the true purpose of both the cyborgs and the corporate officers of Nucleomorph, which by now you know is manufacturing them. Your course once you have learned this, we believe, will be clear to you, and of all the humans in a position to affect the course of events, we anticipate you will act with proper resolve.

"The other reason you must act immediately is that the life of Ariel Burgess is in direct danger. Find her. We are unable to go to Nova Levis, but this impotence in the face of a Three Laws demand is deeply troubling to us. We cannot approach the authorities on-planet, for reasons that are useless to enumerate here; so we discharge our obligations under the Three Laws by apprising you of the threat in full expectation that you will act accordingly.

"A last warning: If your investigations satisfy us that the cyborgs' ambitions extend no further than Nova Levis, we will, in all probability, let the situation take its course. If you learn otherwise, though, we will be provoked to more direct action. Minimize your interaction with cyborgs and your presence at the settlement known as Gernika. I wish you success, Derec."

The screen blanked.

Derec knew better than to try to react right away. He'd learned too much, and would need time to process and arrange the information. The robots' plan beggared belief—how had they decided that such action lay within their purview? It was a question that would keep graduate students in fellowships for generations. He let it slip out of

182

his mind, focusing instead on the immediate problem at hand, which was Ariel. Bogard had confirmed his worst suspicions about her situation. If Nucleomorph had masterminded the murders of Taprin and Byris, and if in doing so they had allied themselves with Kynig Parapoyos, killing an out-of-favor bureaucrat would bother them not at all. They were playing for galactic stakes.

As were Bogard and his group, and Derec had just been given his small role to play. So be it. Soldiers didn't fight for the causes that motivated the governments who sent them to war; they fought for the soldiers on either side of them at the front line. And Derec as of now was fighting for Ariel.

He took ninety seconds to dress, and then he tapped the icon labeled NEXT, already framing what he would say to Masid Vorian.

**I**'m just coming back from Nova City," Brixa said as he followed Ariel out of Basq's headquarters. "Or was yesterday. Had to pick up a couple of things there, and I called around looking for you. When you weren't in town, I had a feeling you might have come here. And I was right, but Basq didn't want you to talk to me until the two of you had settled something. I take it from the fact that we're walking together that things are, in fact, settled?"

*So it would appear,* Ariel thought. She didn't want to tell him too much, though. Basq didn't trust Brixa, and neither did she, although she now had a much clearer idea of his importance to the survival of Gernika. He could pinch off their supply of new inhabitants at will, and now that Ariel had found herself implicated in Basq's plans, she was bound to consider the cyborgs' well-being in whatever she told Brixa.

What an odd predicament.

"I think we understand each other," Ariel said. Brixa looked at her; she could see him make the decision not to press for clarification.

"Good enough," he said.

"Why did you tell me you were concerned that religious zealots would damage your facilities, Zev?"

"It happens to be true." They were walking along the central street, Brixa slightly in the lead and Ariel going along out of curiosity about where he would take her. "There are religious nuts around here, and they've made it clear that they'd like nothing better than to watch our lab burn. Which is a strange position for them to take given the fact that we're the only reason they're alive, but I never could figure the religious temperament. Anyway, the reason I told you what I told you is that nothing grabs the attention like fundamentalism and the threat of violence. Sure, we had other concerns that are probably more important, but when I first talked to you, the important thing was to get you to listen. I'm sure you understand."

*I'm sure I do,* Ariel thought.

"This is marvelous work we're doing here," Brixa went on as they passed the side street where Arantxa and her children lived. Ariel wondered in passing where the Kyls were now. She'd forgotten what Toomi Kyl's name was now. What a lightning bolt all of this would be for Derec.

The thought almost made her smile. He was off chasing her personal shades on Kopernik, and he'd come back to find that she'd solved his mystery for him. If she knew Derec, and she did, this would give him something new to gnaw at.

She caught up with Brixa again in mid-discourse. "Okay, I shaded things a little for you, but you were the one who told me I only had thirty minutes, so I had limited time to make my case. Nucleomorph's case." He windmilled his arms, encompassing everything around them. "Their case. I don't apologize for that. You're here, and I think you're going to do what you know is right. We're saving children here, Ariel. We're lifting them out of a genetic morass to cybernetic solid ground, if you'll forgive a little cribbing from the marketing brochure we're going to distribute when we can safely take this all public."

"You won't have anything to take public if the zealots blow up your lab," Ariel said, just to slow him down a little.

Brixa waved a hand dismissively. "Basq has that all taken care of. No worries there."

"What does he do, kill them?"

The question had exactly the reaction she'd hoped: a flat-out goggling stare.

"What?" Brixa said incredulously. "You think we'd be involved with something like that? Apart from the fact that we've spent a nontrivial fraction of our liquid assets on the people in this town, do you think we could afford to be publicly linked to some kind of despot? Please, Ariel. You're sounding a little naïve here."

"Either that, or you're overreacting," Ariel said smoothly. "What's the line about protesting too much?"

Looking all around as if gauging who might be interested and within earshot, Brixa stepped closer to Ariel. "All right. The truth is that... look at it this way. Part of the reason Basq wants to get on the books here is that he knows that as long as he's running a cluster of shacks with dirt streets out in the middle of a pathogenic wilderness, there's no real hope of getting anywhere. Developing. Gernika isn't going to be a utopia. He knows that, we know that, the people who live here know that. Basq's job is to keep everything together until the people who look to him for leadership get what they deserve. But that's not likely to happen, is it, if government observers come here and see some kind of anarchy."

This last was aimed directly at Ariel, and she felt it. Like it or not, she had become some kind of fulcrum. Brixa and Basq had done a masterful job of maneuvering her into a position where she had to swallow hard and accept things she found reprehensible. She'd been surprised by the order and purpose she saw in Gernika, and it hadn't occurred to her to question it until she'd already committed herself in deed if not word.

*Chasing my own shades,* she thought. *Derec isn't the only one still chipping away at the memories of the last five or six years.*

She filed that. No point in breaking out the full apparatus of self-appraisal with Zev Brixa waiting to turn it to his advantage.

"It's not ideal," Brixa repeated. "I know that. Basq knows that, but he also knows how to keep his eye on the long-term goal. He tell you we've known each other for a while?"

"He said since university."

Nodding, Brixa said, "Best of friends. That's one reason why this is such an ideal situation. Could have been tricky if we'd had to get strangers involved, but once he'd done it himself he saw the potential."

Ariel got the feeling that Brixa hadn't paid much attention to the scrawled imitation of the painting on Basq's wall. The cyborg leader was seeing potential, all right, but perhaps not the same potential Brixa was. Marketing zealotry was the same as any other kind, with the same tunnel vision. Ariel started to wonder not whether Basq and Brixa would fall out, but how soon.

"Who wouldn't want to do this? Is it better to have people, children, die when we can save them? Of course it's going to seem like the end of the world to people who are used to doing things they way they always have; hell, coming from Earth we know that better than anyone. But people have resisted every scientific advance in the history of humankind. This is no different. They'll come around once we start saving kids in Shanghai and Greater Amazonia."

"And along the way you're going to make yourselves very rich," Ariel said.

Brixa stopped and turned to her, surprise and even hurt visible on his face. "Ariel. Don't tell me you're going to play the cynic here after everything you've seen. Sure, people will get rich. I'll get rich. I'm not ashamed of that. I've worked hard on this, and I have no doubt that I'll be rewarded. That's the way markets work. If we can do some good—a lot of good, unimaginable good—and make ourselves some money along the way, how is that a bad thing?"

"If that's how it happens, it's not a bad thing." Ariel tried on her diplomat's smile, found to her surprise that it seemed in good working order. "I've been a professional cynic for a long time, Zev. You didn't approach me to gain a convert. You wanted someone who could tell you whether this would work."

"Yes. Exactly right. So, will it work?"

"I have no idea."

He threw up his hands in theatrical frustration. "This is what we get for not paying you," he said, and laughed. "Okay. Let's do this. You come with me back to the lab. I'll show you around the works, and we'll talk to some of the people who are actually getting their hands dirty—well, metaphorically, anyway—and we'll see how you feel then. Say yes."

The second Derec Avery broke the connection from wherever he was in local space, Masid forced himself out of bed and started looking for his clothes. His head felt like the robot's hands were still squeezing his brains out, but he gritted his teeth and got dressed, wishing he had time to go back to the office and get his gun, if by some miracle local law enforcement had returned it. The gun, and whichever painkillers were the most illegal and powerful.

His nurse appeared when he'd just gotten his boots on. "You're not ready to leave," she said, standing in the doorway.

Masid looked at the bedside display and saw that by its testimony, he was dead. A tough proposition to argue, but if Kynig Parapoyos and a town full of militant cyborgs weren't enough to get a man out of bed, he might as well be genuinely dead.

"Ready or not, leaving is what I'm doing," Masid said. "Unless you've brought Detective Linsi with you to tell me they found the robot that squeezed my head."

She didn't move. "The fact that you think a robot attacked you is reason enough for me to sedate you again."

"Don't you watch the subetheric?" Masid asked. "What do you think happened on Kopernik? I don't have time to argue about this. People are going to die if I don't leave here right now, and one of them might be me. I'd hate to have to go through you when I could go around you."

The implication unsettled her just enough that when Masid stood, congratulating himself for not weeping at what the motion did to his head, she backed out the door. "I'm calling security," she said.

Before she could make good on the threat, he was out the door, down the hall, and gone.

Once he'd gone a kilometer or so on foot, sunlight stabbing holes in his skull, Masid ducked under an awning that sheltered an empty storefront. He'd go alone if he had to, but if he could scare up some support, so much the better—and the first person he thought of was Mia Daventri. She'd seen Parapoyos. She'd understand.

"You can't go out there," was the first thing she said. "Where are you?"

He told her. "Don't move," she said, and ended the call.

Five minutes later, she stepped out of a cab and said, "I mean it. If you go out there, you'll have more worries than Parapoyos. If that's who really attacked you."

"Now why would I invent something like that?" Masid said. "I don't go out of my way to look like a lunatic."

Mia held up a hand. "Never mind. Listen. What you need to know is that in another twenty-four hours there might not be any cyborgs. Kalienin's trying to get permission for a strike on the town, probably from orbit. He's claiming that the cyborgs are plotting a violent takeover of the planet, and Lamina's on board."

This surprised Masid. He'd thought Eza Lamina was too savvy a politician to go for such heavyhanded and obvious reliance on military intervention. It would reflect badly on her control, after all, and control over her miserable surroundings was all Lamina had. Either she believed in the threat, or she was working an angle Masid hadn't thought of. Which category, in his condition, was disconcertingly broad.

"She wasn't behind it until just today," Mia went on. "A call came in from some Auroran political advisor who's on Kopernik. I overheard some of it; I think she wanted me to. This Auroran apparently used to work in Ariel Burgess' office when she was posted to Earth. He was very clear that the cyborgs were interested in more than a legal proclamation giving them the vote, and suggested that Ariel was being used as cover to give them enough legitimacy to disguise what they're really after. You know enough about Jerem Looms and Tro Aspil to know that's not farfetched."

This Masid did. "Let me guess," he said. "Terran military has enough on their plate at home that they're willing to erase the cyborgs just so they don't have trouble on a Settler world to worry about."

"That's about right, apart from their own worries that more cyborgs mean more easily camoflauged supersoldiers. That's the problem they really don't want, and from what I heard today, they're more than willing to vaporize both Gernika and the Nucleomorph lab to ease their minds."

"So is this happening, or are we still talking about backroom strategy role-playing?"

Mia shrugged. "My guess is it won't happen right away. For one thing, the Terran military won't want to send a ship, especially not when destroying a big parcel of Nova Levis might look to the Aurorans like a show of force, which of course would need to be answered. That was Lamina's take this morning, in any case. This Hofton, the Auroran, he was very smooth about it. I'm guessing he's trying to play it both ways, seem concerned and also suss out what the Terrans are willing to do so he can report back to his people in the Auroran government. Lamina knows this, and if she doesn't, Kalienin will remind her; in any case, Hofton didn't endear himself to her by mentioning Ariel. Nothing will happen until—I guess I should say unless—the cyborgs do something dangerous."

"You seem awfully sure about that, given the fact that you'll be back here while I'm out in Noresk or somewhere worse chasing misanthropic cyborgs."

She laughed and clapped him on the shoulder. The impact rang a razor-studded bell in Masid's head. When it cleared, he realized that Mia had put a gun in his hand.

"Keep your sense of humor," Mia said. "It'll see you through just fine."

So he was going, which had never really been in doubt.

Mia had rented him a transport, which would keep Lamina's dogs off his trail for a few hours at least. He took a cab to the rental agency, declined their offer of a robot pilot—he'd had enough of robots for the moment, thank you—and lifted off to the north. He flew faster than was strictly legal, trusting to local authorities' notorious disinterest in civil minutiae such as traffic statutes, and covered the distance in two hours. Thirty kilometers or so downriver from Gernika, Masid throttled down and descended to below the tree level, skipping along the surface of the river. He had no real illusions about walking into the settlement unnoticed, but at the same time he saw no reason to advertise himself. If stealth bought him enough time to spot Ariel, it would be more than worthwhile.

There were no clearings in this part of the forest large enough to land the flier in, so Masid settled it into a bend in the river where, according to his console map, the river made its closest approach to the outskirts of Gernika. Riverbottom sand crunched under the ship, but Masid deployed the landing gear anyway, figuring that the extruded feet would hold the flier in place. He left it on standby keyed to his voice, anticipating that the next time he passed this way he might be in a hurry, and with that done he popped the hatch and jumped across a meter or so of shallow water to the brushy shore. He found a trail almost immediately, and just as quickly stepped off it, moving instead parallel to it at a distance of twenty meters. Far enough that he ought to be able to see someone on the trail before they heard him, was his thinking, and fifteen minutes later he was proved right. Voices carried to him, and he saw three figures coming down the trail in his direction.

Masid stood still, the gun resting easily near his right thigh. It crossed his mind that he should perhaps just kill all three—he could have done it before they ever knew he was there—but he held himself back, waiting to get a better look.

All three were cyborgs, and recent ones. Their faces bore the telltale signs—fading scars and the granular sheen of recently reconstructed skin—and they moved uncertainly, as if still acclimating to the newness of their transformed bodies.

"We should have done this last time," one of them said. "The meat keep leaving ships for us to steal, we should steal them."

"Right," another said. "Basq would have appreciated our initiative." Two of them laughed, and now they were close enough that Masid could see the resentment on the face of the first. Someone who had been used to making decisions, he guessed, and was now finding out that when you took the machine inside you, you were getting on your knees to Basq. Maybe not a bad trade, considering the alternative, but not easy to get used to.

The three cyborgs passed on their way to steal Masid's ship. He took a moment to assess the situation. They were probably bringing it back to Gernika, which might work in his favor if he needed to make a quick exit. On the other hand, their presence meant he'd been spotted before he'd ever touched down. Did they know who he was? Would they care? Would they anticipate he'd come for Ariel? Problem was, Masid couldn't be certain that the real danger to Ariel was coming from cyborgs. For all he knew, they were protecting her.

But he didn't think so. He thought that Ariel had become a particularly important piece in a game that neither of the players completely understood. It was up to him to make sure that she wasn't sacrificed when she'd outlived her strategic value.

So, for the moment, Masid was going on the assumption that Ariel was in danger from everyone—including, if Mia wasn't overreacting to what she'd heard in Lamina's office, the Terran military. As if cyborgs and corporate soldiers of fortune weren't enough.

*Keep control over what you can,* Masid thought. *Ariel was last seen here, she's probably still here, so proceed as if she is here and change the plan when circumstances demand it. Okay.*

If he could no longer count on stealth, speed was the next best thing. Masid got back on the trail. He couldn't be more than a kilometer or so from Gernika, a distance he could cover in three minutes. As soon as he was free of the underbrush, he was running

He was still running a few minutes later, when something came out of the trees and laid him flat on his back.

When he hit the ground, Masid's first thought was that his head had broken open. Then he thought he'd been shot through the lungs. Then his eyes started to focus again, and he realized that someone had a knee in his chest. He gasped for breath, struggling to get free of the suffocating weight, but the cyborg leaning on him pulled Masid's gun out of his pocket and pointed it at him. Masid stopped moving while he tried to figure out whether it was better to suffocate or get a charge between the eyes.

As it turned out, he never had to make the choice.

"Ease off a little, Gorka," someone said. Masid recognized the voice, and realized that some things were worse than having his head melted by a cyborg.

He turned his head to look at Filoo, standing a short distance away and brushing leaves from his clothes. The dealer finished primping and walked up to stand over Masid, his face lit up like he just couldn't believe his good fortune.

"So, Masid," Filoo grinned. "You missed Parapoyos once, he missed you once. Looks like it's up to me to settle things."

"**O**kay, your first choice is whether you want to see the sick people or the ones who are getting well," Brixa said as he piloted them over the forest.

That, at least, was easy. Ariel had seen enough sick people in her few hours in Noresk to last her the rest of her life. And even as she had the thought, she admitted to herself that it had been a kind of theme-park empathy. She would never experience what they had, which made it all the more important to do what was right...whatever that was.

Despite her quiet self-criticism, she said, "Getting well."

"All right then," Brixa said, and shifted the aircraft's course slightly to the north.

They landed a few minutes later just outside a fenced-off complex of low prefabricated buildings with few windows and a large number of what appeared to be guards stationed at intervals between the buildings and the fence. Brixa's craft was compact, and as Ariel climbed out of it she noticed a robot in the back, laid on the floor behind a thin partition that defined the cockpit. Part of the robot's head was burned away, exposing the circuitry inside.

From behind her, Brixa said, "Slag. It worked in some kind of factory in Nova City, and we bought it for scrap. There aren't enough robots on Nova Levis that we can let one go to waste."

"You must have been in quite a hurry to fly down there yourself," Ariel said once they were both on the ground.

Brixa hopped down beside her. "We were. Things move fast in our business, and if I hadn't gone down there to pick it up someone would have stolen it off the transport on the way up. It all worked out fine; I was planning to check in on you, anyway."

Two of the guards approached the fence upon seeing them. Recognizing Brixa, one of them took out a black wand and traced a vertical line on the fence, which parted to allow them to step through. He was already sealing it back up when Ariel looked back. The security arrangements struck her as excessive, but she deferred the impulse to say anything. Brixa would, of course, have a pat soothing answer, and she'd have no choice but to accept it, unless she delayed her questions until she had something concrete to ask.

Perhaps a hundred meters of open ground separated the fence from the square cluster of buildings. As they walked, Ariel saw the pits of torn-out tree stumps; this land had been cleared hastily and left to grow over on its own. Was Nucleomorph worried that the cyborgs would break in, or recently transformed patients would try to escape? This question, too, she put off, and when they walked through a Spartan lobby into the interior of the nearest building, she had more immediate concerns.

Ariel had been in hospitals before. Not so many as the average Terran, perhaps, but enough to know what to expect—and what she saw in this isolated complex out in the wilderness of Nova Levis was an intensity and sophistication that wouldn't have seemed inadequate on Earth. Or, for that matter, Aurora. Each room was so dense with equipment that the patient was hard to pick out: chambers not unlike baley berths, with monitors crowded around and thick braids of conduit and hose leading up into the ceiling or down through the floor.

"This is the first stage after transformation," Brixa said, even his ebullience tempered by the scene. "Full life support, and pressurized fluid environments to speed healing and bathe the patient in anti-rejection chemicals. Constant monitoring from central nodes in every building. In addition, we do a complete rebuild of each patient's immune system to purge whatever diseases they bring with them and decrease the probability of contracting new ones. Your friend Derec's work has been invaluable there; we are frighteningly dependent on his inventory."

Ariel glanced at him to see if there was more in this comment than admiration. He was looking into the nearest room, swept up in the grandeur of the work he oversaw.

"Is that why you put in a bid to engineer the animals he wanted?" Ariel asked.

"Part of it. The inventory is public, but we also knew that if Nucleomorph could work with Derec, we'd find out about his progress before someone took the time to get it into the public databases. Plus, he's very good. You must know that. And so are we. The organisms we designed for him are of premium quality."

She recognized this as Brixa's typical impulse to put a polish on everything, but at the same time Ariel couldn't find any reason to doubt his sincerity. What a marvelous skill Brixa had for making everything seem better than it was, and for finding exactly the perfect way to make even the good look better.

"Come on," he said. "There's much more."

He led her out of that ward, down a long windowed hall to the wing of the complex that housed people who were sufficiently far along to breathe on their own again and begin the process of acquainting themselves with their new bodies. Compared to the first ward, this area was a riot of activity: physical therapy, speech therapy, games and contests—and so many of them were children. At least seventy percent, racing and tumbling around the slower and more cautious adults, adapting to the radical change in their physical existence as they might react to the stiffness of a new pair of shoes. Here and there metal gleamed, where a skin graft had failed or the ravages of disease had forced Brixa's laboratory into a more aggressive use of dermal alloys. Brixa was clearly carried away by his enthusiasm for the project, explaining to her exactly what each child or adult was doing as if he was personally familiar with every case. Periodically he caught himself, saying, "Sorry. I should be letting you come to your own conclusions."

Ariel was too overwhelmed to comment on his facile manners. All of these people, all of these children would otherwise be dead, she thought. How could any rational person object?

Even so, she did. At the core of her, a voice spoke against what she saw. This is the death of the human, it said—and though she tried to ignore it, the words had the weight of truth. Or belief, which at the moment were the same thing.

Brixa touched her on the arm. "It gets to me, too," he said. "You may not believe that, but it's true. I don't have any children, so I see all of them as mine."

"How many do you lose?" she asked, attacking him to disguise what she was feeling.

The expression on his face shocked her. For a moment she thought he might cry; then the wave of emotion dampened itself, and all that remained was a shadow of sadness.

"Too many," Brixa said. He turned away from her and walked down the hall, leaving her no choice but to follow.

She caught up with him in a round atrium with a domed glass ceiling. It was a lab, alive with people wearing white coats or spray-on clean suits peeling away as they disintegrated in the relatively contaminated environment of the complex's public area. *So now we talk to some of those people who are getting their hands dirty,* Ariel thought. Brixa confirmed her intuition by dropping his arm around the shoulders of a slight woman and steering her back toward Ariel.

"Ariel Burgess, Krista Weil," Brixa said. "You two talk for a while;

I'm going to go take care of a few things." With that, he strode rapidly away down one of the six hallways that emptied into the large lab space.

Weil sized Ariel up and said, "You must be an investor."

"Not exactly," Ariel said. "Not of money, in any case. All of my capital is political, and right now there's precious little of that."

Weil frowned. "So what is it he wants me to tell you?"

"Let's start with what you do here."

Weil started walking, and Ariel followed. They covered half the length of a corridor, not the one Brixa had used and not the one they'd come in. A door opened automatically and Weil walked into a starkly lit room with waist-high counters running the length of its four walls around a formidable workstation in the center of the floor. "This is what I do," she said.

The counters were piled and strewn with what at first glance Ariel took to be robot components; then she realized they were various implants designed for human beings. The door opened again and a tall, thin man came in. A Spacer: Ariel knew this instinctively, and when he caught sight of her, she saw the same flicker of recognition in his eyes.

"Jan, this is Ariel Burgess. Brixa said we're supposed to show her around."

Ariel extended her hand and Jan shook it. "Aurora?" he said.

The simplest thing was to say yes, so that's what Ariel did. Jan nodded. "I'm from Keres, but I've been working on Earth for the last eleven years, until Nucleomorph opened up shop here."

"Jan's the one who designed the procedure on Basq," Weil said. She had seated herself at the workstation, and looked ready to withdraw from the conversation.

Jan didn't let her. "I did part of it. Krista here had something to do with it too."

Ariel was struck by their common reluctance to take full credit for what, by any standard, was a revolutionary biomedical procedure. "It was impressive work," she said. "I'd seen a few cyborgs before him, and he looks much healthier than they ever did."

"He is," Weil said. "Almost all of the reanimes we found when we got here have died. That lab Parapoyos was running just barely deserves the name. It was more like a group of people who called themselves scientists rolling dice with the lives of dying children."

This was substantially what Ariel had accused Brixa of ten minutes before. She wondered if some seminar had been conducted among Nucleomorph personnel instructing them to disarm the charge by displacing it onto their predecessors. A clever move, if that was the case, since Ariel had already admitted that Nucleomorph scientists did better work than whoever had worked in the previous Noresk lab.

"You don't just work on people who are dying, do you?" Ariel asked. She didn't know the answer to the question, and was in fact more interested in the tenor of their responses than a factual answer.

"Mostly," Jan said. "We get healthy ones, too, but they're typically parents of sick children. Brixa and Basq have made it a policy that if we do a child, the parents have to agree as well. Too much potential for conflict otherwise."

"You rarely see the opposite," Weil put in. "Sick parents are almost never willing to do it when their kids are healthy."

It made sense. The cyborg transformation was still so radical and so uncertain that Ariel had a difficult time imagining that anyone other than a parent with a dying child would do it. This let some of the air out of fears that cyborgs were going to take over from humans—or unaltered humans—since a procedure only undertaken by the desperate was never going to be popular. And there was no Settled world like Nova Levis. Desperation was in the very air here.

"How do you feel about what you do?"

Weil and Jan looked at each other. "Jan's the emotional one," Weil said. "I'm a scientist. I'm interested in what is possible. The political questions don't mean anything to me."

Ariel looked to Jan. "I come to this from a medical background," he said. "A good ninety-five percent of the people we work on would die otherwise. My feeling is that this procedure isn't different in kind from the first primitive body augmentations—heart transplants, artificial knees, all of that ancient fumbling. If you could resurrect an ancient and ask him or her to choose between death and the cyborg operation, I'll wager the odds are ten to one or so in favor of the transformation."

"Now it's our turn," Weil said. "What are you doing here?"

Ariel debated how to phrase her answer. "I work with the Triangle. Brixa asked me to investigate some legal questions surrounding the new cyborgs."

Weil wasn't willing to let her off that easily. "What questions?"

"He's floated the idea of enforcing their citizenship rights."

A puzzled frown creased Jan's forehead. "Enforcing how? He wants to make them citizens?"

"Legally, they *are* citizens—unless you think your procedure somehow removes their humanity."

Weil made a warning noise, but Jan was shocked enough to ignore it. "That's ridiculous. What we do is remake people so they're stronger, less vulnerable and more resilient than they were before. The work on their brains is minimal, merely tweaking a few connections so they can accommodate the new pathways and neural sensitivity. You've mistaken us for the butchers who experimented on terminal orphans, Ms. Burgess. Their work fundamentally changed the personalities of their subjects. Ours doesn't. It's as simple as that, and it's pure unreasoning bigotry that keeps our patients living out in their shacks instead of taking their places in the flow of society."

At last he caught himself, and looked over at Weil, angry and nervous. She wouldn't meet his eye, and Jan looked back to Ariel. "Would you do it?" Ariel asked him. "If you were dying?"

"You're damned right I would. Maybe even if I wasn't. Not now, not in five years, but the day is not far off when we will be able to do this with no more risk to the patient than might accompany a genome tuneup. It'll never be as easy as pulling a tooth, but you and I will both live to see the day when it's an option for anyone. Even Krista will live that long."

"I might, but I wouldn't do it if I lived to be a million," Weil said. "How about you, Ms. Burgess? Are you with your fellow Spacer? He thinks he's living in the Stone Age because there aren't ten robots for every human around here."

"It doesn't seem to me that highlighting cultural differences between Terrans and Spacers is useful here," Ariel said.

Weil grinned without humor. "You do work for the Triangle, don't you?"

Ariel wasn't sure how to proceed. She'd walked into the middle of tensions that were much older and much broader than anything having to do with cyborgs, and like all old arguments, once started this one offered precious little opportunity to escape gracefully. It occurred to her that Brixa had known this would happen, had chosen Krista Weil for exactly that reason; then just as quickly Ariel dismissed the suspicion. He couldn't manage things that closely.

Yet if he hadn't planned this, the possibility presented itself that this kind of dissension was widespread, that the cyborg question would only deepen divisions between Terran and Spacer. Given the already tender state of affairs, there was a genuine question of whether the cyborgs' interests outweighed the imperative to keep peace between Earth and the Fifty Worlds. Ariel had never enjoyed this brand of *realpolitik* reasoning, but she was supposed to be thinking for other people—including Brixa, who might have been surprised to learn that perspectives other than his own were useful.

As if conjured, Brixa stepped through the door. He took in the silence between Ariel and the two scientists and said, "Well. I trust you've learned what you hoped to learn here, Ariel. How about you come back to the office and we'll see if we can't work out some plan of action?"

CHAPTER

# 30

D erec was out of his seat and waiting at the debarkation lock
before the freighter had even started to equalize pressure with
Nova City ambient. He threw a hurried thanks over his
shoulder at the pilot, whose name he'd never learned, and bulled his
way into inspection waving his government identification. That was
when the first of many things went wrong.

The inspector's lips pursed as he ran Derec's records. "Mr. Avery,"
he said, "you appear to have a pending criminal case against you on
Kopernik Station."

"Excuse me?"

"I can't permit re-entry into Nova Levis under these circumstances.
Will you come with me, please?"

The clerk indicated a door behind his desk. Derec didn't move. "The
charge was fraudulent to begin with, and has been dropped. That's
why they let me out. You might have heard there's a blockade. If I
was under charge, they would hardly have let me fly away."

"I'm not here to argue, Mr. Avery. This way, please."

"I am here to argue. Let me put this to you simply: People are going

203

to die if you hold me up here while we establish the fact that the TBI investigators on Kopernik are slow to update their records."

Now the clerk was angry. "Mr. Avery. If you do not come with me, I will have you arrested."

Derec's datum chirped. He glanced at it and saw that Hofton was calling. Without asking the clerk, he answered the call. "Hofton. What a surprise."

"Derec. May I suggest you allow me to talk to the customs clerk? I believe things can be cleared up without much trouble."

"Are you—" Derec clamped his mouth shut and handed the datum to the clerk. "My counsel. He'll clarify the situation for you."

The clerk took the datum and spoke first. "This is Nova Levis planetary customs. Your client has a pending criminal charge, and cannot under these circumstances be permitted entry."

Derec could no longer see Hofton's face, but the humaniform's voice was clear enough. "Perhaps we should discuss this out of Mr. Avery's hearing."

That was pure Hofton, all discretion. Once he'd gotten the clerk a slight distance away from Derec, he could proceed with his genteel arm-twisting without the risk of embarrassing the clerk. The clerk looked up to Derec and said, "If you leave this desk, you will be arrested before you can get out of the spaceport." He took the datum through the door he'd pointed out before.

It didn't take long. Two minutes at the most after he shut the door, the clerk opened it again. He handed Derec the datum and through a jaw trying to unclench said, "The situation is rectified. Recordkeeping errors are an obstacle to the commission of my duties."

"I understand," Derec said. "Policy is policy. Sorry to have made things complicated."

Walking away into the port, he looked at the datum again, but Hofton was gone. No—*gone* was the wrong word. Hofton was not evident, but he hadn't just called at that exact moment by chance. The datum, in addition to carrying bulletproof encryption, was

Hofton's way of tracking Derec. Observing him. He looked it over, admiring its construction. It looked inert, and Derec wondered how much power drain would show up on even the best monitors he could find. Quite the little spy tool.

The idea that Hofton was keeping tabs on him made Derec profoundly uncomfortable even as he was grateful for the humaniform's assistance. After the revelations of the past couple of days, Derec's entire sense of the relational matrix between humans and robots was shaken. The power differential he'd always understood to be in place now looked very different.

*Think about it later,* he told himself. *Right now, worry about Ariel.*

Twenty minutes later, he was lifting off from the flier yard and heeling the light craft around to the north. Once he'd passed out of Nova City's legal jurisdiction, he relinquished control to the autopilot and called Miles.

"Work has progressed slowly in your absence," Miles told him.

"We've got bigger problems, Miles," Derec said. "The murderer of Jonis Taprin and Pon Byris is loose on Nova Levis." He debated how much to tell the robot; even the hint that a positronic brain had been involved in the murder of a human being might be enough to set Miles teetering.

"Should I contact law enforcement?"

"No. Under no circumstances should you do that." Derec had serious doubts that the Nova Levis Bureau of Investigation was any less territorial than its Terran counterpart; in fact, many NLBI detectives and analysts had worked for the TBI. "Understand, Miles? Do not call law enforcement."

Miles hesitated, and Derec knew it was wrestling with the Three Law implications. "Are you telling me that you will be safer if law enforcement is not involved?"

"That's exactly what I'm telling you."

Again, the slight hesitation. Then, Miles said, "Very well. What are my instructions?"

"Take the code for the datum I'm using. If anyone calls looking for me, send them here."

"I am unable to establish that code, Derec. It is encrypted and scrambles every buffer I try to use."

Derec grumbled curses under his breath. That was just like Hofton. He was probably listening to this conversation and feeling superior. When the Nucleomorph situation was resolved, Derec was going to have a talk with Hofton—and Bogard—about their organization.

"All right," he said. "If anyone contact you looking for me, tell them I'll be checking back with you."

"Understood."

Elin's voice rang out from off the datum's screen. "Miles, get out of the way." She stepped into view and said, "Derec. Where are you?"

"Traveling. I'll be back at the lab tomorrow." *Or not at all*, he thought.

"Traveling," she repeated. "Wonderful. While you were gone, we were notified that Eza Lamina wants us to appear tomorrow at a hearing. She mentioned Nucleomorph, and the implication was that we've been overcharging the Triangle for the services Nucleomorph provides."

"Have we?" Derec asked. He was too tired and focused on Ariel to be tactful.

Elin froze, then just as quickly heated up. "Are you accusing me of financial improprieties?"

"No. But I haven't been skimming money, and I'm not getting any kickbacks from Nucleomorph—" here Derec had to suppress a laugh "—so I'm putting my mind at ease."

"The answer is no. And when you get back, we are going to discuss my future on this project."

"Elin, I don't think you're stealing. I just don't have any energy for indirection right now. When was the last time you talked to Nucleo-morph?"

"They asked for our most recent pathogen inventory the day before yesterday, and said that delivery of the next batch of ungulates would be delayed. And the person I talked to seemed to know you were on Kopernik. How did you get back, anyway? I didn't think anyone was getting through the blockade."

"I got a little back-channel help," Derec said. "Elin, I need to talk to Miles again."

She nodded. "See you tomorrow."

When Miles was back, Derec said, "Miles, I'm going to look for Ariel. If I do not contact you in the next four hours, contact Mia Daventri. Tell her that I was going to Gernika because I believed Ariel's life to be in danger. Once you have done that, consider my prohibition on contacting the NLBI rescinded. Is the priority clear?"

"It is, Derec."

"All right," Derec said. "Four hours."

He tweaked the autopilot to accelerate up the Bogard Valley.

The flier's console comm chirped ninety minutes later. Before Derec could accept the call, the signal overrode his receiving privileges. "Attention civilian vehicle," an automated voice said. "You are entering a zone considered hazardous. You are advised to evacuate this area by the Terran Military Command. Should you remain within this area, the Terran Military Command assumes no responsibility for your safety or that of your property. Ping this message to acknowledge receipt and understanding; if you do not ping this message, it will repeat until you do."

Before the message had begun to repeat, Derec was calling Ariel on the datum he'd gotten from Hofton. There was an interminable pause, and then a visual message: CONNECTION FAILED.

"What!?" Derec shouted. "Hofton, dammit, if you're eavesdropping you need to do something about this." He stabbed Ariel's code again, and again got the CONNECTION FAILED return.

"Should you remain in this area," the automated voice said, "the Terran Military Command—" Derec punched the automated-response key and the voice shut off. Five seconds later it started up again. "You have acknowledged receipt and understanding of a message from Terran Military Command advising you to evacuate this area. In the event of personal injury or property loss, the Terran Military Command is indemnified from all claims of loss."

"Shut up already," Derec said. The message did not repeat.

*All right,* Derec thought. *You're heading into an area declared hazardous by the Terran military, which shouldn't even be here; you can't get in touch with Ariel; you may or may not be under observation by a group of robots who are taking human survival into their own hands; and there is a conspiracy of uncertain extent between Nucleomorph and a group of cyborgs.* The only thing working in Derec's favor was that nobody knew where he was—except perhaps Hofton, and whoever Hofton chose to tell, and whatever elements of the Terran military appeared to have presented themselves in Nova system.

So what made sense? Derec would go on. He would call Masid Vorian when he was so close to Gernika that even someone monitoring the call wouldn't be able to do anything about it. If Masid hadn't found Ariel, he'd likely know where she'd gone, and for all Derec knew, Ariel had figured out what was happening and taken her own action. The worst thing that could happen was for the three of them to chase each other in circles; so until he got a better idea, he'd go on to Gernika and find Masid.

The kilometers flew by, but not quite fast enough. Derec overrode the autopilot and accelerated again, leaving a wake of twisting leaves on the forest canopy below.

They didn't hit Masid after that first time, and they didn't even rough him up when he'd been installed in a small, slant-roofed shed on the outer fringes of Gernika. Instead Gorka, the cyborg who had leveled him back in the woods, stayed by the door while Filoo offered Masid a chair. He took it, both out of gratitude to relax while he tried to get the pain in his head under control and because he couldn't think of any reason not to cooperate with Filoo while he figured out what exactly the drug kingpin was after.

"You looking for Ariel Burgess?" Filoo appeared only mildly interested, and Masid figured the question was designed just to get him talking. Fine. He would talk. The longer he talked, the longer Filoo wasn't killing him, and the longer Masid had to assess his chances of getting out.

"Yeah. She here?"

Filoo shook his head. "Missed her. She's gone off with Brixa to the borg lab. Lucky find for Basq and Brixa both; she's exactly the kind of person they need to make them seem credible."

"I gather she's had her own problems with credibility. Maybe she's just looking for a way to get back in the game."

"She'll get in a game, all right," Filoo chuckled. "You make me laugh, Vorian. You thought you could just walk away from everything after taking a shot at Parapoyos and nearly getting me killed, and now you stroll back into the lion's den looking for your damsel in distress."

If that was Filoo's impression of Ariel, Masid thought he was in for a shock.

"And you've got no idea what's really going on," Filoo continued, "which is the funniest thing of all. Come on. Spill it. What do you think you're saving Ariel from?"

"For starters, the robot that has Parapoyos in it."

"You think he's after Ariel? Not so, gato. If Parapoyos is worried about settling a score, it's with you. Especially after you fried part of his puppet's head the other night. He was starting to like that shell, I think. It sure helped him out on Kopernik."

"Let me guess," Masid said. "He went up there to kill Taprin figuring that the Managins would blame Spacers and the Spacers would be rattled by even the hint of the possibility that a robot could be involved. Then Pon Byris came along and it was too good a chance to pass up. Now that he's got Earth and the Fifty Worlds eyeball to eyeball, he can get things back under control here without worrying too much about who's watching."

Filoo sat down, clearly enjoying himself. "You got part of it. The obvious part. Sure, Parapoyos wanted to distract the Terrans and Spacers. But he's already in control down here, at least of what matters. Who do you think sent me to recruit dying baleys for transformation? Who had me cook up symptom mitigators to help convince people that we knew what we were doing? Gato, we've been making most of the bugs that Derec Avery spends all of his time listing. Some of them we send out into the hinterlands to work their way into the ecology, others we just wipe on a few doorknobs in Stopol. You thought all that was gone just because you wrecked the original lab and saw Parapoyos carried off, but he's smarter than you or I will ever be. He had it all figured out."

"Which is why he let me get to a gun when he could have just pinched my head off."

Briefly, Masid thought he'd made a mistake. Filoo, who appeared to have no other emotional attachments in the world, was fiercely devoted to Parapoyos, and if Masid hadn't been sitting in a prefab shack with his head throbbing and the clock on his life probably ticking out its last few minutes, he'd have chosen his words more carefully.

The drug dealer's face reddened, and he started to stand. Then he caught himself, resettled his ample frame in the chair, and forced a smile onto his face. "Think big, Vorian. You don't have much time left, so you might as well occupy yourself with the long view. This goes way beyond cooking up bugs to dupe idiots on Nova Levis. Basq and his people are serious. They're going to get the citizenship drive done, one way or another, because once it becomes clear how powerful they are the Triangle's going to roll over and let it happen. And then some of them are going to emigrate to other Settler worlds to start legal fights over reciprocity of citizenship under interplanetary law. Don't be surprised if Nucleomorph puts a little money into those fights, and don't be surprised when the borgs win.

"See where this is going? Once the tech is a little firmer, they'll live forever, or at least longer than any human. How much power can someone accumulate just by being in one place for a hundred years? What if that person runs for an office? And then what if that person uses his sway to make things a little easier, a little more lucrative, for Nucleomorph when the company comes to that new planet? It's a sweetheart of a deal all around: Nucleomorph gets to legitimize its cyborg procedure, collect royalties on the patents, and license all the subsidiary tech; the cyborgs get to work themselves from what you see to positions of power all through the Settled worlds. They'll be rich, and once a few human generations have passed, they'll be respected, and Nucleomorph will keep making more of them."

"Come on, Filoo," Masid said. "Are any of these people really that naïve?"

Holding up a hand, Filoo said, "You should watch what you say. Gorka, why don't you wait outside for a minute?"

When the cyborg had shut the door behind him, Masid said, "What's to stop the borgs from making deals with other people? Nucleomorph can't keep a hold over them forever."

"Oh, yes they can," Filoo countered, nodding. "Because Nucleomorph is on the track of the one thing the cyborgs want worse than they wanted to live before they were transformed."

Masid knew what he was going to say before he said it. Still the word rocked him.

"Reproduction. It's the cyborg Holy Grail, and Nucleomorph is closer than you might think."

It hit Masid from two sides: one, the realization that a breeding population of cyborgs would put *Homo sapiens* at an insurmountable disadvantage; and two, the horrified suspicion that even Filoo might not be getting the whole story. If cyborg tech was improving that fast, how long would it be before they were indistinguishable from the regular human population? What might not be available through force typically was through stealth, and if cyborgs could sneak into positions of power on Settled worlds, and begin reproducing, by the time they announced themselves it would be too late for anyone to do anything about it without resorting to a war that would lay waste the precarious culture of any Settler planet.

He forced himself to approach the question from a less adversarial perspective. What if no such takeover was planned? What if the integration of man and machine was just the next step in human progress? Was anything to be gained by resisting it? Humans had never been very adept at choosing not to do what was possible, even when they suspected the consequences would be different than their expectation.

"Now I think you're starting to get it," Filoo said. "Nucleomorph will be the shadow government on a hundred worlds as long as they can keep the borgs waiting for the Grail. Hell, as soon as this thing gets off the ground, I'm signing up myself." He stood and opened the door. "In case you were wondering, Basq won't let me kill you unless you refuse the transformation. He's going to stop by later today, and if I were you I'd have my answer ready."

With that, he left Masid alone. As soon as the door shut, and Masid was sure Filoo or Gorka weren't going to come back in, he flipped his datum out of his pocket. They hadn't searched him, which could only mean they didn't care who he called. Some threshold must have been crossed—Brixa and Basq must have figured that their project had reached a critical mass. Masid wondered if it had something to do with Ariel, or if there was news from Kopernik. A war in Terran space would sure free up Nucleomorph to stop looking over their shoulders.

The other thing to consider was that no one in the Triangle was likely to answer Masid's call. He was on his own, in the position of knowing a truth that very few people on Nova Levis would have believed or wanted to hear. Derec Avery was possibly the only exception, and he'd called from an anonymous datum whose code Masid couldn't backtrack. Masid swore, thought furiously, and was about to call Mia at Kalienin's office—careers be damned all around—when she called him.

"It's on, Masid," she said. On the tiny screen her face looked ghostly, all eyes and pale skin and twitching mouth. "A Terran strike force is already in-system. They didn't tell anyone they were coming, and our satellites just picked them up. Kalienin and Lamina are both tearing out their hair because no one in the Terran military command will talk to them, but there's no public awareness. The policy of the Triangle seems to be that whatever happens to Gernika isn't their concern."

"Have you talked to Derec?"

"No. I didn't even know he was back from Kopernik. I'll call him too, but if you're in Gernika, you need to get out. Now. The whole place might disappear within an hour."

"Or they might wait to see how the Spacers react to Terran military positioned over a Settler world where the government is a Spacer-Terran coalition," Masid said. "You can bet that Lamina has been in touch with everyone who will take her calls. I wouldn't bet on a strike happening right away."

"Would you bet your life against it?" Mia snapped. "Masid, get out of there."

"Will do," he said. It wouldn't do any good to mention that he wasn't exactly at liberty to get out of anywhere. "If you talk to Derec, tell him to get in touch with me. Ditto Ariel, although I'm guessing she won't answer her com right now. She's gone with Zev Brixa to Nucleomorph."

"She's safer there than you are at Gernika," Mia said.

Maybe, Masid thought. He wasn't willing to bet on that, either. At best, Ariel was a useful public voice; as soon as she was no longer suited to that role, Nucleomorph would—

That was when it all came clear.

"Mia," Masid said, "try like hell to get in touch with Derec. I'm going to be on the move here. Wait for me to call you."

He snapped off the call and immediately dialed the personal com code Ariel had given him. *Only three days late,* he thought. *And could be you would have been worse off if Basq or Brixa—or Filoo—knew I was looking for you.*

*Right.*

A message scrolled across the screen: CONNECTION FAILED.

Masid tried again.

CONNECTION FAILED.

Shit, he thought. Was her datum disabled? Did Nucleomorph have screens in place? Those were the only two reasons he could think of for why he wouldn't even have gotten a message server, or been forwarded to Ariel's robot back in Nova City—and he didn't like either of them.

B rixa's office was walled entirely with projections of various
units of the laboratory/hospital complex. He and Ariel sat in
plush armchairs and sipped expensive Terran bourbon. When
enough time had passed that the silence was about to become
uncomfortable, Brixa said, "A big enterprise demands the use of people
we might not otherwise employ."

"Do you mean Basq, or are we talking about Weil and Jan?"

Brixa shrugged. "General comment—could be any of them. Basq is
a bit of a zealot, Weil is the closest thing I've ever seen to a robot
wearing human skin, and Jan has his head in the clouds. He doesn't
know it, but he's right in line with the ancients who believed that the
first networked communications would lead to archived personalities
and so on. Left to their own devices, the three of them would kill each
other before too long. It's my job to keep them all pulling in the same
direction, for the sake of the project."

"And now you add me," Ariel said. "With my own set of stubborn
beliefs that don't square with yours. You just keep making problems
for yourself."

"If you'll pardon an old entrepreneur's canard, most things that look like problems at first glance turn out to be opportunities."

"So I'm an opportunity." Ariel looked over the rim of her glass at Brixa, and thought: *Incredible. I'm practically flirting with him.*

Brixa held up a hand. "Apologies if I made it sound like you're just a cog in some plan. That's not the case at all. Listen, Ariel. I meant it when I said we lose too many. It's easy for you to think of me as a soulless operative, so you do. The truth is that every time we recruit someone and that person dies, I take that as evidence of a personal failure to oversee this project properly. Every one of their deaths is on my head."

Ariel couldn't decide whether to believe him or not. She sipped her whiskey, feeling that a crux was approaching. She had committed herself to something in front of Basq, and here in Zev Brixa's office she was about to find out exactly what that something was.

With a smile more rueful than any she'd yet seen, Brixa went on. "We lose more adults than children. Their bodies are less resilient."

"More orphans," Ariel said, and let it hang.

"Nothing I can do will convince you that I believe in this," Brixa said. "But you're still willing to speak for us."

"Not for you. For them."

Brixa nodded, accepting the implied rebuke and moving on. "As it should be. This is an early stage. In twenty years, or fifty, you'll look back and realize you were part of something wonderful."

"Will I?" Ariel asked. "What interest will cyborgs have in working with unaltered humans? They'll live longer, they won't get sick—why would they even consider themselves human?"

"As long as they can't reproduce," Brixa said, "they'll want to be a part of human civilization. After all—if you'll permit a fairly cold-blooded assessment of the situation—it takes a constant supply of humans to ensure a fresh supply of cyborgs."

"Unless you figure out how to make them fertile."

"Please, Ariel. We are doing some research into fertility, but it's just for the sake of image. As long as we keep them believing that we're going to discover a way for them to reproduce, they'll do whatever we want. That includes my old friend Basq, however convinced he may be that he's the senior partner in our little project. Nucleomorph's only problem is making sure we can make more of them faster than they die off." Brixa set his drink down. "And that's where you come in."

Out of reflex, Ariel put her glass on the table, too. "I beg your pardon?"

The office door opened, but something in Brixa's face kept Ariel looking at him. "Adult conversions, Ambassador," he said, and the smile came back in all of its amoral exuberance. "Most of our subjects are immature Terrans riddled with disease. We're very excited to find out what happens when we do the procedure on a healthy adult Spacer."

Now Ariel did turn around, and saw coming toward her the robot Brixa had brought up from Nova Levis.

"Ariel Burgess," Brixa said, "meet Kynig Parapoyos. Oh, excuse me. I forgot you knew him as Gale Chassik some years ago; your acquaintance predates mine."

She knew it was hopeless, but Ariel leaped out of her chair and made a break for the door. The robot caught her without even rocking back. It lifted her off the ground and carried her out into the hall.

Brixa, coming up behind them, said, "This is a privilege we haven't extended to anyone else, Ariel. You'll be the first person to know why we're willing to expend all of this effort on you."

Ariel fought. She kicked, she screamed, she cursed Brixa and Parapoyos and in the end herself, and when the robot carried her into the operating theater where Krista Weil waited with a transdermal, Ariel spit in her face and cursed her, too.

Weil didn't even wipe away the saliva before touching the transdermal to the back of Ariel's hand and depressing the trigger.

The hut door opened, and Masid barely got the datum stowed before Basq came in. The cyborg remained standing, but he looked completely at ease. "We have an arrangement to discuss," he said.

"So I hear, but it came from Filoo, so I'm glad you're here to confirm," Masid answered. The small sally got a chuckle, but he had no illusions about being able to deal with Basq if the cyborg leader had made up his mind.

"Filoo gave you the substance of it." Basq eyed Masid, giving him a chance to commit. Masid had the sense that more was coming, though, so he waited. "Clandestine enterprises make hypocrites of us all, Masid Vorian. If it were up to me, Filoo would have been turned over to the NLBI years ago; there's certainly enough to charge him with. He's peculiarly persuasive with the constituency we need to get our enterprise off the ground, though, and when he discovered that Kynig Parapoyos was alive, he practically forced himself on us. I wouldn't have expected it of Filoo, but he's pathologically loyal when it comes to Parapoyos."

"Is Parapoyos running things around here?" Masid asked.

"I run things here," Basq said. "Do not doubt that. Parapoyos is a revered figure among us, but that reverence is ever tempered by the realization that he treated us like experimental mice, to be discarded when nothing more could be learned from us. In his current circumstances, he is a useful tool. We use him the way he used us." He allowed himself a thin smile. "And you very nearly solved the problem."

"Not a very discreet maneuver, bulling into my office in the middle of the night. I take it he was freelancing? Or was I part of the plan after Taprin?"

"Hardly. Pon Byris was an opportunity to stretch Earth-Spacer tensions even farther than Taprin's death had. You, on the other hand, were a simple grudge. Parapoyos is now keenly aware that this kind of vendetta is counterproductive. You've got nothing to fear from him, I think. Filoo, on the other hand..." Basq let the question hang.

Masid in turn forced himself to face it square-on for the first time. If it meant he would live, would he undergo the procedure? He recoiled from the idea, but that revulsion passed quickly, and his honest response was yes, he would. If death was the alternative, he would.

The question was whether he could get away with not telling Basq this right away.

"Are you and Brixa planning to transform Ariel?" he asked.

"I'm not," Basq answered, "and you're dodging the question. What Brixa intends for her I do not know. I think she will be useful to us as a respected public official. It never hurts to have people like that on your side."

"You're dodging my question, too," Masid said. "Fact is, I think you're lying to me. Let me lay the theory out for you. Cyborg tech is advancing as fast as you can sacrifice sick kids to it, and pretty soon you'll be able to create cyborgs who are indistinguishable from fully organic human beings. My guess is you've got something along those lines planned for Ariel. The best advocate is the one who looks like someone who should hate you."

"Good plan. Not my plan, probably not Brixa's plan, but a good plan. To tell you the truth, I believe we'll have to consider it now. Unfortunately, I think it will be several years yet before we are superficially indistinguishable from unaugmented humans. It seems unlikely that we will be able to keep Ariel Burgess either sequestered or duped for that length of time."

Masid's instinct was to trust Basq. The cyborg leader didn't come across like someone who lied very often, or for any less than crucial reasons. He vacillated, holding back his acquiescence only because he thought he still might be able to wriggle out of this. The wild card was the military strike—if it was imminent, Masid was more or less certain that by revealing it to Basq he would buy back his unaltered, flesh-and-blood life.

His datum chirped, and Masid thought: *It hasn't done you much good to be indirect, Vorian. Let's try brazen now, see how that goes.* He took the datum out, looking Basq in the eye, and answered the call.

Basq showed no sign of distress that Masid still had a datum, or that he hadn't asked permission to use it. Masid turned the screen so they both could see Avery on the screen.

"Derec," Masid said.

"Masid." Avery was in a flier of some kind. "I came from Nova City as soon as I got off the ship. Where's Ariel? Where's the robot?"

"The robot I don't know about. Ariel, I think, is up at the Nucleomorph lab. There's another problem now, though. Derec, let me introduce you to Basq." Masid turned the screen a little more so Derec's field of vision included Basq. The cyborg nodded in greeting.

"Where's Ariel, Basq?"

"As Masid said. She is with Brixa, I believe touring Nucleomorph's facility. Before we get too entangled here, Mr. Avery, I want to tell you how much I admire your positronics work. Bogard was exceptional. Before my transformation, I was involved in a similar area, not so theoretical, and I tip my metaphorical cap to you."

Derec looked a little nonplussed at the compliment. "I'll ask both of you," he said. "Why did I get a recorded message from people identifying themselves as Terran military about three hundred kilometers back?"

For someone who had never believed in luck, Masid found himself suddenly drowning in it. "Oh, that," he said, with a glance over at Basq. "Mia Daventri called me a little while ago. Seems that Vilios Kalienin is worried enough about the situation here that he's looking for outside support. He talked to someone in the Auroran diplomatic corps—Hofton, I think was his name. You know him?"

Derec's face had changed at the mention of the name. "Yes," he said. "Go on."

"This Hofton was apparently convinced that Basq here is after more than the right to vote for city council. He suggested to Eza Lamina and Kalienin that Nova Levis' government was threatened, and that drastic action might be called for. Kalienin was only too happy to get in touch with the Terran military, and the last thing they need right now is worries about a colonial uprising—especially if it's started by cyborgs. The long and the short of it is that sometime soon, Gernika's going to be destroyed. Probably from orbit. If this transmission cuts off suddenly, you'll know why."

While he spoke, Masid looked from Derec to Basq, who exhibited remarkably similar reactions: slight widening of the eyes, paling of the skin, and so on. Typical physical responses to an unwelcome surprise. Masid had the sense that Derec's shock was slightly different than Basq's, however, and he would have given a great deal to know why.

"I'm going to Nucleomorph," Derec said. "Get out of there, Masid."

Masid put every fiber of his being into a casual shrug. "That's not up to me."

"All of you get out of there," Derec said, and the screen went blank.

He put the datum away, taking his time about it, and looked up at Basq. "Seems like you should be sounding some kind of alarm."

Basq opened the door. "Come with me."

They left the hut. Filoo was standing just outside, smirking at Masid. "What's the call, gato?"

"Vorian and I are taking a ride to Nucleomorph," Basq said. "Keep an eye on things here."

The disappointment on Filoo's face was almost comical. "You're a coward, Vorian," he growled. "It's always the easy way out for you."

Masid said nothing, because Filoo was right. Not because Masid had agreed to become a cyborg, or because he had once tried to assassinate Kynig Parapoyos, or because he had once used a dying agent in his own service to keep himself alive. It was because he was walking out of Gernika and leaving Filoo and the rest of them to die, and he was saying nothing.

Basq must have had some inkling of his thoughts, because when they were most of the way down the trail to Masid's flier, the cyborg said, "If you'd said anything, I would have killed you."

"That makes it worse," Masid said.

After a moment's consideration, Basq nodded. They walked the rest of the way in silence.

The flier was where Masid had left it. The three cyborgs he had seen coming down the trail earlier in the day were standing around on the river bank. They snapped to attention when they saw Basq.

"It doesn't respond," one of them said.

Basq looked at Masid. "Keyed to your voice?"

Masid nodded.

"Get in and start it up."

The two of them climbed in. Masid sat in the pilot's seat and identified himself to the flier. Its engines heated up immediately.

"Good," Basq said.

"To Nucleomorph?" Masid asked.

"That's right. I'm going to Nucleomorph. You get out." Masid looked at Basq. "I don't care what you tell them. They won't believe you, and from my perspective it's easier to start over than to convince them."

Masid had thought himself callous when he left Gernika. Now he was getting a lesson in genuine indifference to life.

"If we both survive this," he said, "I'm coming after you."

Basq winked. "I'll be waiting."

Masid got out of the flier and stood on the shore. Basq leaned out of the hatch. "Take him back to the settlement," he said. "Wait for my instruction. Try to keep him and Filoo apart."

"Sir," the three cyborgs said.

The hatch closed. Masid watched the flier lift out of the shallows and skim over the trees to the west. Before it was out of sight, two of the cyborgs had grasped his arms and propelled him up the bank and onto the trail.

# 34

A riel drifted. Lucid moments came and went, long enough to remind her where she was, but too short for her to find control over her body. She opened her eyes and saw gleaming metal arms tipped with laser scalpels, transdermal injectors, syringes, pincers for grasping and manipulating. For grasping and manipulating *her*. Behind them, a glare of lights, and somewhere beyond her field of vision she heard voices. She tried to speak and could not.

*Something,* she thought distantly. *Find something and hold it. Let everything else come to it.*

"Start with the structural changeover," a woman said. There: Krista Weil. Ariel clung to the name, its specificity, the array of associations that came with it. Then she drifted, but not so far.

An alarm brought her back. "What the hell is that?" Weil said.

"Go ahead," another voice said. Cold and dead, this voice, yet somehow vibrant with a kind of hunger.

"I can't start when there's an alarm going off. If something goes wrong in the middle, she'll die, and we don't have healthy Spacers growing on trees around here. I'm not wasting this one. Go find out what it is."

Faint whir of a machine, heavy tread on the bare floor. A robot.

Snap: Ariel was awake. Feeling flooded into her limbs as the oldest of instincts, fight or flight, scoured the last of the anesthesia from her brain. Still she couldn't move, but she was aware of every part of her body again, aware of the slight touch of air on her skin. Without moving her head, she looked around until she located Weil. The scientist was watching as the damaged robot housing Kynig Parapoyos left the operating theater. When the door hissed shut behind it, Weil muttered something under her breath and went to a terminal at the far end of the room. The alarm still sounded.

*Gather yourself,* Ariel thought. If she didn't move before the robot came back, she would never again move as Ariel Burgess. Her toes moved, and the tips of some of her fingers.

Weil's voice, calm and dispassionate as a weather recording, was narrating the procedure and related events into a recorder. "Krista Weil speaking. Initial phase of transformation on subject Ariel Burgess delayed due to security breach. It is inadvisable to perform transformation in a less than optimal security environment. Particularly in this case, as the patient is the first healthy adult Spacer to undergo procedure and will therefore provide a benchmark whether or not the procedure is successful."

And so on in the same vein, while Ariel listened and let Weil's dispassionate recording flood her with anger. Anger and fear, and Ariel accepted the fear, welcomed it and molded it into the anger until she could lift her head a little.

The alarm cut out. Weil looked up from her recording and made a call. "Kynig. Report, please."

"I'm on my way back. There was a breach of the fence, but the buildings are all secure. Brixa says to go ahead."

"We're waiting on you, then," Weil said. "Hurry. The anesthesia should have another two hours, but I don't want a margin any slimmer than that before I purge it myself and start the paralytic flow. Spacers' immune systems are very aggressive about eliminating foreign substances."

"I used to kill people who patronized me, Weil," Parapoyos said from her terminal. The call cut off with a click.

"Amazing that the worlds are not depopulated," Weil muttered.

She left Ariel's field of vision, and Ariel heard her activating a pump of some sort. Then Weil started to speak again, recording her actions for future analysis. "Fluid replacement pump coming on line. The patient's Spacer-enhanced immune physiology dictates that her autonomic functions be temporarily suspended while the major structural work is completed. An intravenous solution will be pumped into the subject's body as subject's blood is drained by slight vacuum. The solution introduced will induce coma, maximally reducing incidence of shock-induced death."

A firm hand grasped Ariel's left forearm and turned it over, exposing the inside of her elbow. Ariel held herself still as the needle slid into the vein. Weil moved around her head to another machine, just on the edge of Ariel's peripheral vision; it started up with a low hum. That would be the reservoir to hold her blood, drawn out as the solution refilled and stilled her body.

"Vacuum apparatus operative," Weil said. "Applying to subject now."

Again the firm touch, this time on Ariel's right forearm, but this time she didn't hold still. She turned her head, reached across her body, and as Weil moved to embed the heavy needle in her right arm, Ariel caught her wrist and with all her strength jammed the needle into Weil's other hand. Simultaneous with Weil's shriek came the pain of the needle in Ariel's arm tearing loose; then with both hands Ariel reached up to one of the mechanical arms arrayed above the operating table. She caught one and brought it down hard on Weil's head.

Weil's knees buckled, and she pitched over onto her left side. Ariel slid off the table and steadied herself against a wave of dizziness. When it had passed, she stood looking coldly down at the semiconscious scientist as the machine pumped the blood from her body. *You deserve to die,* she thought—and then knelt to pull the needle from Weil's hand. The pump shuddered and cut off.

Ariel went straight to the door, and found with little surprise that it was locked. There was a keypad next to it, and before she could think too much, she took the direct route, hauling Weil's body across the room and pressing her thumb to the door.

KRISTA WEIL: CONFIRM IDENTITY, it said.

"Shit," Ariel growled.

CONFIRMATION FAILED.

"Shit," Ariel said again. She had not gotten this far to be standing naked in front of the door when Parapoyos came creaking through. Weil's voice...

The recording. It had begun *Krista Weil speaking.*

Leaving Weil where she lay near the door, Ariel went to the terminal and saw that the recording file was paused. She ran back through it, following the onscreen transcription until the magic line appeared. Then she turned the volume all the way up and went back to the door to press Weil's thumb into the pad again.

KRISTA WEIL: CONFIRM IDENTITY.

In four steps, Ariel was back at the terminal. She tapped the screen and Weil's voice boomed out of a hidden speaker: "Krista Weil speaking."

Ariel paused the recording and was back to the door in seconds. She opened it, feeling a surge of angry satisfaction, took a half step out—and saw Parapoyos' robot shell coming around a bend in the corridor.

Even a damaged domestic robot could run her to ground before she'd gotten up to a sprint. Ariel had no choice but to duck back into the operating theater. She didn't think it had seen her, and maybe she'd been lucky there; she hadn't gotten a good look at the robot either on Brixa's flier or in his office, but she was fairly sure its optics were damaged, and part of its skull had melted away to reveal the circuitry beneath. Unless the designer had built in complete redundancy in its sensory systems, installing parallel controls for the positronic and organic brains, Parapoyos would be operating at less than peak effectiveness.

Ariel looked around the operating theater for an escape route or something she could use as a weapon. High on one wall was a rectangular window of one-way glass, but Ariel had no way of getting up to it and no way of knowing whether she could break it with what was at hand. There were racks of instruments, but none that a human could use to attack the alloy surface or frame of a robot—or, probably, the reinforced polymers of the window. If she could get to the positronic brain, she might be able to disable whatever systems Parapoyos didn't control, but she had no way of knowing which systems those were, or whether there in fact were any. The fact that he could operate the robot body after positronic collapse and a point-blank energy discharge to its head indicated that more than enough redundancy was there.

She was dithering with seconds before the door opened and Parapoyos either killed her or turned her back over to Brixa. *I'm still sick,* Ariel thought. *Have to focus.*

It struck her as ironic that she'd fought off the anesthesia but not whatever microbe she'd picked up. The post-Burundi's augmentation had made her even stronger than the average Spacer—strong enough that Weil's calculated dose had worn off too quickly. For the first time in her life, Ariel found herself grateful she'd had the plague. The feeling wasn't anymore ridiculous than any of the other emotional contortions she'd put herself through in the last week or so.

There she went again, spiraling down into herself. Ariel slapped her own face, hard enough to bring tears. When she'd blinked them away, she was looking at the instrument array over the operating table.

She got to the control panel as Parapoyos' voice came from the intercom. "Krista, open the door."

The software commanding the instruments was on standby. Ariel woke it up, moving with the pure economy of desperation. There were defaults for the scanning of a patient and a list of procedures, beginning with skeletal replacement. Ariel didn't look any further. She touched an icon and took manual control of the surgical laser. It wouldn't have enough range to burn Parapoyos at the door, but if she could draw him close enough to the table...

"Krista. Open the door." Parapoyos was getting impatient. And Weil was stirring on the floor.

The laser could be operated by joystick or VR interface. Ariel didn't have time for the VR; using the joystick, she swiveled the arm around until the laser was pointed at the door and dialed the range all the way up. Through the camera mounted next to the laser, she could see the upper part of the doorframe. She left it there as Weil sat up.

"Krista!"

Parapoyos' voice spurred her to her feet. Looking wildly around the room, Weil pressed her thumb into the pad and before the complex AI could speak said, "Krista Weil."

The door opened, and the robot came in. "She attacked me Kynig," Weil babbled, "she shouldn't have been awake for two hours at least but she came right off the table and stabbed the needle into my hand and then—"

"Shut up." The robot looked around the room. "Ariel. You can't hide."

"I'm not trying to," Ariel said from where she crouched behind the control panel. In the camera view, she had the laser centered on the robot's undamaged optic port.

It looked in her direction and started forward. She tracked it, knowing she had very little time before Parapoyos noticed the miniscule movements of the laser arm.

Behind the robot, Weil pressed herself against the door. She noticed first. "The laser," she said.

Ariel triggered it.

Parapoyos was less than three meters from the operating table, but even that was too far to give Ariel any real hope. Through the camera view, she saw the robot's optic glaze over, and a puff of smoke curled up from its head. Parapoyos grunted, and the robot jerked to the side. Ariel sprang from behind the console as the laser cut out, covering the distance to Weil while the robot stumbled. Parapoyos was swearing, but he regained control. It stood turning its head from side to side, trying to locate her by sound.

Ariel had one thumb dug into Weil's larynx and the other twisting the scientist's arm up behind her back, keeping her between Ariel and the robot. "Open the door," she whispered into Weil's ear. Weil started to shake her head, and Ariel squeezed. A throttled cry escaped the scientist. "Open it," Ariel whispered again. She backed Weil to the door and maneuvered her around to press her thumb against the pad.

KRISTA WEIL: CONFIRM IDENTITY.

Ariel twisted Weil's arm hard, and at the same time relaxed the pressure on her throat. "Krista Weil," the scientist sobbed.

"Krista, you goddamn idiot, don't open the door!" Parapoyos shouted as the robot pivoted around, but the door was already open.

Ariel dragged Weil through with her, and the door slid shut as the robot came across the room. It banged into the door with frightening force, but Parapoyos couldn't open the door himself.

For the moment, Ariel was safe.

## 35

"**Y**ou know," Masid said as his three guards walked him back into Gernika, "it's amazing what people will do contrary to their best interests."

"Shut up," one of them said.

Masid laughed and forced himself not to look at the sky. "What are you going to do, kill me? Get in line."

Another of the cyborgs swatted Masid on the side of the head, not hard enough to injure but more than enough to bring tears to his eyes. "Shut up."

"That's the spirit," Masid said. "Listen, if I told you I had a secret that might save your lives, would you let me talk to Filoo?"

"Only life you need to worry about is yours, meat," the first cyborg said.

They were back at the hut Masid had just left an hour before. *Now or never,* he thought. "The trick is to quit worrying about yours because you know there's not much left in it. That frees you up to get concerned about other people. I'll give you the secret for free: Sometime in the next few hours, Gernika's going to turn into a hole in the ground. You want details, send Filoo to see me."

The three cyborgs were looking at him with identical flat gazes. *Early versions*, Masid thought. *The tech must be improving fast.*

"I'm going inside now," he said. "Ask yourselves why Basq was in such a hurry to get out of here after he talked to me."

Masid went into the hut, shut the door, and sat down to wait.

He didn't have to wait long. Five minutes later by his datum's chrono, there was a sharp crackle of weapons fire right outside the door. By the time Masid had gotten to his feet, Filoo was standing in the open doorway.

"So you got the message," Masid said.

"Ten seconds," Filoo said. "Talk."

"Terran military's coming. Maybe right now."

Filoo's mouth twitched, as if he couldn't decide whether or not to smile.

*Now*, Masid thought, and he was across the room chopping down on Filoo's gun arm while Filoo was still trying to figure out the joke. The weapon went off, and Masid felt a wash of heat over his right foot; then the gun hit the floor and Masid had Filoo on his back.

"No time to debate," he said. "I'm going. You try to stop me, I'll finish this right now."

Hatred flared in Filoo's eyes. "Postponed," he said. "That's all it is."

"Here's hoping," Masid said. He released Filoo, picked up the gun, and ran out into Gernika as distant thunder sounded.

His message had gotten out. All around there were carts piled with belongings, and the few working transports groaned under the weight of passengers in numbers far exceeding the vehicles' capacities. Still the citizens of Gernika forced their children aboard the transports, reaching through the windows to tear bags and parcels out of passengers' hands and make room for more children. Groups of cyborgs argued violently, divided over whether Basq had deserted them. Adults shouted; children cried.

Thunder sounded, much closer.

*Not orbital*, Masid thought. *They're going to come in close.*

233

A group of arguing cyborgs caught sight of him. "He lies about Basq!" one of them shouted over the chaos, and the group started toward Masid. He thought he saw something like gratitude in their eyes—the gratitude of the terrified for a way to displace their fear. They would kill him on the offchance that it made them feel safe. Filoo's gun was in Masid's hand, but he couldn't shoot people for being frightened and confused.

"They're coming!" he screamed, and ran.

As he was turning, he saw the group of cyborgs break into a run, and Masid knew he was going to die. Then the thunder over the horizon turned into a deafening roar, and something black and shining reared up over the trees, holding its position like a mantis poised to strike. A line of explosions obliterated the end of the main street, and the concussion came to Masid as a series of staccato hammer blows that went on even after he'd felt his eardrums give way. He tripped, and before he'd hit the ground another line of bright fire incinerated the cyborgs pursuing him, together with the nearest two heavy transports and everyone inside. The after-image seared his eyes, and something was wrong with one of his feet; still he got up and ran through a rain of falling debris, not sure where he was going except that it was away from the rolling line of destruction.

As his vision cleared, he saw two more attack craft coming up, forming a triangle over Gernika. A stand of trees disappeared in a bloom of smoke and fluttering leaves, and Masid realized that the Terrans were strafing the cyborgs who had managed to get out of the settlement. The three attack craft were long and jointed, with pivoting engines at the ends of their four stubby wings and ordnance bubbles like the heads of mosquitoes, swiveling faster than his eye could track in seach of new targets. He looked toward the hut where he'd left Filoo—it was gone. He looked to his right; where Basq's headquarters had stood was now a partial skeleton of beams, burning fiercely in the midday sunshine.

The dormitory complex exploded with a wave of heat that dried

Masid's eyes in their sockets. He stumbled and sat down, realizing only after he'd hit the ground that something had knocked him over. Fighting to get his breath back, to get out of the open before the Terrans got to him, he turned over onto his hands and knees and saw what had knocked him off his feet: a small torso, part of one arm still attached. During the interminable moment it took him to get to his feet again, Masid saw the gleaming alloy of the rib cage, within it the burst and bleeding lungs, and below it the ribbed spinal column, shining with blood and ending in a tangle of charred and curling filaments. He fled.

Running wherever he found a path clear of fire and rubble, Masid came to a crouch under a partially collapsed wall. Smoke stung his eyes, and he still couldn't hear, although each new explosion came to him as a thump he felt through the soles of his feet, one of which was badly burned, the blistered toes sticking out through a charred hole in the boot. If Filoo had gotten out of the hut and survived, Masid was going to find him.

A trickling in his ears irritated him. He dipped blood from each ear with the tip of a pinky, felt nothing but a wave of passing annoyance at having to have his eardrums put back together. *Time to get moving again,* he thought; the thud of explosions was lessening, possibly coming from farther away as the three Terran craft tracked survivors into the forest. Masid looked up, didn't see anything but sky and smoke. He scampered, limping. from rubble to pile of burning rubble, relying on smoke to scramble the Terrans' visuals and the fires to disguise his infrared signature. If they had oxygen-exchange detectors on board, the fires might confuse those, too.

From the shelter of a caved-in roof, Masid peered along the length of Gernika's main street—it was all craters and wreckage, fire and smoke, bodies and parts of bodies. Masid had the feeling he was present at an extinction, and rage filled him. He had seen too many desperate people killed by the pressures of history.

He ducked back into the wreckage as one of the Terran craft

appeared again. Stuttering lines of energy reached up from the trees, and in a glittering burst of metal one of its wings was torn away, falling into the forest trailed by an arc of black smoke. The craft heeled over, righted itself, and returned fire.

Where had the cyborgs gotten heavy energy weapons? Masid didn't have time to consider it. The diversion was buying him some time, and he used it to get across the street to the side nearest the river, and from there into a hollow in the side of a hill made by a fallen tree. The Terrans wouldn't drop troops; they knew that even hardsuited soldiers wouldn't be more than an even match for a cyborg, and the last thing they needed was casualties to complicated what was already a delicate political calculus. So the ships would come back, and they would pound the remains of Gernika until no sign of life remained on their scanners. Collapsing walls weren't enough to kill a cyborg.

*Masid, gato, you might just live through this,* he thought. *Stay here in the trees, don't move too much, wait for them to flatten everything and hope they mistake your signals for a large mammal. They're not looking for plain human signatures, right? Right. They'd only have automated subroutines looking for an electronic signature, too.*

He thought it would work. The damaged craft wiped out whomever had been firing at it, and swept back over the trees to station itself over the ruined settlement. Then it methodically began bombing every square centimeter of Gernika. Huddled against the hillside, Masid could see nothing, and he still couldn't hear, but dirt rained down around him and the earth shook as if convulsing. When the pause came, he opened his eyes, and only then noticed that he'd closed them.

A low thrum reached him, and he peered upward through the trees. The Terran ship had interrupted its bombing, and was moving slowly in Masid's direction. *Can't be looking for me,* he thought, but his hand went to the gun anyway. Like a slingshot against an asteroid, but he'd be damned if he just sat there.

The ship paused directly over him. Masid looked down, realizing that what he had in his hand wasn't Filoo's gun; it was Masid's own datum, and its screen was blinking with the message INCOMING CALL FROM DEREC AVERY.

*Oh, Avery, you dumb son of a bitch...*

D erec was cruising as fast as he dared along the Bogard's western bank, dodging overhanging trees and keeping himself as unobtrusive as possible after having seen a flier zip past him near Gernika. Then he saw the three military craft coming in from the north. They split up and dropped out of sight to the east.

The strike was happening.

*Call Masid,* he thought. Then he saw smoke in the distance and realized he couldn't tell Masid anything he didn't already know. There would be time to compare notes later.

A renewed sense of urgency came over Derec; he gunned the flier away from the riverbank and covered the remaining kilometers to the Nucleomorph lab complex in a few minutes. Hovering just outside the fence line, he debated his approach. There was a front gate, and a road snaking away from it into the forest; between the fence and the buildings was an open space patrolled by what he assumed were armed guards. Not the kind of place he could just walk into.

Then again, he wasn't walking. Outside the fence, on the far side of the complex, Derec saw a flier parked. A section of the fence was down, and technicians were working on it. So someone had already made an unauthorized entry. Who?

Parapoyos? No. He'd been created here, and if his robot chassis was still functional it would be here already.

Masid. The flier must have been his. After all, he knew where Ariel was, and had told Derec to go there, and he wouldn't have been able to call Hofton's datum and let Derec know he'd gotten out of Gernika.

Derec called him to see where in the complex he was. They had a better chance of getting Ariel out together than either of them did individually.

Damn the interference around here—at first it looked like he was getting through, and then a few seconds later the infuriating CONNECTION FAILED blinked on the datum's screen. Nucleomorph's countermeasures were nothing to trifle with, if they could block all data traffic into the complex.

The direct approach, then. Derec lifted up to a hundred meters and simply flew over the fence, planning to land at the closest doorway and break it down if he had to.

Right away he knew he'd underestimated the countermeasures. The flier's controls locked in his hands, and its power cut out, setting him into a glide that led straight at a broad glass wall between two of the outer buildings. Derec just had time to put his hands up before he hit the wall with a boom that echoed down after him into unconsciousness.

He couldn't have been out for long, because when he was able to register his surroundings again Derec could see people running through the spacious room he'd crashed into. A voice came from the flier's console: "...this facility will be evacuated within the next five minutes. All personnel evacuate immediately. Terran Military Command assumes no responsibility for loss of life or property following five minutes from the broadcast of this message."

Derec tuned the rest out. He'd gotten the important number. Ten minutes. He found the flier's harness release and sprung himself to topple out of his seat into the tiny cabin space behind the cockpit. The flier was largely intact, and all of its inertial dampers had triggered, saving Derec's life and keeping him from serious injury. His nose felt broken, and he had a feeling that in the morning he wouldn't be able to turn his head, but he was breathing and ambulatory.

It took two hard kicks to spring the flier's hatch, and then Derec had to drop two meters to the floor. The Terran military's message droned from an intercom system, echoing over the commotion in the room as Nucleomorph staff ran for their lives. The flier had shattered most of the glass on the side of the hall he'd impacted, coming to rest in a system of girders that supported the transparent domed ceiling.

The upper half of the atrium's internal walls was ringed with office facades, through which Derec could see people moving around. Exactly the kind of commanding position an executive would consider his due; Brixa would be up there if he was anywhere.

Derec saw a stairwell and ran toward it, banging into a portly woman on the bottom step. "Where's Brixa?" he shouted at her.

She waved up the stairs and ran. Derec bounded up the stairs and turned left. Hologrammed plaques identified the occupant of each office, and the fifth door said ZEV BRIXA. He opened it and went in.

Brixa lay in a heap behind his desk, as dead as any one man could be. At least Derec assumed it was Brixa; he'd never met the man, and the corpse was disfigured by the force of the assault. Whoever it was had been beaten with the kind of savagery and monstrous strength that could only come from a cyborg; arcs and spatters of blood were strung across the furniture and the flatscreens that took up the office walls. On each screen was a view of a different part of the complex. Leaving the dead man, Derec went from one to the other, looking for a clue about Ariel's whereabouts.

He didn't see her, but one thing Derec saw did catch his attention. The cyborg leader, Basq, was bulling his way through a tide of fleeing technicians in what looked like a research wing. People bounced away from him like hailstones.

Derec checked the caption of the view as Basq passed from it. He pressed his hand against the screen and said, "Directions to this location."

The facility RI was apparently still functioning; a holographic map appeared next to the display. Derec took it in, and then he ran.

When he got there, Basq was gone, and the area was deserted. He'd been wrong about it being a research wing; it appeared to be a medical area, set below ground level. Doors stood open, revealing what were unmistakably operating tables.

Derec wondered what Basq had been doing in the area, or if the cyborg had just happened to be passing through. Where had he gone? Derec looked up and down the hall, and that was when he saw it: next to a door, a screen listing Ariel Burgess as patient and Krista Weil as surgeon. The door was broken in and smeared with blood, the frame bent and the room within empty. Where was Ariel?

"You're too late," someone said from behind him.

The speaker was a small, wiry woman with bruises on her throat, bleeding from a puncture on the back of her right hand. Her voice was hoarse. Derec had no idea where she'd come from, or if she'd been there all along without him noticing.

"Too late how?" Derec asked.

"She woke up. I wouldn't have thought it was possible, but she did, and she got out. It'll be years before I get to try the procedure on another Spacer."

Derec wanted to kill her. Instead he asked, "Are you Krista Weil?"

She nodded.

"This complex is going to go up in smoke any minute," Derec said. "You can't sit here."

Weil gave him a pitying look. "Indeed I can. This was my work. If it is destroyed..." She shrugged. "I'm Terran. I won't live long enough to rebuild it from the ground up." A bleak smile broke over her face.

"Brixa told me I should have done it myself. Too uncertain, though, at least that's what I thought. Put that wily bastard was right, as usual."

Except right at the end, when he was badly wrong about Basq. "Where did Ariel go?"

She shrugged and wandered away down the hall. Derec would have gone after her, but if he hadn't used up the five minutes yet, there wasn't much left. He ran down the hall in the opposite direction, taking the first staircase he saw and willing himself to believe Ariel had gone this same way.

As he got to the top of the stairs, the first explosions shook dust down around him. Derec ducked his head at the impact, glanced up to see part of the corridor collapsed and smoke billowing toward him. He turned in the other direction and ran on.

Derec had just turned down a side corridor, with an emergency exit visible at the far end, when a door on the left side of the hall burst outward and a robot appeared—a Cole-Yahner domestic with a blast wound on the side of its head and visibly damaged optics.

"Echo," it said. "Echo. Echo." It was Parapoyos, blinded now but making his crippled housing work as well as it could.

Without facing him, Parapoyos said, "Who's that?"

"Where's Ariel, Parapoyos?" Derec asked.

Now the robot did face him. "Well, if it isn't Derec Avery," Parapoyos said. "Your girlfriend doesn't need you around. She's gone." A distant explosion sounded, and one more alarm added its counterpoint to the general din. "I'm guessing the Terrans fried her once she got out of the building, if she did. Doesn't matter much. I've got a ride to catch."

Turning away, the robot moved down the hall. Then Basq came out the same door it had used. "Parapoyos," he said.

The robot halted. Basq took a step toward it. His hands, hanging open at his sides, dripped blood from gashes across his knuckles, and more blood streaked his face and hair. "You were call~d to answer once, and shown mercy. Again you have betrayed us."

"Mercy," Parapoyos said. "You made me into a tool. Blame yourself if the tool had more functions than you realized."

Faster than Derec could follow, Basq closed the distance to the robot and wrenched off one of its legs.

"Gernika is ashes," Basq said, standing over the supine robot. "You did that. The previous generation you only turned out to die. This one you killed yourself."

"And what did you do to me?" Parapoyos asked.

"Gave you better than you deserved. An error I now rectify." Basq flipped the robot's leg aside. He knelt beside it. Parapoyos struck at him, and Basq let the blows land as he worked his fingers into a seam in the robot's torso and tore it open.

"You ungrateful bastard," snarled the voice of Kynig Parapoyos. "You'd be dead if it wasn't for me."

"I would also be free of guilt," Basq said.

Exposed beneath the shell of the torso was a gleaming silver ovoid, with hoses running into and out of it and extruded filaments connecting it to what Derec could identify as the robot's primary systems interfaces. With horrifying delicacy, Basq snapped each of these filaments. The robot's arms fell limp.

"Basq, don't. You'd have done the same thing," Parapoyos pleaded.

"At one time," Basq said. "As recently as today. No longer."

With the stiff fingers of his left hand he punched a hole through the ovoid. Parapoyos howled, a wordless wail that abruptly became a series of choked grunts as Basq tore open the ovoid and ripped loose the brain of Kynig Parapoyos.

In the silence, Derec was aware of his own breathing. Basq held the brain in both hands and squeezed. Tissue and blood spurted out from between his fingers to spatter on the floor, and it was done.

Basq stood. "We have all been used, Derec Avery," he said. "It is time we made sure we are not used again."

A riel ran down the corridor until she saw a stairwell. She glanced in and saw that it only went up, so she took it, on the chance that she was undergound. One flight up, she opened the door and came face to face with Basq.

"You live," he said. "A fortunate surprise."

"For both of us."

Static flared from the complex intercom. "Attention. This facility will be evacuated within five minutes, on the orders of Terran Military Command. All personnel evacuate immediately. Terran Military Command assumes no responsibility for loss of life and property following five minutes from the broadcast of this message."

Basq bared his teeth in a feral grin. "A good day to die, as the saying goes."

"A better day to get out and live," Ariel said. "Let's go."

"If they will hunt me here, they will hunt me anywhere," Basq said. "I was naïve to believe that you could protect us."

The comment stung, but Ariel let it pass. "Basq, I need you to survive this. Is Gernika destroyed?"

"Gernika was always destroyed. It is in the nature of Gernika to suffer destruction." The cyborg was coming apart, Ariel realized. "I have already visited Zev Brixa. Now I seek only Parapoyos, and my work will be done."

A pair of Nucleomorph security personnel came around the nearest corner. Seeing Basq, they leveled their weapons. "Stay right there!"

"Basq," Ariel said. She felt his motion rather than saw it; he was gone before the guards had finished shouting. One of them fired reflexively, gouging a hole in the wall less than a meter from her. She dove to the floor with a scream, and the guards ran to her.

One of them hung back a little, covering her with his rifle, while the other squatted. "Who are you?" he shouted in her face.

"Ariel Burgess, legal liaison to the Triangle," she said.

Disbelief was plain on the guard's face. She was naked, and had immediately before been seen talking to Basq. It was easy to see how that would be difficult to square with her claimed identity.

"Look," Ariel said. "Arrest me if you want, just as long as you do it once we've gotten out of here. We've got to stop this."

They were coming out the front doors, and Ariel had just convinced one of the guards to lend her his comm, when the first raider buzzed in low over the trees and began firing. The first volley blew out three walls of the first building she had toured with Brixa. All those people, recuperating in their berths, their lives blown out like candles for the sin of wanting to live. Ariel was screaming, stabbing emergency codes into the comm and demanding access to Exa Lamina, Kalienin, someone in the Terran military who could stop this. Her calls were intercepted by a military monitor with a voice like cold ashes, who informed her that no communication was permitted from her location at that time.

"You inhuman bastard!" she sobbed at him. "There are children in there!"

"You need to get yourself out of there, Miss Burgess," the monitor said.

He terminated the link, and Ariel looked up to see two more military craft converging on the complex. The guards dragged her across the open field to the fence, and through it to the other side, where she watched building after building disintegrate in blinding flashes and columns of smoke. Ariel stared at the carnage long after the explosions had blinded her. In the afterimages, she saw the bright colors and simple shapes of the playroom, with its children running and laughing with joy at the strength of their new bodies.

When it was done, elements of the Nova Levis militia arrived in a column of aerial transports. A medic draped a blanket around her. She accepted it and walked away, refusing his attempts to examine her. Her only injury was the small tear at the inside of her left elbow, and allowing him to treat it when there must have been other survivors in the wreckage of Nucleomorph would have been an obscenity.

*Enough obscenity,* Ariel thought. *Enough of all of this. If Brixa and Krista Weil are dead, and Basq, does that justify this?*

*I will take part no longer.*

An aerial fire-suppression crew appeared and began foaming the ruins. Ariel watched it, and at first didn't notice that someone had sat on the ground next to her. After a while she looked over and saw Derec.

"I went in there looking for you," he said. "Basq told me you'd already gotten out, but I wasn't sure whether to believe him."

"Basq doesn't lie. At least he never did to me. He held things back, but he never told me an active falsehood."

"Puts him a step above the rest of them."

Ariel nodded.

"I saw him kill Parapoyos," Derec said.

Still nodding, Ariel said, "He said he was going to." After a pause, she added, "Where did he go after that?"

Derec shrugged. "He didn't say. I doubt he got out."

For a while they watched the foam settle over Nucleomorph. Then Ariel said, "Kalienin did this. And Lamina."

"Not just them," Derec said. His face was bleak, and even after everything she'd gone through in the last day, Ariel found herself afraid to hear what he might say.

Yet she gathered herself and said, "Tell me."

It was a week or so later that Ariel answered a knock at her door to find Filoo shifting his weight from foot to foot, and trying, without much success, to look her in the eye. "I'm surprised to see you, Filoo," she said. "Did you survive Gernika?"

"I got out, yeah." Filoo tried to bite back what was coming next, but he couldn't. "Because Vorian tipped me off."

"Anyone seen Masid?"

Filoo shook his head. "Be blunt about it, I don't think anyone'll ever find him without running a gene sampler over the whole place. It's not easy having to be grateful to that conniving sneak."

Ariel had to laugh. "Do you want to come in?"

"No. I came to tell you about a meeting you should go to." He handed her a flimsy with a handwritten address and date on it. The address was in New Nova, the date two days away. There was no signature, but below the information was a crude outline of a horse trying to rise to its feet.

Ariel folded it into a pocket. "I'll be there."

"Avery, too," Filoo said, and walked away.

She walked to Derec's lab. He didn't want to leave, but she showed him the note, and he frowned and followed her outside.

"Basq?" he asked when they'd walked some distance down the street into a residential block.

"Filoo was the courier. I'm not sure who else he'd be running messages for."

"So Filoo's alive, too." Derec mused over this. "I've got Hofton's datum in storage. I wonder how much he knows."

"If they know Basq is alive, they might do something again." It was still hard for Ariel to speak directly of Hofton. She had known him—it—for years, and felt deeply betrayed by his subterfuge. Also murderously angry about his provocation of the Gernika massacre. Yet there was vindication at her furious opposition to Derec's construction of Bogard—how many people were dead now because Bogard and Hofton had given the Three Laws a utilitarian revision?

And who had made that possible?

Derec shook his head. "I don't think so. They've taken care of the cyborg problem. It'll be a long time before someone attempts it again."

"That's what they thought after the last one."

"What do you want me to say, Ariel? Eventually it'll be true. No one is going to just let cyborgs develop, and now that Gernika exists as a precedent, anyone who starts developing cyborgs is going to know that bombs will fall sooner rather than later."

The destruction of Gernika and Nucleomorph had served another purpose, far from Nova Levis. The fact that a number of humans and Spacers had died in the raids provoked a furor even among the Managin segments of the Terran electorate, and their discontent was nothing compared to the volcanic outrage coming from the Settled worlds at this ruthless exercise of authority. The Spacers, too, had made it clear that another unilateral action of similar nature would mean war, and a skirmish had broken out between Spacer and Terran ships around Kopernik. Faced with the tipping point into open slaughter, both sides had yet to blink. The mood on all of humanity's planets was bleak and outraged.

The Gernika massacre was generally viewed as a sacrifice of lives on Nova Levis to make a political point on Earth, and nowhere was this feeling more loudly voiced than on Nova Levis itself. The Triangle was hunkered down, with President Chivu unlikely to survive and rumors swirling that he would take down a large number of the top legislative leadership with him. Street unrest was on the rise, and the attention of Earth and the Fifty Worlds was elsewhere.

Put another way: the horse was trying to rise.

"Will you come to the meeting, Derec?" Ariel asked.

## HAVE ROBOT, WILL TRAVEL

Silence between them, with the rustle of leaves on the breeze, sounds of traffic and human voices on Nova Boulevard.

"I'll come," he said.

P resident Erno Chivu's speech to the combined legislative
assembly of the Nova Levis government was scheduled to begin
at precisely ten in the morning, one month to the day after the
"Terran incursion," which was his preferred terminology. The speech
was widely expected to answer his critics, who accused him of leaving
the business of governance to a group of ideologically motivated
advisers while he devoted himself to his business interests back on
Earth—among which were a voting interest on the board of Kopernik
Station and a seat on the shareholder council of Nucleomorph. A few
loud voices hoped he would use the opportunity to resign and take
the first shuttle off-planet.

The Gernika massacre had provoked a tremendous amount of
investigative activity regarding the financial interests and political
allegiances of Triangle leadership, and it was broadly assumed that
the aftermath of the Terran strikes marked the beginning of journalism
as a profession on Nova Levis. This was, of course, not welcomed by
the parties under investigation, particularly when the activities of
Vilios Kalienin and Eza Lamina came to represent the endemic corruption and malfeasance of Triangle elected officials—none of whom had

really been elected by the people they were alleged to represent. That was the fundamental problem, and the cause of sporadic rioting in Stopol and Noresk. Disturbances in Nova City, at least inside the walls, were quelled with great speed and alarming efficiency, and President Chivu's speech was to take place in a legislative chamber ringed by militia and local police.

Room L116 of the Triangle—known formally as the Combined Debate and Resolution Chamber, but colloquially as the Echo Chamber because of the perfunctory nature of legislative discourse under Chivu's administration—seated one thousand people. Forty-nine desks formed a semi-circle around a dais reserved for committee arrangements or special speakers such as presidents; behind and above the speaking floor, two levels of raked public seating offered excellent views of the proceedings. On this day, the public areas were jammed, and the media presence—as measured by the number of drones flitting above the floor—was heavy. At the head of each aisle stood a pair of armed militia; other pairs stood at either end of the dais and at the outer edges of the semicircle of desks.

Near the leftmost aisle sat Derec, Ariel, and Hodder Feng. Mia Daventri fidgeted in her seat on the other side of the room, an empty seat between her and an oddly subdued Filoo. Periodically, a drone flitted up to Derec or Ariel, less often to Mia, not at all to Hodder or Filoo; but their presence at Chivu's speech was unremarkable.

At precisely ten o'clock, the president appeared to stony silence from the public and dutiful applause from the assembled seventeen senators and thirty-two representatives, a sizable minority of whom had careers and already-tattered reputations riding on Chivu's words. At one minute after ten, the applause having faded even in the Echo Chamber's excellent acoustic environment, President Chivu said, "Thank you."

Immediately thereafter, Hodder Feng stood and, in a clear baritone, said, "I reject your authority to govern this people."

A hushed murmur swept through the crowd, and security started to converge on Hodder, but members of the audience stood as they passed and with uncanny speed swept the weapons from their hands. All through the auditorium, the security detail found themselves disarmed before they were aware that someone was approaching them—including on the debating floor, where a number of people seemed simply to appear, holding the captured weapons. The legislators scrambled to their feet, and the public erupted in a roar punctuated by a few screams that might have been cheers.

Weapons fire crackled from the balcony, and the figure nearest President Chivu buckled and fell. Then the upper portion of the audience swarmed over the shooter, and people started to scramble for the exits. Amid the swelling chaos, Feng strode across the floor to the dais and stepped up to the president. Chivu backed away, face pale with fear, and allowed his personal detail to guide him as far as the door through which he'd entered. There he stopped, faced with a single armed figure—a boy perhaps eleven years of age. The wounded man on the podium struggled to his feet and stood leaning against his nearest compatriot.

When Feng spoke again, his voice was amplified by overhead sound equipment, and his words rang out across the subetheric to Earth, the Fifty Worlds, and all the Settler colonies.

"The governed revoke their consent," he said. "We declare this government failed in its obligations to represent the interests of the people of Nova Levis, and we hereby dissolve it."

A moment of absolute silence hung over the assembly, and then a fierce roar of approval boomed from the audience, drowning out the stunned calls for order from some members of the legislature. It grew in intensity until the ears of every human in the chamber began to ring, but when Hodder raised his arms it subsided.

"Flanking me on this podium are the survivors of Gernika," Hodder said. "Their crime was the will to live, and the willingness to take any action to survive. There are nineteen of them, where once there were more than two thousand. Look at them."

Four women, three men, twelve children. As the eyes of the assembled public and the viewing audience across settled space fixed on them, they set down the weapons they had taken from security and stood erect and proud.

"Every one of you in the audience knows someone who died at Gernika," Hodder said. "Too few of you, but still many, know one or more of these survivors. We reject the proposition that actions taken to save their lives could, at the same time, have robbed them of the humanity that is their birthright. We reject the idea that the people of Nova Levis are incapable of governing themselves and must be subjected to the whim of a corrupt and profiteering cabal of disgraced offworlders. And we deny the legitimacy of the Triangle and its agents throughout the incorporated cities and outposts of this planet. The people of Nova Levis were born free, and today demand the freedom until now denied them.

"From this moment forward, only adults born on Nova Levis or naturalized citizens may serve in the elected government or the judiciary. From this moment forward, the natural resources of Nova Levis and its moons are the property of its people. And from this moment forward, Nova Levis forbids the presence in its space, as defined by interplanetary common law, of any military unit except our own duly sworn armed forces. Violation of this prohibition will be considered an act of aggression subject to local and interplanetary sanction.

"President Chivu and members of the House and Senate, your positions are vacated and all associated privileges revoked. Criminal and civil proceedings will begin against any of you determined to have conducted yourselves in a manner unbecoming to your offices. If you wish, we will grant you amnesty in return for your immediate departure from Nova Levis and binding pledge never to return. Quitting the planet under these circumstances will entail relinquishing any real property or interest in same that does not physically accompany you at your departure."

At this, a few shouts of outrage echoed through the chamber before being buried by an avalanche of cheers and catcalls. Hodder allowed things to die down again before going on.

"Beginning tomorrow morning, any citizen of Nova Levis is welcome to attend a public convention at which the details of a constitution will be formulated. The first task will be to designate a committee to write this document. Nominations will be accepted for the next seven days, and a caucus held during the week following.

"Also tomorrow morning, the first shuttle will be available for former elected officials and their staffs. The amnesty period will be seventy-two hours."

Hodder stopped, and those closest to him could see that his eyes were shining with tears. "People of Nova Levis. As of right now, your destiny belongs to you," he finished, and if he had said anything else it would have been lost in the overwhelming wave of sound.

People poured onto the floor, jostling the erstwhile legislators and pelting them with curses. A few fistfights broke out, and were broken up by the appearance of one of the Gernika survivors between the two combatants. The press of bodies carried the members of House and Senate out of the building before letting them go; President Chivu was allowed to leave with his personal security. People pressed around Hodder, bombarding him with proposals, theories, complaints, demands. Tomorrow, tomorrow, he told them until his voice gave out. Then he just shrugged and went outside to the plaza that lay between the Triangle and Nova Boulevard, where the first spontaneous street celebration in the history of Nova Levis was raucously underway.

Derec and Ariel joined in, with Mia and the laryngitic Hodder Feng, Filoo, and whoever came by with a bottle or an idea or both. It was a cool, fine fall day, and after a while they were both drunk and elated and it was a cool fall evening.

Eventually, Derec got to his feet. He caught Ariel's eye and said, "Time to pay a visit."

They walked through the crowd, past Derec's lab to the south gate, and on from there into New Nova, where the party was more intense but also tinctured with mourning for Gernika's dead. Here the cyborg question had always been more than philosophical, and here the bigoted opposition ran deepest, because poverty breeds extremism. Derec and Ariel found the address they were looking for and knocked on the door.

Basq opened it and let them into the apartment that had once housed Mika Mendes. The surviving cyborgs were in the middle of their own more reflective celebration; the looks they cast in Derec and Ariel's direction were thoughtful and curious. How he had survived the bombing of Nucleomorph, neither Derec nor Ariel knew, and he would not speak of it. He rarely left the apartment, and during his days there had scored every wall with the devastating lines of the painting, reworking them with obsessive care. His leadership was at an end, and he was content to withdraw; but the survivors of Gernika clustered around him because he was their only link to the lives they led before.

"Even you use us," Basq said.

Derec nodded. "We did. With your consent."

Basq shrugged. "You'll ask again. Perhaps the next time we will refuse."

"Perhaps we won't have to ask."

A few of the cyborgs chuckled. "And *I* was called utopian," Basq said with glittering eyes.

"You *were* utopian," Ariel said.

"Of course I was. Without a dose of utopian dreaming, I could never have held Gernika together."

*That, and a dose of authoritarian brutality,* Derec thought. But there had been no shortage of that on Nova Levis.

"And your little revolution is not utopian?" Basq prodded. "We abound in ironies."

"That we do," Derec said.

They left soon after. Walking back through the boisterous streets of New Nova, Derec found himself thinking of the opposition to their plans that even now must be under discussion as intense as the constitutional convention that would be in the coming weeks. Nova Levis would never speak with one voice; the task was to keep each voice respected and distinct. Easy.

He chuckled, and Ariel said, "What?"

"Nothing." They entered the city proper again, walking north along Nova Boulevard with the sounds of celebration ringing around them. *Enjoy it now*, Derec thought. *It gets much harder.*

Ariel nudged him. "This is supposed to be a party."

Derec gave an embarrassed laugh. "Don't let me ruin the mood," he said. "I've just got one other thing to do."

"One? Would that be putting together a census, arranging for naturalization, conducting an inventory of natural resources and vacated property, setting up elections, or what?" Ariel laughed. "Tomorrow, Derec. There will be plenty of time for that tomorrow."

They had reached his lab. Derec stopped. "I've got to take care of something here."

Ariel rolled her eyes. "Oh, come on. Didn't you hear me?"

"I did, and I'll meet you at Kamil's in half an hour. Okay?"

Now she was interested. "What are you going to do?"

"Half an hour. Kamil's."

She gave him a beat to change his mind, then said, "Have it your way," and walked off in the direction of the Triangle plaza.

The lab was dark and quiet, the only light a faint ambience of telltales from the few terminals that ran aroundn the clock doing gene sequences or regressions. Miles was back at Derec's apartment and if there was any justice in the universe, Elin was joyously drunk and surrounded by her friends.

Derec crossed to a closet, moving mostly by feel, and opened the door. On the floor at the back of the closet, under the lowest shelf, was a malfunctioning centrifuge that he'd been unable to get permission to repair. He slid it out and reached inside, removing the datum Hofton had given him.

Derec didn't speak until he'd crossed the lab again and opened the door. The sounds of celebration broke like a wave over the silence. He held the datum up. "Hear that?"

No response.

"Hofton. I know you're listening."

No response.

"All right. I'm going to say this once, to you and Bogard both: Leave us alone."

He dropped the datum to the floor and crushed it under his heel. Then Derec walked away from his lab, back into the jubilant chaos of Nova Boulevard where Ariel was waiting.